TONY THOMPSON

DRYVER'S FIELDS

DRYVER'S FIELDS

This is a work of fiction. All of the characters, names, incidents, organizations, and dialogue in this novel are either the products of the author's imagination or are used fictitiously.

iUniverse books may be ordered through booksellers or by contacting:

iUniverse
1663 Liberty Drive
Bloomington, IN 47403
www.iuniverse.com
1-800-Authors (1-800-288-4677)

ISBN: 978-1-5320-7377-9 (sc)
ISBN: 978-1-5320-7376-2 (e)

Library of Congress Control Number: 2019942726

Print information available on the last page.

iUniverse rev. date: 05/31/2019

For my wife Denise, my children Alex, Alyssa, and Tyson. Ten years of dreaming, two years of typing, and it here it is.

PROLOGUE
TRUCE

Wolf & Deer

The two animals, one **predator**, one **prey**, met in the open field just before the coming of dawn on a warm, summer morning. They met, not to continue that constant struggle often demanded by nature, but instead to offer a truce to one another. The meeting place had been agreed upon in the voice-less fashion of animals. It had been communicated out of desperation and the need for the protection and the survival of each of their own species.

Meeting in an open field, away from the depths of the forest and the threat, which now lurked within, the two animals circled each other warily. They were far more concerned with the long shadows cast by the nearby forest of oak trees than the dangers each might offer the other.

Fear gripped both of them. The gathering snowflakes, from the previous evening, had long since melted away in this part of the woods.

Each, both predator and prey, was acutely aware that though they were more than thirty yards away from any of the nearby growth that distance might not be enough to provide the reactionary time needed to flee, should they be attacked. Outwardly, both seemed calm. Both projected the animalistic strength typical of their kind. Both also were nervous about the possibility they were being hunted.

The wolf and the deer, with their hearts racing, calmly moved towards each other.

It was an oddity, this meeting in the fields, during the waking of day. That was sure. Never, had two enemies in nature met without one trying to hunt the other. Never, had two enemies in nature agreed to refrain from the 'animal instinct.' This instinct demanded one consume the other.

As the strongest in her pack, the Alpha female wolf was breaking a time-honored tradition which had been initiated by her ancestors thousands of years ago. Snow-white tipped hair glistened in the morning light as the sun tried to peak above the horizon through the sporadically arranged oak trees of the forest. Majestic Scarlet Oak lined the nearby forest, battling other trees and shrubs for the much-needed resources of the soil. Broad leaves twisted in the sunlight like upwardly cupped hands reaching to the skies in prayer.

Ice-blue eyes locked onto the eyes of the buck. They did not project a sense of hunger, but projected instead something akin to a quiet desperation.

Aware that never, as long as there had been wolves hidden deep within the forests of Southern Illinois, unseen by man for hundreds of years, never had wolf and deer ever met to create such an alliance. Dire times called for dire actions. Bristling with fear in the morning light she moved closer to the buck as if to whisper her thoughts and keep them a secret, hoping they would be unheard by the demon which had recently come to her woods.

That it was her woods and the woods of her pack was a surety. Hundreds of years had imprinted on all of them, at least all those who remained, something must be done. Fleeing was not an option, especially since this is where her ancestors had made their home after the great migration.

What the facets of the alliance would mean neither animal was completely sure. The necessity to survive had caused each of them to push aside all nature had taught them. Failure most likely would end with their deaths. Failure would most likely lead to the destruction of both wolf and deer alike.

The buck, a fourteen pointer, had lived far beyond the expected life span of a deer its size and age. This was true especially in the age of man, with hunters of all sizes and shapes routinely invading the woods hoping to bring home a trophy. The buck had continued to elude both man and wolf alike through hundreds of hunts over a multitude of years. The giant antlers spread atop its head reminded the wolf of the oak tree branches and their leaves. The rack, coveted by man, gave the buck an almost regal quality. Majestic.

The buck moved closer no longer afraid of the leader of the wolf pack. A Beast had recently come to their forest. The two must find a way to counter it quickly.

In modern times, *demon* would be the name given by man, if one had had the misfortune of meeting the beast in the forests while hunting.

The animals feared the beast more than they did the knives and rifles of man. If a hunter and the beast entered this clearing now, at the same time, they would have run towards the hunter. It would have not mattered if the man was armed with a weapon. The demon would have torn them limb from limb drinking their blood, grinding their bones with its teeth and devouring their souls.

If one of the farmers had met the demon while driving one of the machines used to rob the earth of its bounty, it would not have mattered. The demon would have leaped into the machine and dragged the man out screaming.

In years past, the previous men who had inhabited this land, those who were nomadic and travelled from place to place, those men would have called the beast *Wendigo*. Modern man believed, incorrectly of course, the natives of old followed the herds of animals that migrated across the bountiful land in order to maintain a steady supply of food. However, the animals knew the truth, even if they had never seen a demon of the forest before. The natives were nomadic to avoid *Wendigo*. Fear, not hunger, had driven the Native Men to a nomadic lifestyle.

The two animals, unaware of the names given by man in modern times and in ancient times agreed the name given by the animals, the Beast, would suffice. What else but a beast, would devour all in its path not caring whether it was predator or prey, injured or sick, young or old, weak or strong. Both animals stared unblinking at each other. Both thought about that first attack which had occurred a few weeks ago.

It had entered the woods and hunting fields without warning, without invitation, bringing with it an insatiable appetite for flesh and blood. From where it had come, none of the animals knew, but they quickly learned the only way to survive was to avoid the Beast at all cost.

The Beast glided on two legs, similar to that of a man. Long, matchstick thin legs, which crackled and popped as it ran. It also had two arms, as most men had, and had attempted to cover itself in the fashion of man. The wolves had seen hunters, as they hid in the forests, enough to make an accurate comparison.

Paper-thin cloth, yellow and brown, stained by years of use and smeared with blood and dirt covered its chest and extremities. What might have been moccasins covered its gangly feet. Beyond that all similarities to man ended.

It had come across the fields of growing corn and soybeans, through unplowed pastures blossoming with prairie grass and other weeds, over the creeks which snaked to and fro from the Kaskaskia River which meandered southwest across the landscape to meet the mighty Mississippi. The Beast had come without warning; startling both wolf and deer alike with its ferocity and its power. It had come to wreak havoc, death, and destruction on both predator and prey alike. Moreover, it had come to feed.

The first meeting with the Beast had shaken the wolf pack to its core. It had come unannounced one evening as both predator and prey were locked in the never-ending battle which drives those hunting and those being hunted. It had moved with power and speed, graceful as any deer and powerful as any wolf, ripping asunder all in its path.

It was an unnatural moment couched in a natural event, which had been occurring since the dawn of time from the moment predator had hunted prey.

The pure elation, evident by the gaping smile stretched across its leathery brown face from ear to ear, shined brightly in the gleaming eyes and the bloodstained fangs in the coming moonlight. The first deaths were the hardest because they had been completely unexpected. The beast had not distinguished predator from prey in its attack.

Fear had hammered itself into the heart of the wolves, especially those who had witnessed the first attack. That it did not distinguish between wolf and deer, between predator and prey, while it sought the flesh and blood of others only added to the confusion and the fear.

In that first attack weeks ago the lone deer became the first to realize that something unnatural had entered the forests. The deer was able to do so because of its keen sense of smell.

The pervasive odor of death and rotting flesh floated across the forest, through the fields, and over the creeks.

Oftentimes, not knowing the source of a smell, the deer would simply flee in what might be the opposite direction, hoping to avoid the source of the putrid odor. However, this smell was too pungent. It was not something the doe had smelled before.

In the forest, deep in the woods, there were numerous smells, which were to be avoided. This one shook the deer to its core.

Shivering, not because of the coming of night, the deer discontinued chewing on the grass at her feet and lifted her head. Its big, brown eyes searched the surrounding trees for any signs of movement. Its ears perked up listening for any sounds, which might help it figure out the source of the new odor coming from the nearby woods.

The smell permeated the woods. The deer became confused. The odor was not coming from upwind, yet neither was it coming from downwind. It was everywhere.

Appearing on the first hunt of the summer season the eight members of the pack were excited to begin. They began to encircle the deer hoping to trap it. If all else failed, they would be put in a position to run the deer to the point of exhaustion.

The arrival of the Beast immediately altered the animals of the forest. The views of nature imprinted within them eons ago became irrelevant. The Beast pushed the survival instincts of all animals in the forest to new limits.

On that day, the pack was not whole, but there were certainly enough wolves to hunt and kill the doe. The deer, confused about the source and direction of the smell of death, which hung thick in the air like a blanket in the wind, continued to turn her head confused.

It had picked up the smell of the wolves, too. However, the addition of the unknown odor confused the doe enough to prevent it from knowing which direction to flee. She was old enough to know not to panic, but had been unnerved enough to know the foul stench of death could be in any direction she chose.

Members of the pack had smelled the stench of decay, also, but had sighted the deer almost at the same time. The thrill of the hunt drove them forward not realizing the deer had something more than them to fear. They moved into position hoping to catch the deer unaware. They were mindful, though, that the deer most likely had caught their odor and was plotting a path to escape. There were eight of them. Their strength in numbers had always afforded them the strength needed to finish the hunt and would continue to do so.

The small deer, a female, smelled the wolves, too.

Clearly disoriented about the direction from which the wolves might be coming the doe knew it would have to wait for the hunt to begin and hope whichever direction it led her she would be safe from the source of the foul stench now permeating the air.

Lifting her head high the doe circled around nervously wondering from which direction the first attack would occur. Hooves pawed listlessly at the dirt and grass, hoping to create a small crevice from which the deer could initiate its first leap. That first leap might mean life or death depending on how much of an opening, how much separation it provided between the doe and the pack. Though only seconds had gone by it seemed an eternity in the quiet forest. The other inhabitants of the forests, the birds and the insects, and even the wind, had gone quiet.

Separating into two the pack of eight became two packs of four. Noiselessly the two packs moved into position through the dense undergrowth of the forest floor. Each instinctively knew its part to play. Whether it was through years of training, or whether it was something passed down from wolf to pup instinctively, the members of the wolf pack had grown into the dominant predators in this forest.

Those to the north of the deer circled ahead anticipating the others to the south would eventually drive the doe towards their path. They glided noiselessly ahead taking up positions, which would allow them to either continue or end the hunt.

The wolves hoped to drag the deer to the ground after it ran out of energy. The hunt would begin soon. Hunger and the thrill of the hunt mixed to an almost unbearable level in the younger members of the pack. The less experienced knew, though, they were to wait until it was initiated by the more experienced wolves.

Years of instinct and training had allowed the pack to survive in a changing world.

The doe inhaled sharply again, still unsure about the direction from which the wolves might begin their assault.

Snorting and blowing steam into the evening air, the doe also quickly realized its immediate survival required pushing aside any fears of the unknown odor. The hunt would begin at any moment. Pawing the ground, again, the deer lifted its head even higher trying to look for any sign of movement from the wolves.

The deer knew it would be no match for a pack of wolves if it became trapped or if it fell during the pursuit. Its only hope was to flee, bounding around trees, and hoping to make it to the edge of the forest into the open fields. One or two wolves versus the speed and grace of the deer were an even match. However, the smell of numerous wolves hung in the air and the doe knew the chances of survival were slim. It could feel the beating of its own heart quickening with every second and knew it was time to act. To the doe, every second counted and it would be most unwise to wait any longer.

The deer bolted quickly, bounding over a rotted log hoping the path chosen would be one that led to safety, to survival. Long-strides would have to help it gain some space. That distance might be enough to allow the doe to outrun the pack.

Two of the wolves, in the group to the south must have had some warning the doe was going to spring into action. Almost instantly, they bolted towards the doe, each working together to herd her to the north. Two more wolves sprang from nearby bushes clearly hoping to guide her in the direction they wanted her to travel.

Flashes of black, grey, and brown seemed to flit through the trees picking up speed. Flashes of color bounced around the trees, weaving in and out, as the wolves began the hunt.

Some of the wolves ran in silence, some snarled, some snapped at the deer with sharpened fangs as white as snow. None of the wolves howled, though. This specific trait had been passed from one generation to the next in this pack, located in the woods of Southern Illinois. The sound of wolves' howling would be carried for miles on the open wind. After the great migration, the leaders of the pack had decided their survival depended on secrecy. The survival of the wolves, who would not howl had ensured to this very day no one knew that a pack as strong as theirs hunted in this very forest.

For an instant, it seemed if the young doe was going to have enough space to run around the enclosing circle of wolves. The instant was only a fleeting one. Two wolves inched closer, tightening the invisible noose even more.

She turned and fled to the north hoping her stamina and the strength of her legs would be enough to save her. She was young, though, and did not realize the pack was going to be this relentless in its pursuit.

The wolves would continue to hound and pursue her. If there were a moment at which the four wolves would begin to tire, based on instinct and training, wolves to the north would pick up the pursuit. They would track the doe until her energy ran out and her heart had felt as if it were going to explode. Then, as she slowed enough, the pack would close in and one of the wolves, if not all, would move in for the kill.

If though, she could put enough of a distance between herself and the pack, they might become discouraged, at least that is what the deer had hoped. The plan was sound except the doe soon realized there were new smells up ahead.

The smell of death and decay once again mingled with the smell of the wolf pack. The doe frantically scanned the nearby shadows ahead.

Instinct told her the smell came from some of those shadows up ahead. That smell should be avoided at all cost.

A pair of unknown eyes peered at the deer as it fled through bushes and around trees. The stench was overpowering.

The doe was not sure why the wolves continued the pursuit. Surely, they could smell it too.

Losing its focus the deer nearly tripped over a broken log. It recovered quickly and continued running.

How did they not smell what was all around them? The deer was not sure if the shadows of the forests trees were alive or dead.

Eventually, it became evident this hunt was nearing its end and would most likely end in death.

The doe knew it was doomed, but nature demanded it continue to flee bounding along away from the snapping jaws that pushed it further and further north. Both predator and prey knew exhaustion would overcome them at some point. The energy of the deer was gone. It had been sapped from the relentless pursuit of the pack.

As those wolves to the south began to tire and their pace seemed to slacken, the deer seemed to pull further and further ahead, but if only for a brief moment.

That moment respite was not enough, though.

It did not provide the deer with a false sense of comfort. The wolves may have noticed, but did not seem to show any despair.

There was the understanding with the pack members ahead, those to the north. These wolves would take up the pursuit and continue the grinding pace pushing the deer to the limits of its stamina. The southern part of the pack slowed their pace, their job finished. Their brothers and sisters in hiding places to the north immediately took up the pursuit. Eventually the deer slowed tiring from the relentless pursuit. Three of the wolves were all that remained of those chasing the deer. The fourth, new to the chase had run into a tree, disorienting it long enough for the deer to bound away from its sight.

The doe finally made it to the edge of the forest, bolting from between a mass of trees and shrubs. Clearly, the open-field offered the opportunity for the deer to pick up its pace and separate from the pursuing pack. Nevertheless, the doe sapped of its strength from the long pursuit slowed and the predator, re-energized by a fresh set of legs felt the finality of the hunt and picked up speed. Both knew the struggle was almost over. One wolf, a young male, eager to make its first kill moved in quickly coming up behind the doe. The jaws of the young wolf clamped down tightly on a hind leg and both predator and prey collapsed to the ground in a pile of exhaustion. The wolf clamped down tightly shutting its eyes. It held on knowing if it could hold the prey long enough others in the pack would soon arrive.

The two remaining pack members trotted towards the tangle of deer and wolf, weaving through the trees.

They were startled as something bolted past them, almost shoving them aside in its rush to get to the deer first. The Beast exited the forest, a wide-gaping smile, which seemed to spread across its leathery face from ear to ear. It took two bounding strides leaped into the air and landed squarely on both wolf and deer alike.

The speed with which the new predator had moved caught the two young wolves off guard. The initial reaction had been one of survival causing them both to retreat slowly, a few steps. Growls of anger and frustration filled the forests as the wolves realized what they had done. They moved forward slowly growling loudly hoping to warn the intruder away. It was their task to help their brother and preserve the kill for the pack.

The wolves barked a warning to the lone wolf. Its fangs still clamped on to the hind leg of the deer, eyes shut, holding onto the deer so it could not escape. They realized their fellow pack member was unaware there was now a new beast, another predator.

The final leap of the Beast brought it squarely onto the back of the young, male wolf. Eyes popped open, the wolf expected to see the other members of the wolf pack there to help finish the kill. Instead, the wolf looked up into the bloodstained eyes of a Beast.

These eyes had no soul. For the first time in its young life, other than when it had been a pup, the wolf knew the meaning of fear.

The wide-gaping mouth filled with razor-sharp fangs glistened even in the waning light.

A forced whine from the wolf as it quickly released its hold on the deer was the only sound, which filled the night.

Turning to flee, the Beast seized the wolf in both hands before it could leap away. One hand locked tightly around the back of the wolf's neck.

The Beast had grabbed the wolf behind its head with one hand and with the other hand clamped down on the wolf along its lower back. Vice-like fingers squeezed tightly, the talons of the Beast piercing through the thick hair of the wolf. The yelp of the wolf, which lasted only a brief moment, floated through forest to the other members of the pack.

Its long fingers squeezed tightly, the beast rose to its full height of more than seven feet. It lifted the wolf above its head and began stretching each arm in opposite directions.

The beast smiled with elation squeezing the wolf's neck even more tightly. The sound of crunching bones lifted through the forests. Claws dug into the wolf's pelt snapping the neck of the young animal. The beast continued to hold the wolf above its head as a sadistic laughter filled the forests.

"Haaaaaaaaaa Haaaaaa! Heee Heeee!!!" screamed the Beast as it raised the wolf and tore it into two.

It turned on the two approaching wolves, both who were too young and had never before heard laughter, especially after a kill.

Startled, they again cowered and retreated a few steps.

The Beast immediately crawled over to the deer and sank its fangs into the neck. The Beasts' eyes glowered with delight. It stretched both of its arms out and grabbed the two halves of the dead wolf. Lifting its head towards the sky, the Beast opened its mouth widely. It began to feed. It began to devour the remains of the wolf.

Emboldened once more the two wolves charged. They began to growl at the Beast, jaws snapping. Made reckless by the anger felt at one of their pack killed and by the threat of losing the deer.

The Beast responded by standing up to its full height towering above the charging wolves. The Beast, with blood dripping down its leathery face, met their charge with an open almost welcoming stance, elated at the prospect of having more to eat.

The fangs of any wolf should be enough to disembowel most animals. These fangs were met by razor sharp talons, which protruded a few inches from each of the leathery fingers.

These fingers grasped the legs of the wolves as the two had simultaneously leaped at the Beast. The Beast clamped down with its fingers backed by powerfully muscular arms on a front leg of each. The beast whirled and flung the wolves hurling them twenty feet across the field. Neither wolf was injured by the collision with the ground. They both rolled to a stop and leaped up again, facing the Beast.

Both immediately reasoned they were not a match for the Beast. They fled the field seeking out the remaining wolves to warn them about the dangers of the Beast, which had come to kill and to feed.

The Beast's eyes glowered in the night air, its jaws widening with delight as it turned once again and began to feed on the remains of both predator and prey. Lapping up blood, chewing through skin, tearing through muscle and chomping through bone, the Beast ignored the other sounds of the forests. Oblivious, as it fed, it did not notice the arrival of the Alpha male.

The Alpha had observed the hunt from a distance. It exited the nearby forest a few hundred yards to the south hoping to find its pack feeding on the doe.

The Alpha male had caught the scent of the Beast far before actually seeing it.

It neared the kill and saw the remains of the young wolf as it was being devoured. Anger and fear leaped into his heart. The Alpha slowed his pace and paused about fifty yards away.

The Alpha knew the other wolves should have been here at the kill, but were obviously keeping their distance.

It knew something unnatural had entered their territory. There were eight pack members in this hunt, but the Alpha knew none of the wolves dared go any closer to the Beast otherwise the pack would have already done so.

Unnerved by what it was witnessing the large, grey wolf backed away slowly. Growling, the Alpha barked a command at the others nearby and the pack immediately dispersed, loping quietly and quickly away from the feeding frenzy of the Beast.

The Beast smiled, giggling with delight as it continued to feed on the remains of the wolf and the deer.

It had been nearly six weeks since the *demon, the beast, the Wendigo,* had come into forest at the beginning of summer. Nearly six weeks since both wolf and deer had begun to share one commonality.

Both were now being hunted. Both were being tracked down in the dead of night.

Both were being killed. Both were being eaten. Both were being devoured by the Beast in the woods.

The death of the Alpha male, a week ago, as well as the death of three other members of the pack, all devoured by the Beast, and the death of countless numbers of deer had forced each of these species to look for options. Neither wanted to leave the lands of their ancestors.

The two animals, one **predator**, one **prey**, met in the open field just before the coming of dawn. They met, not to continue the constant struggle nature demanded, but to offer a truce to one another. They met for the protection of their species before the Beast devoured all.

As the dew of morning evaporated and rose in blankets of steam into the morning sky, the wolf and deer made a pact, a truce, for the protection of both. No longer would they be enemies created by nature's struggle, but would work together for the common cause of both species' survival.

The unspoken bond hung in the air. The dominant buck and the Alpha female eyed each other clearly understanding if they were going to survive, they must work together.

It would not be enough to run, to hide, or to fight. Both had agreed the Beast would eventually find them. It would only be a matter of time. The Beast would hunt them into extinction.

They must find a place where even the Beast might fear to go.

If sanctuary were available, they would have to find it. They would have to find it quickly. The appetite of the Beast was insatiable.

Both knew, as they looked to the east, remembering what lay beyond the woods and through the fields and over the creeks. Both knew there was only one place to which they could go.

Their instinct to survive had caused both wolf and deer alike to avoid this place for more than a hundred years.

The place called to them, a sanctuary. It was only used desperate times.

The wolf turned away intent on gathering the few remaining members of its pack. The deer also turned with the hopes of gathering the remaining deer in the forests. They would meet together on the edge of the forest, in the morning. They would meet where the forests bled into the fields planted by the humans.

Those who were still alive would meet and together they would seek the refuge.

They would meet together wolf and deer, predator and prey, enemies in nature, for the common survival of all.

If sanctuary did not exist, if the knowledge passed from one generation to the next was not true they were all in trouble.

The knowledge that this place of safety might be available to all who were brave enough to find it was etched into their very DNA.

This place was safety, but it had also been forbidden for hundreds of years. If in the forbidden place, there was no sanctuary, then they were all doomed.

PART I
WHAT WAS BEFORE

ONE

THE GREAT MIGRATION

*Gather around me children. Huddle closer to the camp-fire with your friends and family as I re-tell the story of **what was before** and what comes after. Remember always the lessons to be learned. Remember always the traditions of our ancestors. Remember always the ghosts of our fathers and their fathers before them. When thinking about the '**what comes after**' remember always your obligation to re-tell the story of what was before and what must always be.*

Eons ago, long before the deer bounded over open fields of prairie grass which stood high enough to cover a full grown man from foot to head, long before the bear dipped its claws into the waters for salmon in ice-cold streams, long before the wolves decided for their own protection that they would no longer howl, long before the elk and the rabbit, long before the squirrel and the birds, long before the rivers meandered through the land, and long before the lakes provided life sustaining water, and long before the trees provided shelter and shade, and long before the sky rested above the world, there was the Great Father.

As he looked down upon the land from above, nestled in his tepee warmed by a multitude of stars the Great Father smiled with tears of joy. Those drops of tears fell like meteors crashing down into the land creating the lakes and the rivers. Laughing with joy at what had happened, the great father hit the land with his hands. The mighty force of those hands broke apart the land creating deep valleys and creating gigantic mountains and gently rolling hills. As he looked down upon the land from above, the Great Father smiled once again, happy with what he had done.

Gentle rays of light, provided from the stars above, glistened off the shimmering waters and he was glad. The Great Father realized that the only way to add to this wonder called Nature was to add the plants and the animals. With a wave of his hand all of the animals and plants of nature sprang up around the world. Again the Great Father was pleased with what he had done.

As he smiled with pride, the Great Father's light of happiness brought color to the land. Green grass, purple flowers, yellow feathers, and red lava, it did not matter. The colors of the rainbow were born. He was so happy with the colors provided by the light of his smile that the Great Father reached into his own mouth and plucked out one of his teeth. He stuck it in the sky, so that it might provide light to the creatures of nature in the daytime until the end of time.

Looking down from above, at the animals and the plants that he had created, the Great Father was once again pleased with what was before. He immediately realized that only one thing could make nature even better. With that he plucked one of the hairs from his eyebrows laying it gently in his palm. Nai Pa Ta was created. The Great Father gently blew on Nai Pa Ta and in doing so breathed life into the mighty Sauk warrior. The Great Father then placed Nai Pa Ta gently down among the forests surrounding the five Great Lakes in the north. And once again the Great Father smiled pleased with what he had done.

So that Nai Pa Ta would not wander the earth alone, the Great Father plucked another eyebrow and placed the Great Mother Na Na Pe upon the earth to live alongside Nai Pa Ta. The Great Father was pleased and watched with enthusiasm as these two learned to live as one with Nature. He was especially pleased when he saw that the two had grown to love one another and had children who had children who had children. Once again, the Great Father smiled a knowing smile because his work here was almost done. The Great Father then withdrew silently to his place among the stars to watch forever as the children of Nai Pa Ta and Na Na Pe grew into a family, blossomed into a clan, and might someday develop into a great tribe.

Even now he watches all of you children, you who are descendants of Nai Pa Ta and Na Na Pe. He watches you as you rise in the morning. He watches you as you help your mothers with your chores or as you help your fathers gather and hunt in order to provide for your family, and your tribe. Each evening he watches you intently as you gather with your parents around the camp-fire to learn about What Was Before and What Comes After. He watches pleased to know that you respect your elders and you love your family. He watches pleased with each of you. As you lay your head down to sleep know that the Great Father is pleased with the work you have done today.

Great Lakes Region Indian Tale of the Great Father

CATAMOUNT

Life in the Great Lakes Region of North America, in the thousands of years prior to the arrival of the white-skinned, yellow-skinned, and brown-skinned people from the other side of the oceans, had been a spectacular sight to behold. Thousands of years before the land was invaded by Europeans and Asians, the Indian Tribes of the Great Lakes region lived in peace with each other one day and then warred on each other the next, depending on the availability of resources, and the season. That they all were descended from the same ancestors who had crossed an ice-bridge between the continents, millennial years before, did not matter.

Those common ancestors had migrated from one continent to the next crossing rivers and mountains and desert looking for new homes. As they explored the new continent these groups splintered apart, created new clans, and blossomed into news tribes. And then when the local resources were stretched to their limits they splintered again. North America, with its vast areas of wilderness and wildlife provided homes to hundreds of Indian tribes and hundreds of thousands of people.

Thus, in the early years when the white men arrived in their heavy ships, floating up river to explore the supposedly uncharted lands they were met with a wide-array of Native American Indian cultures many of which were unique and vastly different from one another.

The Chippewa were an Indian tribe located in present day Michigan, Wisconsin, and sporadically settled in parts of modern day Canada. Their cousins were the Potawatomi, those tribes who would attempt, years later, to force the white-man out his fort and back towards the East, from where they came.

The Huron Indians occupied parts of similar territory in the north, often-times coming into conflict with the Chippewa and their cousins. They were a large tribe and would routinely attempt to exhibit a heavy influence on the other tribes and their movements.

Lesser influential tribes such as the Miami were forced south and east and their migrations led to them into settling into present day Indiana. The Sauk or Sac and their cousins the Fox were smaller and lesser known Indian tribes of the Great Lake Region.

The land near the Great Lakes in those days teemed with life. Forests of green trees were filled with animals of all varieties. Herds of deer numbered easily in the hundreds of thousands, if not the millions, and provided ample opportunity for the tribes to be well-fed. In addition to the deer, the bear and the rabbit, the elk and the fox, the squirrel and the ground hog, a wide and varied group of animals inhabited the great forests of North America. The Great Lakes teemed with fish of all varieties. Atlantic salmon could be caught along the banks of any of the Great Lakes on any given day. Indians who skimmed across the lakes in canoes were able to catch the trout, the chinook, and other types of fish. Life, in the Great Lakes region, while constantly a battle with Nature and a battle with each other, was good.

The Great Lakes region was settled either through peaceful means or through combat by the various Indian tribes that competed with each other for those resources. The fields were vibrant with colors of bright blue, and green, and purple and red. Flowers blossomed in the spring and provided pollen to the millions of bees which pollinated them each summer. On a clear day the azure sky seemed to float overhead like an ocean of air. The resources of the Great Lakes Region were ample for life to exist.

One day, early in the 1600s, a boat arrived and brought with it white men whose scruffy beards and odd manner of speech and dress both awed the Indians and caused a fear of what was to come. As they came into contact with the various local Indian tribes it seemed the heat of a slow pressure cooker had been turned on. It would only be a matter of time before the Old World and the New would clash causing the pressure cooker to explode. Initially, the white man few in number appeared easily managed. The encroachment onto traditional tribal land was dealt with individually, but swiftly. Some men were allowed to stay and to trap for furs. These men made the necessary adjustments by learning the languages and manners of the local tribes. These men often traded with the tribes and offered respect for the cultures with which they were interacting.

Others, though, were dispatched immediately by the various local tribes of the Great Lakes. These men struggled to understand that the Indian tribes were a part of Nature and should be revered and respected. These men were dispatched and their goods confiscated for the good of the tribe. Their journey into the Great Void had little impact on Indian life.

Thus, the Indian tribes adjusted to the introduction of the Europeans without much upheaval in their everyday lives.

Eventually, those Europeans, the whites who had invaded the Indian lands grew in numbers. Their populations grew and it became clear they meant to colonize the lands of the Indians. Cabins were built. Eventually these cabins grew into forts for their own safety and protection.

One of these forts, Fort Dearborn, as it was known by the Europeans, or the Wooden Village, the name given by the Indians, finished being built in the early 1800s. Initially, the Indians expressed their complaints to the local military leaders of the whites. When those complaints weren't heeded, the local Potawatomi tribe, supported from warriors from a few other tribes attacked the fort, slaughtered the soldiers and drove off the remaining settlers. The fort was burned to the ground.

One of the local tribes, a sub-tribe of the Sac Indians, refused to offer warriors to participate in the attack on the fort. The Chief Kai Ta had many misgivings about what would happen when the whites eventually returned. And return they would, at least that had been his prediction.

The other tribes, though, weren't happy with this refusal. A series of skirmishes between the tribe and others within the Great Lake Region followed, eventually slowing as the tribes returned to the ever-present battle with Nature for resources.

By 1812, word was brought to the leaders of each tribe that the Europeans had returned in force and were beginning to rebuild Fort Dearborn. Emissaries from the nearby tribes arrived at the village of Chief Kai Ta to requests support for another attack.

It became immediately clear to Kai Ta that this was not a request, but was a demand. Either the Indian tribe would provide warriors to attack the new fort or the nearby tribes would send their warriors to wipe out the tribe. Kai Ta was distraught about both choices.

Eventually, out of the pressure provided by the powerful Huron and other powerful tribes of the Great Lakes region, and the fear of an oncoming conflict with the encroaching whites, Kai Ta made the decision to take his people and migrate away from the pressure cooker of the Great Lakes region.

Chief Kai Ta gave the warriors within his tribe the option to flee with his clan or to remain and help with the attack on the newly built fort. Some members of the tribe splintered away and fled east hoping to find available territory along the eastern portion of one of the Great Lakes. The remainder of the tribe, led by the Chief Kai Ta, took a different route and headed south.

In the dead of the night, the tribe slipped out of their tepees and headed towards the south. They decided to travel by night hoping to avoid conflicts with other Indian tribes. Especially those whose territory they were going to have to cross.

Kai Ta made the decision to move the whole tribe south, towards the lands near the St. Louis region. While the St. Louis region was occupied by nearly 8,000 residents from Europe, life towards the east was still primarily controlled by the local Indian populations. In the months before, returning cousins, from the south, had described how many of the forests teemed with life and conflict with the whites over land and resources had been almost unheard of. The Europeans had settled mainly along the Mississippi river banks.

Thus, in the middle of the night, the Indians packed up all of their belongings and fled, travelling by night time, by the light of the moon, leaving the home of their ancestors.

On the end of the third night of their journey, Chief Kai Ta quietly gave the signal for the tribal members to halt. The other members of the tribe responded to the signal by moving to settle into a nearby thicket of trees to wait out the coming day.

He swelled with pride knowing the men, the women, and the children of his tribe had traveled quietly through the unknown forests without complaint. Strict discipline had been imperative if they were to move unscathed through the lands of unknown and possibly hostile tribes.

Kai Ta was completely aware he had pushed what remained of his tribe almost to the breaking point. They had walked south using the stars as a guide. They travelled only at night hoping to avoid other Indian tribes.

On this night the sky lit up brightly with a full-moon hanging over the heads of the tribe in the waning hours of the March night. Stars dotted the sky adding to the luminescence. Silently, his warriors positioned themselves around the perimeter of the rest of the tribe. In each cluster of warriors a few settled down to eat while their comrades grabbed some much needed sleep. The others, in pairs, would remain awake until their shift was over.

The women of the tribe handed out pre-made breads to each member of the tribe. They walked to the warriors first, offering up food, water, and smiles. Kai Ta smiled at his wife who had brought him a pouch of water and a snack. She reached down rubbing his head and moved on to others.

"She is a good woman." He thought to himself.

Leaning back on a small birch tree he watched his fourteen year old son Cha Kai Ta who was walking amongst the other warriors offering words of encouragement. His other son, Nai Pa, was only eight years old and had already settled at his father's feet to sleep out the day.

Cha Kai Ta, a young warrior already much too tall for his age, frowned deeply looking down at his brother. The older brother's dissatisfaction wore heavily on his face.

"He should be helping the others." He thought to himself.

After staring at his sleeping brother for a few seconds Cha Kai Ta turned towards his father.

"This is no way for the son of a chief to behave." He said to his father. He gestured with his head at his brother who lay sleeping at his father's feet.

"Good evening, my son." The Chief said. He reached up and shook his son's hand as Cha Kai Ta nodded at his father.

The younger warrior moved on clearly happy that his father had acknowledged him.

The howls of coyotes filled the air. With the remaining minutes of darkness winding down the sun broke ever so slightly above the horizon to the east. Kai Ta closed his eyes knowing that one of his warriors would wake him in a few hours to take his turn guarding the perimeter.

The sleek, brown cougar limped along gingerly through the three feet high prairie grass. It continued to trail the tribe of humans who only seemed interested in travelling during the night time.

The large cat had been trailing the humans for two days and two nights hoping to pick off one of the younger ones. More than one of his meals had come from other tribes and their little ones who had strayed away too far.

The catamount limped on, acutely aware of the throbbing pain in its front right paw. Three days before the three year old male had been running down a small beaver which had left the water for a brief moment. In the chase it had been unaware that the hunt would take it dangerously close to a thorn patch.

The momentum carried both the beaver and the cat into a thick grove of bushes. Clamping down on the beaver with its fangs the large cat recklessly stepped its paw onto a broken plant stem. Its paw was pierced deeply by a thorn which ended up being wedged in between two of its toes. The sharpness of the pain grew and within a few hours it became apparent the traditional way of catching food wasn't going to work. Most animals were too quick and the big cat needed stealth and quickness in order to hunt.

Barely able to put weight on the paw the cougar had cleaned the wound with its sandpaper-like tongue. Eventually the thorn was removed, but the pain remained. The result was a throbbing pain and a growing hunger.

The young cougar knew it did not have the strength and speed to catch anything to eat. It was getting very desperate, almost to the point of madness, when it smelled the humans. Crouching down in a nearby tree it watched them closely.

They moved in a large group methodically across the fields of grass and trees. In the darkness its big brown eyes, which were adapted to night-time hunting, easily spotted the little ones who walked in the center of the traveling group. The mountain lion's hunger made its stomach growl. It drooled heavily thinking about catching one of the little ones.

It was at that moment desperation took over and the big cat knew it would have to trail these humans, and hopefully, one of them would move away from the group long enough. It could then have itself an easy meal.

That was two days ago. The cougar was becoming overly frustrated.

The humans seemed to be packed too close together for it to launch an attack. The smaller humans were kept to the interior of the group while the larger ones, the males, especially those who carried sticks and other things in their hands, patrolled on the outside of the group.

The group travelled at night and then when the sun began to creep up towards the edge of the horizon they would settle down in a grove of trees. The group was much disciplined, seemingly intent on protecting the most vulnerable ones from attack.

On this day, as the group settled in, the cougar flattened its body down as low as it could towards the ground and slowly, very systematically, began a belly crawl towards the humans. Its body was hidden from anyone's sight within the grass of the forests. It crept forward silently slithering along the ground like a giant snake.

One of the females of the group, the one who had moved around from human to human, passing out items and smiling to others in the group, said something and started walking towards the perimeter. One of the males, the one who had been sitting with his back against a tree, said something to a younger one who picked up an item and began following the woman. The cat flattened its body closer to the ground. Changing direction it began moving silently towards the path of the small, brown-skinned woman.

After checking on all of the members of the tribe, Me Na Te, the wife of the chief, was happy that everyone seemed to be in good spirits after another difficult night. The tribe had moved silently, and slowly, southward towards their new home. She completely supported her husband's decision to move the tribe, but she had not realized how much of a strain the journey would be both physically and mentally. As the Chief's wife it was on her shoulders to be cheerful, to be happy, and to be strong. That was not an easy task.

"*I might have to be strong,*" she thought, "*for the sake of the tribe.*"

That did not mean she could not sneak off away from the others and while relieving herself she could shed some tears. That's what she had decided to do.

She briefly made eye contact with Kai Ta, smiled, and gestured with her head towards the nearby bushes. She wanted to let him know she was going into the woods to pass water. The Chief nodded in agreement made a quick statement to their oldest son and leaned his head back up against the bark of the tree.

She saw him close his eyes hoping to get a few moments of rest. Before doing so he had glanced down at his younger son, Nai Pa who seemed fast asleep.

In reality, the eight year old was wide-awake and taking in all that was going on. He continued to do his best to fool everyone into believing he was fast asleep.

Kai Ta had been aware his youngest son was actually awake. He had been impressed at the curiosity and the quick wittedness of his eight year old son and had decided not to address it. He had thought for a moment of telling his son to quit pretending to sleep and to go help his mother.

Rather than chastise his son, though, he simply smiled to himself and drifted off to sleep.

Cha Kai Ta nodded to his father, immediately picked up a bow and arrow, and began to follow his mother.

She gave him a quick, stern look, which said, "*I am still your mother and you better give me my privacy.*"

She turned quickly and headed towards a thicket of bushes and trees which were about fifty yards from the group. Her fatigue was evident, not to others, but definitely to her. She hurried her pace hoping to get a few moments respite from the demands of being the wife of the Chief.

Cha Kai Ta slowed his pace, hoping not to anger his mother, but also wanting to follow his father's orders to guard her. The safety and discipline of the tribe required anyone who left the camp do so with another person.

The safety restrictions were in full effect though, ensuring anyone who needed to relieve themselves would be free to do so knowing they were being guarded and protected by someone else in the tribe.

At fourteen he was tall for his age. He was at least two hands lengths taller than the other fourteen year olds in the tribe. He had grown taller than his father and would often swell his chest with pride when his mother praised how big and strong he had become.

Both his father and mother agreed he had not quite done growing and would probably sprout up a few more inches.

As his mother quickened her pace the distance between the two of them widened.

His mother picked up her pace even more as she came to a clump of bushes. She circled around to the right moving around the bushes and between a few trees.

Cha Kai Ta was about fifteen seconds catching up to her and was surprised to hear she was being so noisy while on the other side of the bushes. The clump of bushes she was behind began to shake furiously as if his mother were purposely trying to shake off all of its leaves.

While he lay on his bedding the eight year old boy listened intently to the sounds of his mother who moved around to the members of the tribe.

It was clear to the boy she was the Chief's wife and felt an obligation to ensure everyone was getting the necessities before they settled in to sleep out the oncoming day.

Nai Pa had become very adept at pretending to be asleep and so far he felt like he had done a pretty good job of fooling everyone who came near him. He had heard the disgust in Cha Kai Ta's voice as he neared their father and could almost feel his brother's piercing stare. Even then, though, Nai Pa continued his deception.

Years ago, when he was about five seasons old, he had decided to practice the art of feigning sleep. His eyes, seemingly closed, were actually opened a sliver.

He had learned to listen carefully. He learned to read lips even with his eyes almost closed. Nai Pa had done so in order to listen in to the discussions many of the adults of the tribe would have whenever they came to his father's teepee each evening.

The aching of his muscles from the long journey would not allow him to settle down and actually get the much needed sleep his body demanded.

His brain filled with excitement from being on the journey.

He lay on his pad continuing to feign sleep. He listened to his older brother bark orders, to his mother while she offered words of encouragement, and listened to the sounds of his father breathing deeply while sleeping against the tree.

He watched his mother begin to walk towards the edge of the group and then he noticed his older brother pick up a bow and a quiver of arrows. He watched as Cha Kai Ta began to follow her.

Nai Pa rolled over slowly, stood up, and began to quietly follow his brother. If his brother was going to protect her then he was going to protect both of them. It was only fair.

The cougar lay in wait underneath the very bushes the small, brown-skinned woman was coming around. His body flattened out beneath the bushes, the cat watched her movements intently.

The big cat knew she, so far, had no idea he was hidden beneath those very bushes. His razor sharp claws extended from his paws and he slowly position himself to pounce on the woman.

She stopped a few feet from him and unknowingly turned to face him when she started to squat down. It was a split second before she realized they were face to face. Their eyes met for a brief moment each acutely aware of the other. That is when he pounced.

Me Na Te rounded the bushes hoping her older son would heed her wishes and give her a few minutes of privacy. She needed the time to shed the tears she had held back for the last two nights.

Turning to face the bushes, knowing Cha Kai Ta was just on the other side, she began to cry without making a sound. She started to squat down, but immediately froze.

Her eyes met the eyes of the catamount, widening for a brief instant. They both became aware of what was about to happen.

The big cat sprang like a coil launching itself the few feet needed to close the distance between them. She reacted by raising her arm, aware that its goal was to clamp down on her neck and snuff the life right out of her.

Me Na Te was mindful of the danger to her life and the danger to the tribe if she cried out loudly. As the wife of the chief and for the sake of her two children she decided to take the attack without making a sound.

Me Na Te absorbed the weight of the big cat courageously, but was knocked backwards onto the ground. She silently kicked and rolled the two of them into the bushes fighting for her life. The cougar clamped down more tightly on her forearm.

"Mother?!" Cha Kai Ta whispered, probably too harshly, hoping to remind her they were to maintain silence in the woods. The bushes continued to shake rapidly without any let up.

Cha Kai Ta decided it did not matter if she was his mother. His father had left strict orders and he needed to make sure they were followed. He walked forward towards the bush. He wasn't able to peer through since the leaves were so thickly clustered.

He turned and circled around the bushes following the path his mother had taken only seconds before.

He came around the bush ready to defend himself from his mother's fury and he was caught completely by surprise. A large cougar was straddling his mother its fangs clamped down on her right arm. His mother was doing her utmost to keep those same fangs from sinking into her throat as she silently fought to keep from succumbing to the dangerous predator.

Without thinking Cha Kai Ta reached to his side pulled his flint knife out of its sheath and jumped on top of the two of them. The big cat had been so caught up in its prey it did not see the young man who had leaped onto its back and stabbed with fury into its side. It immediately released its hold on the woman and squirmed its body into position to take on this new danger.

The catamount and Cha Kai Ta rolled over back and forth in a struggle to see who would have the upper hand.

They were briefly separated giving the cat the opportunity to reach up and take a large swipe at Cha Kai Ta with its good paw.

Large claws ripped three giant gashes into the right side of his face.

Everything seemed to be moving in slow motion. He saw his blood splatter onto the ground next to him.

Slowly, Cha Kai Ta looked to his mother who was lying motionless on the ground near the bushes.

"I'm going to die." he thought to himself as he fell backwards knocked to the ground by the massive paw of the cougar.

The cougar immediately sprang onto Cha Kai Ta and the two became embroiled in the same furious struggle which had been fought only a few seconds before between the cougar and the mother.

Slowly, the strength of the mountain lion began to win. Its fangs moved closer and closer to Cha Kai Ta. The gash in his face oozed blood. This seemed to embolden the catamount even more.

Curiosity got the best of Nai Pa when he saw his brother quickly circle around the shaking bushes that his mother had gone behind a few seconds before. The eight year old ran to the bushes and followed his brother.

Nai Pa tripped on the bow and arrow quiver Cha Kai Ta had dropped. He reached down and picked it up quickly.

Moving the rest of the way around the bushes he exhaled deeply as he saw a mountain lion knock his brother to the ground.

The big cat leapt onto his brother, completely unaware of Nai Pa's presence. His mother lay un-moving on the ground a few feet away.

Without thinking, he notched an arrow, pulled the string of the bow with all of his strength, and released the arrow.

His eyes widened. He saw the arrow strike the big cat on the side of the neck.

The oozing blood, the silent strength of the cat, the pain in his face, his mother lying motionless, all of these forced Cha Kai Ta to admit to himself that he was going to die.

Slowly, the fangs of the cougar moved closer to his face. His two hands were pressed around the neck of the cat, pressing outward with all his might in order to keep those fangs away from him.

He closed his eyes aware he would be helpless, regardless of what strength he had left, to prevent the inevitable. It was only when he heard the silent twang of an arrow being released that he opened his eyes.

The arrow pierced the neck of the mountain lion causing it to lose its grip on Cha Kai Ta.

The shaft of the arrow jutted out on one side while the arrowhead protruded from the other side of the big cat's neck.

As the life of the cat quickly died away and its weight sagged onto his own body, Cha Kai Ta looked over to see his eight year old brother breathing heavily holding his bow. Another arrow had been notched, but it was not necessary since the big cat had already died.

TWO

1818

SETTLERS

Early in the year 1812 the United States was a still a fledgling country comprised of eighteen states all located east of the Mississippi River. The tiny country had experienced the traditional growing pains which often come when one group of people throw off the yoke of oppression and tyranny forced on them by another.

Clearly, though, the British Empire carried a deep resentment toward its former citizens who now were the citizens of a newly created country in the New World. The English had not yet shrugged off the residual effects of the American War for Independence; or as it was known in Britain as the Colonial Uprising.

Out on the open seas, away from the Continental United States, American ships were being routinely boarded by the stronger British navy.

That this was an insult might have played into it, though the British saw it as an opportunity to enhance the ranks of sailors on British naval ships. American sailors were simply arrested by the British only to be impressed into service immediately as sailors on British naval vessels.

This was done to fill needed manpower aboard the ships of war for the British navy. This impressment was also meant to send a signal to the American citizens, who a few years prior, had been citizens of the British Empire.

The message, "You may have defeated us on land, but on the open seas, we still reign supreme."

America was determined to be too weak to intervene on behalf of its own citizens. This was evident since the pace of the impressment seemed to increase with the outcries of anger expressed by the American diplomats in London.

The result of these impressments, in the eastern part of the United States, was an immediate cry for war.

Many American citizens, though, did not want to directly challenge the supremacy of the British Empire. Many felt the impressments were a slap in the face to the former colonies, now independent.

The leaders of the country debated in the largest of America's cities, and in the nation's capital, for a response to the British insult to American sovereignty. Congress debated loudly while the newspapers of the eastern cities, such as Boston and New York, printed bold headlines which stoked the underlying anger and promoted the calls for war.

Articles were written which described many married women now left to fend for themselves and their families. All this while their husbands were forced to sail around the world Prisoners in all but name onboard British ships.

Many of the leaders in the country, which included the President James Madison, feared the country was in no position to protest too loudly since it could not match the strength of the English military.

America might be an independent country. It might be an insult to the sovereignty of the country, but backing up the outrage with military responses was another issue. President Madison was keenly aware America did not yet have a military to force the British to rethink the practice.

In the cities, though, the citizens of America were filled with a national pride which typically rears its head when there is a perceived insult by another nation.

Many continued calling for immediate declarations of war against England. The War Hawks in Congress demanded Congress immediately declare war and continually expressed their feelings in the newspapers against President Madison and his reluctance to fully engage the British. Congress, though, had enough War Hawks to tip the balance and as a result, the country began to prepare for the worst, another war with Great Britain.

In those years the tiny country of the United States of America stretched from an area west of Chicago in the north, with a population of about two-thousand five-hundred people all the way down to New Orleans in the south, along the Mississippi River.

The Atlantic Ocean made up the eastern boundary of this country. A country clearly on the brink of its second war in twenty-five years.

While the bigger cities in the East, such as Boston and New York beat the drums of war, further away from the east coast, the villages decreased in size and so did the population.

The farmers in the western part of the United States might have agreed with the notion that the actions of the British were atrocious, but there were far less cries for war. These farmers, many of whom were attempting to settle lands west, towards the Mississippi River, vaguely paid any attention to the goings on back east.

The western part of the United States in 1812, near the Mississippi River, was still pocketed with blankets of forests and large swaths of Prairie grass which seemingly ran for miles at a time.

Most of the people of the United States, who had moved west, had chosen to settle in the larger cities. Chicago, at that time, was mainly a conglomerate of hardy men and women whose lives were based on trade along the rivers. There were safety in numbers as small groups of settler villages opened up out on the current western frontier.

In 1812 British infantry divisions invaded the United States and marched unabated into the nation's capital of Washington D.C. President Madison barely escaped and fled into the nearby hills. Watching in silence as the symbol of America, the Presidential Manor was burned by British soldiers, the President wept openly in front of his staff.

The President's wife, Dolly, fled after her husband only staying long enough to save the Presidential Paintings, including the portrait of George Washington. Thus preserving some dignity for the United States and its President.

The War of 1812 brought the United States into another war against the strength of the British Empire. The battles would be fought in the east and the south, but those who had moved out west in search of farm land largely escaped the effects of war.

To these settlers the life they chose continued unabated by the War to the east. Many of them continued to move slowly further west looking for rich farmland on which to plant crops and build homes.

This movement westward brought many of them into conflict with the local Indian populations. The War of 1812 would continue to drag on for almost three years though it went largely unnoticed by the settlers.

In the United States, in 1815 the expansion west continued. During the War of 1812 many Indian tribes, who had learned of the war to the east, used the opportunity to force settlers back out of what they considered their lands.

Without American soldiers to support their claims on the Indian lands the settlers had the choice of fighting and probably dying, or giving up their cabins, their farm fields, and sometimes their livestock. The hardiest of these settlers, though, were not to be deterred and continued to move into land claimed by the Indians.

By 1818 Illinois was admitted into the United States, but the vast majority of the state's population was in the north in Chicago, or distributed around the state mainly in tiny villages. There were about thirty-five thousand '*Illinoisans*' counted at that time. To the south of Chicago, most of the land included vast stretches of prairie grass most of which continued to be home to many various Indian tribes.

The original settlers, as they passed into Illinois, were not impressed by the prairie grass and seemed completely unconvinced the dirt was capable of growing crops on a large scale.

Those settlers who were willing to try to build cabins and cultivate the land did so in opposition to the local Indian tribes.

Richard David Dryver was a thirty-six year old Irish man who a year before had picked up his wife and six children and loaded them onto a boat bound for the United States.

Family members, who had already made the journey, wrote back to describe the boundless land available to those brave enough to risk the journey. Richard looked at his pregnant wife and told his children they were going to the New World.

His seventh child was born on the ship which carried them across the Atlantic Ocean, a two-masted ship named the *Corinthian*.

Richard was so thankful his daughter was born healthy and alive. He immediately named her Corin. His wife, who recuperated for the remainder of the trip, exited the boat on her own two legs. Richard immediately gathered his children, ages six days to sixteen years and walked off the ships and into a bustling American city.

The culture shock, experienced by the immigrants such as Richard, soon wore off and he immediately went about buying supplies and three wagons.

Richard's goal was to also raise cattle. He hired a ranch hand, bought eleven cows, and one bull.

With the family and the wagons loaded the Dryvers headed west looking for a place to settle in the interior of America.

With hard work, though, the rewards could be great. Richard explained each evening, as the family sat around the campfire.

"Everything will be worth the trip, as long as we stick together."

"Everything will be worth the trip as long as we all work hard."

In 1818, Richard David Dryver and his family pulled the reins on the wagons and settled on a remote spot in the south of a newly approved state called Illinois.

Richard and his family immediately set out to cut down trees and within three weeks a cabin was built. It was a two room cabin, furnished with a few chairs and a wood burning stove.

Richard, the ranch hand named Tom Brown, and his oldest children quickly set about building a small barn with a room up top for Tom to live.

Each morning the family would run the cattle along the river to feed and water them. Cattle pens were going to be built and eventually, after a month or two, the farm looked to be in good order.

One morning, early before the rest of the family woke up; Richard Dryver took one of his sons outside to check on the cattle. Hearing a noise, the soft sound of feet running on grass, he rounded the cabin with his son.

"What was it Pa?" the son asked, clearly upset by the look on his father's face.

Richard Dryver looked at the footprints near the cabin and said, "Indians."

THREE
A WARRIOR'S COUNSEL

Gather around me children, for I have a tale to tell, that is as old as the dawn of time itself. Many years after the Great Father ascended into the heavens, to sit in his teepee near his ever-burning fire, to watch his children from above, their came into the world the father and mother of us all.

Content with watching, the Great Father was pleased to see Nai Pa Ta and Na Na Pe give birth to children whose children and whose children's children began to populate the forests near the Great Lakes. He was pleased to see the children continue the customs and ceremonies passed down from Nai Pa Ta and Na Na Pe from one generation to the next.

As the Great Tribes evolved and grew in size, many separated and moved from one lake to the next, populating the forests until finally, eleven strong tribes inhabited these pristine lands. Many strong warriors sprang up, and many often had conflict with the other, but the Great Father resisted the urge to intervene.

Ultimately, these tribes learned to live in harmony with each other, sharing nature's bounty, rather than trying to steal from each other. Wars had quickly become a thing of the past, and the warriors of the tribe respected the peace passed on to them from their ancestors. Though each tribe was unique with their languages and customs, they listened to their elders, knowing they had a kinship, which stretched back generations for as far as the eye could see.

Though each tribe fractures, splinters, and grows distant from their cousins, they are all linked together by their link to the Great Father. No matter how far they roam, no matter how many years go by, the eleven Great Tribes will be forever a part of the same family tree.

Great Lakes Region Indian Tale of the Great Tribes

COUSINS

It was a warm, summer morning.

Much of the tribe had finished breaking their fast from the previous evening when the cousins to the Sauk Indian tribe arrived unannounced. They sent an emissary asking for permission for four of their warriors to enter the village.

They were granted permission by Kai Ta, chief of the tribe, and welcomed with enthusiasm and genuine affection.

The four warriors gathered around the fire with the chief and the other warriors of his tribe hoping to swap stories of recent exploits. Following the typical formalities, which were a matter of tradition more than anything, the warriors finally offered the reason for their visit.

They notified the chief that white settlers had been spotted on their tribal lands along the Little Silver Creek. These settlers originally consisted of two families both of whom had built two cabins and were now raising cattle and growing crops.

The visiting warriors had been able to harass and scare off one family who packed up their belongings and headed back to the east. The other family resisted the efforts of the Indians to scare them away and was firmly entrenched.

The warriors of Kai Ta's tribe asked many questions, which also included the number of family members and how heavily each family was armed.

Sitting behind his father, the eldest son Cha Kai Ta, who was also known as Crow became furious. He leaned forward to whisper into his father's ear.

"Father!" he almost growled. "These settlers must be dealt with immediately."

Silently, Crow also cursed his cousins for bringing the information. Not that the settlers did not need to be dealt with, that was for sure.

However, it also meant their cousins had been trespassing on lands which were not their own. This offense raised an even bigger question. Surely, his father meant to deal with them too.

If they had been only passing through an emissary would have been sent to get permission from the Sauk. That had not been the case.

Crow was now convinced they had been hunting on Sauk Lands.

How they knew about the settlement was not raised in the conversation.

Yet surely, his father understood it could only mean they too had encroached on the lands of the Sauk Indians. They would have had to have been hunting on territory that was not theirs.

Crow sat silently fuming. He realized the encroachment by his cousins was another issue. That would be set aside and dealt with later. This issue would have to wait until a better opportunity presented itself.

If Crow had expected anger from his father, he was severely disappointed.

His father had not exploded with rage, as Crow knew he would have done if he were the chief. His father had not skinned his cousins alive. They had all but admitted they too had encroached on the Sauk Indian tribal lands.

His father had not shown any emotion about the settlers.

Crow's father, Chief Kai Ta, had been the chief of the tribe for more than twenty-three summers. He stood still and listened attentively as their cousins described the cabins and the families who had begun to settle in near the forests of Little Silver Creek. There were fields of maze planted growing taller daily in the sunlight.

Chief Kai Ta listened respectfully to the visitors. Known as Kai to his immediately family, he had learned patience many times over.

Crow immediately demanded his father kill the settlers, but only after dispatching the warriors who had brought the news. Obviously, they had themselves been encroaching otherwise they would not have known about the settlers.

Crow leaned in repeatedly to point out what he thought should happen.

Kai Ta, chief of the Sauk Indians, had chosen to ignore the advice of his eldest son on how to deal with the messengers.

The great flight south, which happened more than a few years ago before still burned in his soul.

The fear of being landless and the fear the tribe might not find a place to settle resonated in what his son had said. Yet, to bring the wrath of the whites and the soldiers who eventually would follow also meant this decision must be thought through with care.

He surprised his son with his next response. His lack of emotion during the meeting with his cousins had convinced Crow nothing was going to be done.

Kai Ta surprised Crow when he sternly ordered his son to gather the remaining warriors of the tribe for a Warrior's counsel.

Crow had wandered from tepee to tepee angry at being sent like some errand boy, but silently hoping his father would make the right decision.

He shouted at younger and older warrior alike, demanding the warriors quickly gather in his father's home. He made sure to insinuate war was at hand and each warrior's duty demanded he help guide his father into making the right decision.

The warriors of the village had gathered in his father's tepee to discuss the news, each hurrying to get a spot closest to the chief. Each warrior sat in silence waiting their allotted turn to offer advice or ask questions of the chief.

"We should kill them, father!" Crow demanded, ignoring protocol, which allowed the other elder warriors to speak first.

Mumblings of assent and of dissent swept through the tepee. It was clear the younger warriors, many of whom had grown up with Crow, supported the idea of killing the messengers and then killing the settlers.

The older warriors of the tribe, though, clearly were disturbed. Crow had ignored protocol. His disruptions wore on the harmony of the tribe, overlooked most-often because he was the eldest son of the chief. However, his boisterous behavior was increasing and clearly, something would have to be done about it.

As his father turned to the eldest warrior, Crow raised his voice, "I said we should kill them father." The agitation on his face was clear for all present to read.

His father ignored the outburst and looked around his eldest son toward one of the other warriors, an elder.

Crow's friends attempted to curtail any further attempts to break the protocol of the tribe. The warrior to his right put a hand on his shoulder hoping that the contact would be enough to encourage his friend to calm down.

Crow brushed the hand away angry his father was ignoring his counsel.

The warrior to the left offered soothing words, "Brother Cha Kai Ta," he whispered, hoping to grab Crow's attention by using his given name.

Crow would have none of it.

Crow jumped to his feet, standing in his father's tepee, furious the elder chief refused to heed his advice.

The air in the home seemed electrified with the emotions clear on all of the warriors' faces. Even the younger warriors, those who supported Crow, knew that he had gone too far. They were not prepared to stand with him, to stand in the face of this type of disruption to the traditions of the counsel.

"No, my son," the chief responded firmly, his deep voice resonated throughout the tent.

Deep creases on his forehead became evident as the rest of his weathered-face deepened into a scowl.

"He must learn to control his emotions." the Chief thought.

Heavy shoulders sagged with the thought his son might not be the person to lead the tribe upon his death. That had always been a possibility, he knew, becoming even more evident as Crow had grown from a child to a man and had increased in his level of hot-headedness.

But his father, who had been counseled by his father before him, in the same fashion, held out hope that Crow would mature.

Kai Ta stared at his son with obvious disappointment.

The settlers and their encroachment offered one challenge. He also feared his son's affection for a violent response would lead to warfare with their cousins.

As chief, he was obligated to avoid violence if possible. His son though seemed completely oblivious to the repercussions of such a war.

"As a future chief he needs to learn how to see the whole forest, not just the weeds that grow within."

Crow would not be deterred. He continued with his insistence the warriors who brought the message should be killed. He was very angry about the encroachment on their lands by the white men, but even angrier his own cousins had been encroaching, also.

He continued to press his father hoping to have the elder one agree to his pleas.

Blood fused into his face. In the darkened tepee, lit only by some glowing embers, his face resembled one of the evil leathery masks used by the women of the tribe to frighten children near the campfire at night.

Crow's sun-brown skin melted into the darkness of the tepee while his white teeth shone like the fangs of a predator. His father, held speechless by the illusion of his son being a beast from the recesses of the darkness, finally put a hand out in front of him hoping to silence his son and further discussion.

"The discussion is ended. We will send our cousins back to their families with gifts."

The sincerity of his voice and the frustration caused by Crow's disruptions did not go un-noticed by the other warriors in the counsel.

Each knew Chief Kai Ta had reached the limits of his tolerance. They also knew the possibility of violence between father and son existed and could happen at any moment.

Each warrior prepared to make a decision, which would affect the tribe for many years, should violence come to fruition.

Many in the tribe supported the chief. They respected Kai Ta. He had been a great warrior and a great chief. He had kept them safe especially during the migration from the north, into new lands, which oftentimes held unknown dangers.

Kai Ta had led them through lands of other tribes often moving at night to avoid an open conflict. His guidance and wisdom had brought them to these new lands. A little less than six years ago, the tribe had fled the threat of warfare.

With the help of many of some of their cousins, the tribe had settled in and had been thriving with the abundance of resources available.

If violence between father and son did occur, each warrior within the tepee would have to make a split-second decision about whom to support or whom to defend.

Fathers and sons would have to decide those decisions might force them to kill members of their own family or members of their own tribe. All of them were very wary of committing the ultimate sin.

The tension of the moment was almost too much.

Most warriors clearly would die for their chief.

These warriors knew they might be required to kill their brethren if those tribal members rose in defense of Cha Kai Ta, also known as Crow.

Each father quietly prayed he had raised his own son to make the right decision. They did not take that decision lightly, but also believed for the good of the tribe, Crow must not be allowed to win.

Crow, had been gently pulled back down by the warriors to each side, still rose to protest this decision. He wanted to explode at his father. He wanted to show the rest of the tribe he was not afraid to lead them.

This decision, which would make the tribe much stronger, was not just his opinion; it was a fact. A few of his friends rose with him, not to protest the decision, but to attempt to keep him from making a decision which could negatively impact his standing within the tribe.

The damage had been done, but it had not reached the point where it could not be undone.

Before he could respond, the Chief held his hand up, again, to silence him. He had reached his limit with his son's protesting.

"You will accept my decision. If you feel the need to continue with argument, go out and join the women. They will better serve your purpose."

Silence melted into the tepee like the darkness once a flame goes out.

Crow sat down stunned at the admonition from his father.

Other members of the tribe sat silently as the father and son ended the discussion.

Some of the elders nodded in agreement, respecting the way the chief had handled the dissension.

Others glared into the coals, afraid to give any indication as to which side they preferred. A few close friends of Crow's scorned the chief's decision, but held their tongues, fearful of what further dissension could mean.

The warrior's counsel had ended.

FOUR

ENCROACHMENT

Gather around me children, for I have a tale to tell. In the early years immediately following the ascension of the Great Father into the stars, three great warriors were born into our tribe on the very same day.

The first was the Warrior Courage. The second was the Warrior Strength. And the third was the Warrior Respect.

When he was born, Courage refused to cry even as he was taken from his mother's womb. Not a tear was shed and he was passed from woman to woman to be inspected for vitality. Even though these strange faces had struck fear into the hearts of other newborns, Courage smiled back at them. The women complimented his mother and Courage was proud.

When Strength was born it was in the middle of a Thunderstorm. His mother had gone into the woods with her daughter to pray to the Great Father that the baby might be healthy. During the storm, his older sister had become trapped beneath a fallen limb. The stress of the moment caused his mother to give birth to Strength, who immediately walked over and lifted the limb from his sister. The members of his tribe immediately complimented his mother and Strength was proud.

When Respect was born, he did nothing, not wanting to over shadow the other accomplishments of the other infants who had been born that day. The members of his tribe congratulated his mother on his birth, and Respect was thankful.

When he was five, Courage used a bow and arrows to fend off a pack of rabid wolves. They had attempted to carry off his younger sister who was busy gathering firewood for her family and the tribe. Standing tall, feet firmly planted on the ground, Courage faced the six snarling wolves. He shot six arrows striking six wolves. The wolves ran away whimpering into the forest. The members of the tribe complimented his mother and Courage was proud.

When he was five, Strength went with his mother to the river to bathe. There, he witnessed his mother being attacked by a Grizzly bear on the banks of the slow moving water. Standing tall, Strength jumped on the back of the bear and wrestled it to the ground. Waiting for his mother to run to safety, Strength held the bear firmly only letting go when the bear had tired. The members of his tribe complimented his mother and Strength was proud.

When he was five, Respect did nothing spectacular, not wanting to overshadow the accomplishments of his two friends and other members of his tribe. On his fifth birthday, the members of his tribe complimented his mother on his growth, and Respect was thankful.

When he was fifteen and allowed to become a warrior of the tribe, Courage stepped forward, holding his flint knife to the sky and yelled aloud, "I am the Great Warrior Courage." The members of his tribe complimented his mother on his becoming a warrior and Courage was proud.

When he was fifteen and allowed to become a warrior of the tribe, Strength stepped forward, holding his flint knife to the sky and yelled aloud, "I am the Great Warrior Strength." The members of his tribe complimented his mother on his becoming a warrior and Strength was proud.

When he was fifteen and allowed to become a warrior of the tribe, Respect stepped forward, holding his flint knife to the sky and said, "I am Respect and I thank you Great Father for the life given to me and I thank the other warriors for accepting me as a member of our tribe." The members of his tribe complimented his mother on his becoming a warrior, and Respect was thankful.

On the day of the twentieth birthdays of Courage, Strength, and Respect, the Chief, who had now moved into his elder years, gathered together all of the warriors of the tribe. They all knew the time had come for someone else to become chief of the tribe.

"It is time to elect a new Chief since I have no son," he declared. He looked from warrior to warrior knowing that the next chief would come from this group.

Many in the tribe argued for the warrior Courage to become the new chief of the tribe. They reminded others that to be a great Chief Courage would be a requirement.

Many in the tribe argued for the warrior Strength to become the new chief of the tribe. They reminded others that to be a great Chief Strength would be a requirement.

After all of the arguments were made, the Great Warriors Courage and Strength stood silently in front of the other warriors. In their hearts, they knew that one other deserved to be the Chief of the tribe.

They said in unison, "We know that to be a Great Chief Courage is a requirement. We know that to be a Great Chief Strength is a requirement. We also know that even with Strength and even with Courage, unless a Chief can show and have Respect, he will not be a Great Chief. We feel that to be a Great Chief Respect is a requirement."

With the words of his friends, Respect became the Chief of the tribe.

In those days, as is true today, all of the warriors and all of the chiefs of the tribe must have Courage, they must have Strength, and above all, they must have Respect.

Remember this always.

Great Lakes Region Indian Tale of
Courage, Strength, and Respect

The Mission

The eight, painted warriors of the Sauk Indian tribe trotted softly along a narrow trail, which had been created by the many animals of the forest. Both silence and a stifling heat hung in the air as animals of all sorts hunkered down into nearby holes, dove into hollowed out logs, or scurried into the tops of the pristine trees hoping to go unnoticed by the eight.

The heat of the summer seemed to envelope the forest with a merciless kiss of burning wind. Even within the shade of the forest, along the trail, the heat was stifling. Gentle fingers of wind caressed each warrior while they ran, but that gentle caress was not enough to bring a cooling relief.

The inhabitants of the forests, both animal and plant, did not greet the warriors with enthusiasm. While the animals scattered, hoping to flee to safety, the plants fought and scratched the warriors with fervor. Thorns scraped along the warriors' legs and leaves rubbed against their bodies depositing secretions, which were designed to cause discomfort.

The animals and the plants were safe for the moment though, as the eight continued their methodical pace towards the east. Clearly, they were on a mission and would not be deterred from the course on which they had been placed.

Each warrior had learned, through years of training there were trials, which would often demand he put aside any physical limitations. This trek, this relentless pace set by the leader in their group, was one of those trials. To complain, to fail, to stop was not an option.

Trotting along in silence each ignored the pain in their muscles. They ignored their lungs gasping for air. They ignored the thorns in their calves and the itchiness caused by the leaves of some of the plants as they brushed up against them.

What each warrior thought about the task ahead was not asked. The chief of their tribe had sent them on this mission and regardless of the dangers they would not be deterred.

There were dangers, which lurked in every interaction with the whites, the settlers, those who would encroach on Indian land. Very few Indian tribes had prospered when the whites had arrived. Those that did work with the whites only saw prosperity for short periods. Eventually, the arrival of the whites meant the Indians would have to choose to fight or choose to flee.

White settlers had been seen on their lands, building settlements and raising cattle along the Little Silver Creek. This encroachment could not be tolerated and the eight warriors had been sent by the chief to warn the settlers to move. Most of the warriors in their party believed they should meet the encroachment of the settlers with violence, the Chief had decided to take a different path. He had ordered the eight warriors to approach the settlers with an offer of peace if they agreed to leave.

The warriors trotted in silence, saving their energy for the grueling pace, which had been set by the leader of their party, and for the miles that lay ahead of them.

The message that settlers had come from the East and were building on their lands had come from a nearby tribe, cousins to the Sauk Indians.

Years before, when they had fled south from the lands of their ancestors, south from an area the whites had named Fort Dearborn, seeking new lands, many of their cousins had taken the journey with them.

Initially, they were parts of the coalition of Indians who had wiped out Fort Dearborn. However, the whites began to return to the previously burnt down fort. Pressure from the Huron tribes to the north began to grow, and the Sauk knew that it was time to flee to the south.

As they settled into areas south, East of St. Louis, away from larger tribes, into lands largely unoccupied, the groups had disbanded each claiming a territory. The tribes, while cousins, agreed to respect each other's rights and each other's land.

One of these sub groups of Sauk Indians, a tribe a little to the north, had brought the message of the white men's arrival. They had arrived at the village and had called for a meeting with the Chief to explain what they had seen.

The memory of that meeting, a warrior's counsel his father had called it, burned like fire in the mind of the leader of the eight warriors. He was the elder son of the chief. He was a warrior named Cha Kai Ta, after his father, nicknamed Crow by the seven other warriors who ran with him now.

He ran in total silence hatred and anger driving his muscular legs to continue the long trek to the borders of their lands. His anger consumed him yet none in his party would have known it because outwardly he had so well hidden it, thus far.

Kai Ta had given his eldest son Crow a chance to redeem himself. Actually though, it had led to Crow despising his father and now his younger brother even more.

The younger brother, included in the group of warriors, made nine. However, Crow did not see him as a warrior. He was more a nuisance than anything. He had hated his younger brothers for years, now.

Crow's lips curled into a snarl as he ran. His legs pushed his body along at an unrelenting pace. Muscular arms accentuated broad shoulders. Running in moccasins, his long legs pushed his almost seven-foot tall frame ahead of the rest of his party. He towered above the other warriors and almost seemed an adult running ahead of chasing children.

"They will have to keep up," he thought to himself. Pumping his arms forward and backward quickly, he picked up the pace.

His white teeth, which were exposed because of the snarl on his face, resembled the fangs of a wolf. His mouth gnashed open and closed as he struggled to inhale enough air to help his body keep up with his own pace. The group continued running in silence.

The other warriors ran in silence each knowing the best way to avoid Crow's wrath was to do as he did. Since he ran in silence, they did the same.

They darted past trees, quickly brushing aside branches and limbs, which hung in their way. If the warrior behind did not pay enough attention he would be slammed with a branch released by the one in front. More often than not, one in the group would be struck, have to slow down, and then have to quicken his pace to catch the others. Crying out in pain and stopping were not options.

Crow was setting a pace, one in which he planned to keep, hoping his younger brother, would collapse and quit. Possibly, even collapse and die.

"I hope he dies," he thought to himself, smiling at the prospect.

He was twenty-one summers old and the distance of seven years had created a valley between the two of them, which could never be bridged. Crow hated his brother almost as much as he hated his father.

The hatred for his father had grown over the years. He had done his best to hide the hatred from others. Routinely, Crow felt his father refused to take chances for the good of the tribe.

"He's become a coward." This knowledge only caused more resentment.

As the leader of the eight warriors, he not only set the pace, but also had an obligation to push on and continue to ignore the searing pain in his own lungs, which were forcing him to gasp for oxygen.

His soul burned with the hot inhaled wind of the summer and with an anger, which drove him relentlessly towards the settler's cabin. He knew what his father had asked him to do was not what he intended.

He had already decided to disobey his father.

"No it isn't," he thought, smiling to himself.

Eventually, he would have to stop and let the other warriors know of his plan. Until then, he was buoyed by the knowledge he would ensure the settler's would not return, at least not this group, to encroach on Indian land.

How could they when they would all be dead?

He trotted along, caught up deep in his own thoughts and emotions.

Crow remembered how his father had reacted when his tribe had been brought the news about the settlers. He remembered being shamed in front of the other warriors. He remembered how the blood had rushed into his face and his eyes.

Later, after his anger had subsided, his mother had come to him to plead with him to listen to the counsel offered by his father.

"Please my son," she implored, putting an arm around his waist.

"Your father is a great chief, as you will be someday, too." The anger subsided, caused by the soothing quality in her voice, which always brought him back to reality. His rage quickly died out.

"Mother, I was angry, embarrassed," he responded.

The realization he had pushed his father too far became apparent in his eyes.

"He will never forgive me."

"Yes he will, my son. He was once your age. Besides, I will talk to him, on your behalf, as I have always done." His mother patted his arm and left him.

Crow, running with the group, was brought out of his reverie by the cry of a bird somewhere off in the distance. Without a word to his group, he increased the pace. His long legs increased the distance between himself and the warrior behind him.

Once again, he was caught up remembering the last conversation he had had with the Chief.

It had not taken long for his mother to convince his father to give him another chance. The chief, who might have done so grudgingly, approached Crow with the task of going to the settler's with a warning to move on.

"They aren't to be harmed, in any way." Kai Ta told his son.

Crow wanted the opportunity to return to his father's good graces, and even though he disagreed. He nodded in agreement.

He turned to leave anxious to gather the seven warriors in his band and begin the trek to see these settlers.

"Wait, my son." Kai Ta said.

Crow turned and faced his father. "I wish you to take Nai Pa." Blood rushed back into his face and Crow looked at his father incredulously.

"A child... You want me to take my younger brother who isn't yet a warrior." Crow used enough restraint to keep the thoughts from bursting out of his mouth.

A multitude of protests exploded into his mind. Yet, Crow held his tongue.

"Nai Pa?" He stared blankly at his father, hoping he was kidding. The chief nodded.

"He's almost of age. I would like him to run with experienced warriors. To see what it's like to meet with white settlers, and most of all, to see our tribe can react to this kind of threat without using violence." Kai Ta stared unblinking at Crow waiting for an argument.

Crow took a controlled breath, exhaling slowly. "I agree. The experience would be good for him."

The memory of that conversation burned in his soul. Crow continued the pace, in silence, remembering those words, letting his anger push him onward.

The ninth of the warriors, one who was small and young for the group and small for his age, also trotted along in silence, but he was energized by the excitement this mission offered.

Nai Pa ran with the other warriors in total silence. His chest almost burst more from the excitement, which coursed through his veins rather than the lack of oxygen from the exertion. He was completely aware his brother did not view him as a warrior though he was well along enough in age he should be considered one.

At fourteen seasons of age, he was the youngest of the group. He had been sent by his father, along with his older brother Crow to warn the settlers they must move off tribal lands.

His father had done so hoping the two of them would mend any animosity they might have for each other. Crow's mother had begged the Chief to give Crow another chance to prove he could handle responsibility. It also allowed the opportunity for the younger brother, Nai Pa, to demonstrate to his brother he was growing into a reliable warrior.

Nai Pa replayed the events, which led up to the decision to warn the settlers, over and over in his head. Obviously, his older brother disagreed with their father's decision.

That his father had given him another chance was also evident. Nai Pa being sent along also meant his father wanted to have another set of eyes to see how Crow handled the peaceful mission.

Though unspoken, Nai Pa knew he would not let his father down and would accurately report on Crow's actions.

These disagreements, between Crow and their father, seemed to be happening more frequently as Crow matured and grew stronger.

"My father had better be careful," he thought. *"Crow's dangerous."*

He could sense his brother's animosity toward the task they were given and towards the fact the chief had allowed his younger brother to be a part of the mission.

Nai Pa had witnessed firsthand the blood infuse his older brother's face the moment his father added him to the group. Crow's brown face had flushed deep purple, then to red, and then back to brown as the Chief had insisted on his attending the warning party with his brother.

Crow knew better than to openly disagree and finally accepted the direction from his father without complaint. Looking at his younger brother with mild disgust, but masking it so his father had not noticed, he turned and began trotting towards the east. The other warriors fell into line.

Nai Pa had slipped into the sixth position, both because of age and because he did not want to be too close to his brother and his rage.

The nine warriors plodded on neither stopping for rest nor for water. Crow insisted they get as close as possible to the settler's cabins before camping for the night.

Mile after mile they continued their silent trek through the forest. The shadows slowly began to lengthen and evening began quickly to cool the forest. As they cleared an opening through the forest, a billow of smoke could be seen beyond the next stand of trees.

The settler's cabin lay straight ahead.

FIVE

MASSACRE

Gather around me children, for I have a tale to tell. The history of our people, our tribal customs, our tribal ceremonies, must be learned and must forever be passed from one generation to the next. The strength of our people requires a dedication to our past. Our history is entwined with Nature and with the world.

Why, might you ask? Why is it important to learn of our ancestors who walked these lands hundreds and even thousands of years in the past? Of what importance is it that the lessons of the Great Father be passed down from grandfather and grandmother to father and mother to son and daughter and on into eternity?

This history, these customs, these ceremonies are the essence of who we are and how far we have come. It is important to learn the mistakes of the past so that they don't become the mistakes of the future. When you are older, and much wiser, and your own children ask, "Why? Why must we learn of our ancestors?"

You may respond with pride and with conviction, "Because that's what we have always done. And that's what we will always do."

Great Lakes Region Indian Tale of the Importance of History

A BROTHER'S HATRED

In the hours just before the coming sunrise; that moment in a forest when the pre-dawn light is barely enough to dispel all of shadows which mask the contents hidden beneath the trees, that moment when all of the inhabitants of a forest are preparing for the coming day, the ant colony sent out its first group of foragers.

This first group of the tiny ebony insects fanned out in every direction, spreading out in a seemingly disorganized approach to finding the necessary resources which would help ensure the survival of the colony.

To the uninitiated observer, the plan had neither rhyme nor reason. Yet, the ants had a plan. They hoped their efforts would bring an abundance of resources for the growing colony. The ants moved silently along the forest floor with the intent of gathering for the colony. They were forever vigilant with their task.

Most groups of foragers were comprised of three to four ants crawling across the forests floor. They moved around, over, and through the various obstacles placed in their paths during the darkness of the previous night. A few hapless ones wandered into the path of a spider or another of the early morning predators. These obstacles did not stop the ants from continuing their trek through the limitless boundaries of the forests floor.

The ants though used to the terrain, had to make the necessary adjustments as freshly blown leaves, sticks dropping from branches above, logs falling from rotting trees, or the remains of dead animals killed by the nightly predators of the forests now littered the landscape. Most of the dead animals would become food for these ants the moment the rest of the colony arrived on the scene.

Three of the carpenter ants, having left the safety of the rotting tree trunk in which the colony which was currently housed, moved in the same direction they had followed for the previous three to four mornings.

Their efforts had proven fruitful and these three began their trek in good spirits. The leader of the three refused to hesitate to rest pushing the group to the brink of their endurance. This ant, as the leader, realized the sooner they found food the more likely it would be their efforts would pay off and other members of the colony could follow their trail to help gather the food. They could then safely return to the colony before the coming of night.

After crawling for about five to six minutes, the leader paused for a brief second. The miniature elbowed-antennae located at the top of its head searched the air for pheromones.

Picking up on the minute changes to the air current, it immediately led the other ants towards an item which loomed in the horizon.

Approaching cautiously, the three ants crawled over a dead animal clinging to the fabric encasing most of its body.

The movement of the ants had gone completely undetected and the three continued searching for the source of the pheromones. Slowly, as they reached the face of the animal, it became clear to the leader what they had taken as a dead organism was actually one which was just fast asleep.

The pheromones being expelled into the surrounding air must have been the remains of some sugary substance previously consumed by the animal.

The ants detected, but ignored the movements of other animals who were similar in size and shape to the one lying in the grass. These animals moved closer to this animal, then moved away all in total silence.

The movement of the others was uncanny. These animals were doing so purposefully with the obvious intent of avoiding waking this animal. The ants continued following their leader towards the opening from which the pheromones were coming.

Moving, stopping, probing, listening, the ants began to leave the safety of the cloth as they reached the organism's neck.

They continued their trek realizing their passage thus far had hardly been enough to be noticed by the sleeping animal.

The lure of the sugary pheromones was too much for the ants to ignore, though. They could perhaps gather some of it and return to the colony with something to show for their efforts.

Crawling in and around the hair follicles, the three ants slowly inched their way up to the face. They paused repeatedly, waiting patiently to ensure their movements had not awakened the animal and put them all in peril.

The lead carpenter ant moved again, its comrades moving in single file in the same path it had taken. Slowly, just as they reached the tip of the nose of the animal, the three froze in place, sensing a change in the breathing pattern of the giant creature.

Slowly, the lead ant turned and looked directly into the animal's eyes.

The sleeping animal had awakened without any notice. It did not seem fixated on the ants or the itching they had been causing with their movements. The eyes, of this animal, were wide open and looking past the ants crouched at the tip of his nose. The animal was staring wide-eyed at the other animals which had now surrounded it.

Nai Pa had opened his eyes.

Nai Pa was fully aware he was dreaming as the ants moved their way across his neckline, up along his head, through his hairline, and out to the tip of his nose.

The movement of the ants had been guiding his dream.

He was standing in a forest surrounded by Crow and the other warriors who had accompanied them on this mission. The warriors had circled around him silently. Each held a flint knife at his side. It must have been a dream. When Nai Pa had attempted to run away, he found he could not move forward.

His feet felt encased in the earth holding him tight. Crow was standing in front of him smiling. The evil in his eyes struck terror into the heart of his younger brother. Crow's face had become hideously contorted into a wide-mouthed smile pocketed with razor sharp fangs.

Crow also held a flint knife in his right hand. The knife and hand were hanging at his side. In his left hand, he held a cup.

Slowly, Nai Pa watched as his brother's left hand stretched out away from his body stopping above his head. Crow's hand and cup hovered for a few seconds above Nai Pa's head and the contents of the cup were spilled across his brother's hair.

Thousands of tiny spiders poured out down along his face. They crawled into his ears and up into his nose. He tried to lift his hands to brush the spiders away from his face, but could not do so. The harder he tried to swipe them away the more of them seemed to be crawling down from the top of his head.

Crow laughed aloud as did the other warriors. Nai Pa wanted to run away to find his father, to see his mother, but knew he could not move, His arms felt pinned to his body. They were weighted down with heavy stones.

The spiders all moved as if in command to the front of his face and then gathered at the tip of his nose. The itching became intense and then almost unbearable.

"*Wake up,*" he wanted to scream, but something had been preventing his mouth from working.

In the dream Crow continued to grin at his brother, and slowly, on command, all the warriors, including his brother, raised their knives and pointed them at Nai Pa.

As his eyes popped open, Nai Pa's thoughts about the itching on his nose fled. He immediately realized his body was restrained because he was staked to the ground.

Both of his arms, as well as his legs and feet, were tied away from his body by strips of leather fastened to wooden stakes. Each stake had been pounded into the ground about a foot from his body.

"How?" he thought, wondering why he had not been awakened by the efforts which had gone into staking him to the ground.

Ignoring the itching caused by the ants was easy since his attention focused on the group of warriors all standing near his feet each with a flint knife unsheathed in their hands.

His brother glared at him angrily and Nai Pa knew from experience no amount of pleading or begging was going to satiate that anger. He knew he was doomed.

"WHA!!..." he tried to scream, but the noise was barely audible.

A wide strip of leather had been wrapped around his mouth. It prevented him from making much in the way of protest. One strip lodged between his teeth while a second wrapped around again covering his entire mouth. He took gasps of air through his nose. He realized he was helpless.

He twisted his head side to side hoping the eight warriors would come to their senses and realize they had gone too far by binding the son of the chief.

His gesticulations, though hindered by his being bound brought little change in the face of his older brother, or in the face of the other warriors who were looking to Crow for a final decision.

Looking to each warrior and then back to Nai Pa, Crow whispered, "It's decided."

He turned and faced Nai Pa, holding the flint knife at his side the blade facing the ground. The handle gripped tightly.

The seven other warriors moved in unison aware he was awake. They began circling the teenager. Each of the warriors took a place inches away from Nai Pa. His brother Crow stood near his feet, unwavering in his anger. Beads of sweat poured down his war painted chest.

Nai Pa looked into his brother's eyes and realized his end had come. He stopped twitching having decided that if this was to be his last moment, his end, he would exit this world with the dignity of a chief's son. He would go out a true warrior, without fear, without anguish. He stared into his brother's eyes with a look of calm.

He tried to mouth the words, "Brother, I forgive you."

The passive look angered Crow almost to an intensity beyond his control.

Without making any sound Crow kneeled down and straddled his younger brother's torso. He looked down into Nai Pa's eyes, lifted his right hand and plunged the flint knife deep into Nai Pa's chest. The thud of the knife striking the body echoed through the trees.

Crow removed the knife and plunged it again, and again, watching the life ebb out of his younger brother. The one he hated most in the world.

Nai Pa continued looking at the older warrior without anger or fear. Crow used the knife to create a hole in the younger warrior's chest. Dropping the flint knife, Crow reached in, with his right hand, into the chest of his brother and ripped out the heart.

Silently, filled with a bloody elation from the kill, Crow smiled. He held the bleeding heart over his head towards the waning stars. Slowly, deliberately, he brought the heart to his mouth and took a bite.

Each warrior kneeled next to Crow and the lifeless body of Nai Pa, leaning forward to take a bite of the heart now offered by their leader.

After each had taken a bite, Crow stood above his younger brother looking at his lifeless corpse. He spat on Nai Pa, threw the heart to the ground, and turned towards the direction of the settler's cabin.

The warriors fell in line behind him aware the Massacre of the settlers was about to begin.

In the eerie morning light just before the sun poked up over the horizon, the eight warriors trotted along silently, exited the forests and entered the clearing of the land around the small cabin.

The rays of the sun cascaded through the trees shining the light of the coming day onto the quiet cabin.

The animals of the forests had attempted to warn the occupants with an offering of silence. This should have been enough, but the occupants were just stirring out of their slumber and were completely unaware.

Some of the occupants had already been up at the crack of dawn. The mother had been busy cooking breakfast. A ranch-hand Tom and one son, eight year old David had already left for the morning. The two of them had gone to check on the cattle gathered together in a clearing about a half-mile away.

Richard Dryver, the father, was in the process of getting dressed quietly while the younger children continued to sleep, oblivious to the happenings inside the cabin and those outside.

The first settler killed by the small group of warriors was a fourteen year old boy, Len. Len, being one of the older boys, had gotten up earlier to help his mother for a few minutes with some of the early morning chores.

He had gone outside for a few and had just exited the outhouse, having relieved himself. Len was slowly walking back toward the cabin, hoping to prolong the break in order to avoid the number of additional chores his father was going to give him to accomplish. Len was felled quietly by an arrow which pierced his chest and another followed quickly imbedding itself into his neck. The young man died completely unaware of who had killed him.

As he lay on his back, looking up at the night sky and the stars, he scarcely noticed the eight warriors glide by him. None had stopped to look at the kill. None had stopped to retrieve the arrows embedded in Len's now lifeless body.

The warriors rushed towards the cabin, in total silence, though the elation of the kill was evident on all of their faces. Wide-toothed smiles carried no sounds as five of the eight reached the door of the cabin. The other three took up positions on each remaining side of the cabin, should anyone attempt to escape through a window.

The mother was just turning, having placed some bread into the wood-burning oven, when the door to the cabin was flung open. She smiled turning, expecting to see Len returning for breakfast when a flint knife was flung across the cabin taking her in the throat. She fell lifeless to the floor. The five warriors silently entered the cabin. They quickly crossed the floor, flung open a door to another room, and entered quietly.

David Dryver, who just happened to be putting on a boot, turned, startled and yelled, "What in God's na...."

His exclamation was cut short by Crow and another warrior who pounced on him, driving their knives into his upraised forearms. Stabbing violently, the two were relentless in the assault on the man, whose lifeless body had long stopped attempting to fight back before their attack had ended.

The other three warriors bounded to the beds of the children and stabbed each of them to death in their sleep.

Crow, elated by the violence, screamed aloud with satisfaction, "EEEIiiiiiihhh!!!"

He raised his hand clutching the knife above his head and screamed again. The warriors returned his call with cries of elation in return.

Each warrior grabbed a lifeless victim and dragged them outside. They returned a few times until all of the settlers, the father, the mother, and the children lay immobile on the blood soaked ground in front of the cabin.

"Burn it," Crow said, sternly.

The anger, flared heavily in his nostrils.

Six of the eight warriors stood in a circle quietly enjoying the weariness which follows a heavy physical exertion. Their leader, Crow, the one to whom they had pledged their lives when they were younger, smiled with an elation he had seldom felt.

The other two warriors had been ordered by Crow to search the perimeter of the nearby woods just in case any of the settlers had made it out alive. Crow searched the woods with both his eyes and ears unable to discern much of anything in the early light.

His warriors were patting each other on the backs aware Crow was watching them as well, looking for any signs of weakness, any signs of regret. Each of them wore the smile he had expected and whether or not they had any regrets, all knew never to show it.

Not only had they killed the settlers, going against the order of the chief Kai Ta, they had also participated in the torture and killing of his youngest son.

Crow had assured them they would blame the death of Nai Pa on the settlers, being sure to include they had been attacked and had to defend themselves.

Crow was turning towards his warriors to congratulate them when he spun around in the direction of a noise coming across the field. The returning two warriors were dragging a small boy, of about eight, between them across the grassy fields. The boy was obviously frightened, and seemed to be pleading with the two to release him.

The two warriors pushed the boy to the ground between the circled warriors.

He made no effort to run, obviously aware it would be futile. They explained to Crow they had found an adult and this young boy with some cattle on the other side of the clearing. They had killed the adult and brought the boy back to Crow, so he could decide what to do with him.

Crow's grin grew from ear to ear as he looked down at the terrified boy.

"Stake him," he whispered.

The warriors moved quickly, staking the boy to the ground, just as Nai Pa had been. They then circled up watching Crow, who had moved quietly, but with purpose, to the boy's feet.

The boy had tried to scream, but was quickly silenced with a blow to the side of his head and a leather strap wedged between his teeth.

As the rays of the sun poked through the trees cascading over the warriors and the terrified boy with an intense light, Crow removed his flint knife from its sheath and stepped between the boy's outstretched feet.

SIX

A FATHER'S TEARS

As we awake in the morning and give our thanks for another beautiful sunrise,

We remember the Great Father and honor his memory.

As we hunt for our meat and gather food for our tribe,

We remember the Great Father and honor his memory.

As we gather around the campfire in the evening and laugh with our friends,

We remember the Great Father and honor his memory.

As we settle into our tepees with our families and say our thanks for another star filled night,

We remember the Great Father and honor his memory.

As we hold our dear children in our bosoms and deep in our hearts,

We remember the Great Father and honor his memory.

As we kiss the foreheads of our elderly parents as they lie down for sleep,

We remember the Great Father and honor his memory.

Great Lakes Region Indian Song of Honor for the Great Father

THE ULTIMATE SIN

Crow raised his flint knife above the chest of the bound child, the one who continued to look into his eyes without any signs of emotion. He had been hoping to see the fear that he had not witnessed in his brother. Nai Pa had been similarly bound and staked to the ground. This child's emotionless expression angered Crow.

His anger was quickly replaced with elation as he relished the thought of driving his knife into this child's chest.

The child reminded him of his brother, who years ago had embarrassed Crow by saving their mother from the lion. *"I hate you,"* he thought. He had wanted to scream it aloud for the entire to forest to hear.

"It should have been me!" he yelled, causing the child to flinch.

Crow's warriors looked on in silence though a few were confused about his outburst. They were wise enough to hide their confusion. None voiced the questions running through each of their heads.

Even without the hoped for fear from the young child, the flinch had been enough. Happiness spread across Crow's face showing itself in a grin which seemed to reach from ear to ear.

Just as he had done with Nai Pa, he prepared to strike hoping to drive his knife into the chest of this interloper. He looked down with disgust at this child hating him more by the minute.

His knife did not get to finish its mission.

A split second before he drove it downward into the chest of the eight year old boy Crow paused, hearing the whistle of a stone being thrown. Before he could turn to see the cause of the noise, the stone hit him in the left temple knocking him unconscious. He collapsed on top of the bound kid completely unaware his father and other warriors from the tribe had arrived.

Kai Ta stepped out of the woods surrounded by twenty-five warriors. These warriors moved quickly and subdued the seven warriors who had come with Crow on this journey.

Kai Ta exited the forests, along with three other elder warriors. These were three of his most trusted counselors who always offered sage advice to the Chief.

He searched for his youngest son keenly aware Nai Pa was not with Crow and the other warriors. He pushed the thought out of his mind realizing this moment was critical. His reaction might push the warriors who had accompanied him into violence against Crow and the seven warriors or it might cause the fathers of these very warriors to react in a less than peaceful manner towards the Chief and the others.

Kai Ta hated to tests their allegiance not wanting to put them in a position to have to decide. The smoke from the burning cabin wafted into the air, floating in gentle waves between the warriors. Kai Ta moved over to the cabin looking with sadness at the pile of bodies that had been put together by Crow and his warriors.

It was clear to him from seeing the young boy staked to the ground, a child who could not be more than eight years old, that Crow and his warriors had abandoned the peaceful mission and had slaughtered all of the other settlers.

The stench of death and decay was already heavy in the air, even though it had occurred very recently. Swarms of black flies had begun to cover the bodies feasting on the death.

"He may have brought destruction upon us all," Kai Ta thought to himself. He watched the cabin continue to burn in the morning light.

The seven warriors, who had accompanied Crow, did not put up any resistance when they were subdued by the other warriors in their tribe. Many of them felt assured since their fathers were present and would protect them from even the wrath of the chief.

Also, while they had pledged to support Crow, they knew better to fight against the chief and their own fathers. They allowed themselves to be tied up without complaint. Each warrior withdrew into his own mind to contemplate how this might play out.

Each of Crow's warriors was bound with their hands behind their backs. Their feet were quickly bound together. It was apparent, the anguish each father felt, at this moment. Kai Ta, who had ordered Crow felled by the stone, had done so only when he realized the warrior was about to kill the young child.

"He's a fool," Kai Ta thought, shaking his head as he continued to scan the surroundings for his youngest son.

Kai Ta did his best to mask his emotions as any good warrior must do. The other fathers did their best to mimic their chief hoping all would be well after they found out what happened with the settlers.

Each knew, though, the chief feared the worst for his youngest son. In their hearts they mourned for Nai Pa even without proof of his death. Nai Pa's absence from the group could only mean one thing.

"Where is my son?" the chief demanded looking sternly at the seven warriors as they sat silently near his feet. Crow was still unconscious, unmoving. He too had been bound and dragged over to the other seven warriors.

All seven of the warriors looked at the ground refusing to make eye contact with the chief.

A father angered at his son for not answering stepped forward and harshly slapped his son on the back of the head and screamed, "Answer him!"

His son remained silent refusing to look up at either of the men.

Kai Ta felt as if he had swallowed a stone so heavy the stress of the moment seemed to weigh on his spirit crushing his hopes. The pit of his stomach churned, yet he continued to put on a brave face while he paced around the warriors.

He was waiting for his eldest son to awaken. Blood drizzled down the side of Crow's face where the stone had struck him.

"I will get answers from him when he wakens," he said, quietly. He looked at the other warriors who had come with him.

"Search the area," Kai Ta stated firmly.

Ten of the warriors spread out in different directions looking in and around the cabin quickly. When it became clear Nai Pa was not with the bodies of the settlers the warriors fanned out in all directions, some into the woods, some further away into the areas where the cattle were located.

Kai Ta waited stoically knowing the news which would be brought to him would not be good.

Minutes passed and the silence of the forests continued to hang like a stone weight around the Chief's neck. Most of the warriors had begun to return to the others. These warriors reported they had found nothing

Crow was just beginning to arouse, still groggy from the blow of the stone.

Kai Ta had leaned over his eldest son, waiting patiently for his awareness to return when two of the warriors came running up to him. The fear and anguish on their faces was evident as Kai Ta stood up and turned to face them.

"Have you found him? Have you found my son?" he asked quietly.

The two warriors nodded in assent. Both turned and pointed towards the woods from which they had just come.

"Why isn't he with you?" Kai Ta asked knowing the warriors would have brought Nai Pa with them if he were still alive.

One of the warriors leaned in and whispered quietly to his Chief; so quietly the other warriors could not understand what was being said.

It was clear to the others the warrior was asking the chief not to go to the woods even while he explained what they had found. He offered to take care of Nai Pa's body. Stoically, Kai Ta turned and faced the warriors of his tribe.

The chief turned to the warriors and said, "I need all of the fathers of these warriors to accompany me into the woods." He turned and began to walk in the direction from which the two warriors had just come.

Seven warriors walked quietly with the chief each realizing they had been chosen because the news must have been bad. A few began to realize what had been found involved their own sons.

The Chief stood silently above the lifeless body of his youngest son Nai Pa.

He grieved in silence holding back tears. He shook his head from side to side hoping he would be able to maintain his composure as he looked at Nai Pa, whose body was staked to the ground. Nai Pa's heart lay near the body. Pieces had been torn out of it. The animals of the forests had already been feasting on his son's heart.

The warriors who had accompanied him, many who had been his lifelong companions, gasped when they came upon Nai Pa's body. Many had seen death in battle countless times. Even these men were shaken to their core.

"My Chief...my friend," one of the father's stated, "don't stay here. Go back to the others. We will give your son the proper rights and prepare the body."

The warrior knew Kai Ta would not do that. He would not have agreed to the offer either and it made him proud to be a friend of his Chief.

Bending over the body of Nai Pa, the chief used his flint knife to cut the leather straps which had been used to stake the young man to the ground.

Delicately, Kai Ta cut and removed the straps of leather which were bound around his youngest son's face. He looked at the face of his youngest son, a face which had seen much laughter and joy over the years. A face which had now been robbed of any life.

"Never to laugh, never to hunt, never to run again into the arms of his mother."

"My son," he whispered.

Kai Ta wracked by emotion leaned forward and sobbed over the body.

Tears flowed down his cheeks unabated by his ability to keep his emotions in check. The warriors all stood silently aware each of their own son's, the other warriors of the tribe, had taken part in the atrocity which was now before them.

Kai Ta picked up what remained of his son's heart and placed it upon the chest of Nai Pa.

Standing, he looked at his warriors in silence, allowing the tears to flow even more freely down upon his face.

"I have now witnessed a horror unimaginable." he said somberly. "My son has been tortured and killed by members of his own tribe, by his own friends, by his own brother."

He waited for what he said to sink in before continuing. The other warriors continued to stare at the body of Nai Pa. Many of them grieved along with their chief.

They knew he had been a good son, full of spirit, full of humor. They all remembered their own interactions with Nai Pa, a child who had brought laughter into their hearts many times. Many knew to be taken away in this manner was a sin against the teachings of the tribe.

"The task of a father, of a warrior, of a chief is not an easy one. I task each of you with making a decision about what should happen to your own children, to the warriors who participated in this killing."

Kai Ta waited allowing his words to sink in.

Each warrior stood silently, weighing in their head what they would have done if they were chief, what they would ask the members of their tribe to do had their own son's been the one bound, tortured, and killed. Each of them wore the embarrassment for the actions of their sons heavily on their faces.

"I go now, back to those who committed this atrocity. I will not ask you for your judgement and I will not judge you for the choice you make. It's not an easy decision...I am sure."

"I will make my decision for my oldest son alone."

Kai Ta moved quietly around his warriors and exited the forests. Walking slowly, with tears still streaming down his face, Kai Ta removed his flint knife from its sheath.

The seven warriors of the tribe stared quietly at the body of Nai Pa, youngest son of their Chief Kai Ta and their friend.

When they were young, barely Nai Pa's age, they had taken a blood oath to follow Kai Ta just as their own son's had done for Cha Kai Ta. They had fought many battles alongside Kai Ta. They had hunted and fished for many moons, had seen many sunrises, and had taken their oath very seriously.

They were proud warriors. All seven were ecstatic when their own children had grown into warriors and had taken the same oath to follow Cha Kai Ta.

Now, as they stood in silence, faced with the atrocity which was before them, anger and rage filled their bosoms.

Nai Pa, a young boy who was so close to joining the tribe as a warrior. He had his life robbed from him. Their own son's had violated one of the most sacred bonds of any tribe. They had taken the life of one of their own.

Worse, they had taken the life of Nai Pa in a manner which was not fit for a warrior.

They had staked the young man to the ground, had tortured, and killed him.

Each father was weighing in his mind the look of his son currently bound at the Chief's command. Each of them would have made the same decision in order to bring the massacre to a halt. This would also allow the time needed to find out what had occurred between the settlers and the warriors.

In unison, they all looked at each other, and without speaking nodded in agreement. They turned to follow their chief, their friend.

SEVEN

A FATHER'S WRATH

Gather around me children, for I have a tale to tell. It's a tale deeply imbedded in our relationship with Nature and to the mother Earth. Years ago, after the Great Father ascended into the stars to watch and observe all of HIS creations, a great disagreement arose between Sun and Clouds. The Great Father, as most parents do, decided he would not interfere and let his two children settle their differences without interference.

On a calm summer morning, Sun and Clouds had decided to go visit their good friend Nature. Walking amongst the plants and trees of the forests, a disagreement began about which of the two was most important.

In a moment of hubris, Sun proclaimed, "Dear Sister, I and I alone am most important to our special friend Nature."

Equally prideful, Clouds proclaimed in response, "You are wrong dear brother, I am most important to our special friend Nature."

Turning away from their journey to visit Nature, the two siblings agreed to a contest. They were determined to see which was the most important to their dear cousin.

They agreed each of them would spend twenty-one days away from visiting their cousin. And by doing so, each would see which one their cousin missed the most.

For twenty-one days, Clouds refused to visit her cousin Nature. Sun visited, and each time Nature asked where Clouds was at Sun just smiled and would not answer. In those twenty-one days, without a visit from Clouds, the grass dried up, turned brown, shriveled and died. The trees lost their leaves and many of the animals died from lack of nourishment. Sun was confused, but never said a word.

Then Clouds visited, bringing with her much needed rain, and things returned to normal.

Later, for the next twenty-one days, Sun refused to visit his cousin Nature. Clouds visited, and each time Nature asked where Sun was at, Clouds just smiled and would not answer. In those twenty-one days, without a visit from Sun, the grass was covered with water, the trees were soaked, and the plants all died. Many of the animals died from lack of nourishment. Clouds was confused, but never said a thing.

Following the contest, as things returned to normal, Sun and Clouds decided to finish their journey and visit their cousin Nature together. They explained their contest, both confused about which one was most important to Nature.

Nature smiled and said, "I cherish you both equally. Without both I could not survive." Sun and Clouds hugged their dear cousin. As they left her home, they put their arms around each other, happy and proud their dear cousin adored them both.

> *Great Lakes Region Indian Tale of the importance of Sun, Clouds, and Nature*

PUNISHMENT

When he returned to the group of warriors, eight of them bound and quietly sitting in a circle with the remainder standing guard over them, the Chief reminded himself he would accept the judgement of his counselors and friends for their own children.

Those seven warriors had remained in the forest behind him, standing over the body of his youngest son. They were now talking amongst themselves in his absence.

"They are my friends and I have put too much of a burden on them," he thought.

"Yet, they stand over the body of my youngest."

The sadness he had felt by discovering Nai Pa's body bound continued to show itself. Tears streamed down his face. Stoically, he returned to the others without saying a word.

The other warriors, even those bound, had never seen Chief Kai Ta show sadness publicly. All were in awe at witnessing such a demonstration of emotion.

They were taught as children the code of the warrior.

A strong warrior kept his emotions in check by day letting them out only when he was alone or inside his tepee with his family. Other than happiness, rarely did the tribe see emotional responses from each other, especially sadness. The exceptions were the death of a loved one, but even then most hid their sadness.

Rather than see it as a form of weakness, though, they all knew the Chief was giving them a great gift by allowing them to see his tears. Silently, the warriors standing thanked the Great Father for the honor being done to them. Those sitting kept their eyes to the ground realizing their actions had been the cause of those tears.

Many of the standing warriors shook their heads disapprovingly. They looked to the eight warriors bound at their feet. They were just beginning to realize the seriousness of what must have been found in the woods.

Kai Ta had ordered no talking be allowed until he returned. The standing warriors enforced his order without question; even as they realized Crow was glaring at them with hatred and contempt.

Chief's son or no, he would bow to the orders of his father. One warrior had lightly cuffed Crow on the back of the head when he tried to offer words of encouragement to his seven comrades.

"Have faith bro…" he did not get to finish what he was going to say. The light cuff on the back of the head was enough to get his attention.

"No talking," the warrior stated.

"He will pay for that," Crow thought. He turned away and looked down at his bound feet.

It was in those few moments as he neared the group of warriors Kai Ta noticed the eight-year-old boy who was still staked to the ground. He frowned at realizing his fate was to have been the same as his son Nai Pa. This thought only saddened him more.

He turned towards the little boy and gestured to a few of his closest warriors.

"Untie him," he said.

Two of the warriors moved to cut the child loose. At first, the little boy lay prostrate, not moving. He did not know how to take being cut loose. He continued to stare at the Indians immobilized by fear.

He had been asking himself, repeatedly, *"Am I going to die?"*

Slowly, the little boy named David sat up and rubbed his wrists. They were aching, but not bleeding, which he had expected. The leather straps had dug deeply into his skin and it would be a while before the imprint would disappear from his wrists. They had been rubbed raw by the leather during his struggle to get loose from the bindings.

Crow, who was now completely conscious, said loudly, "Father, don't do it. These settlers attacked us in the middle of the night. He deserves to die as the others did."

Kai Ta responded firmly, "Did he deserve to die as your brother did?" The question was double-edged and Crow looked back to his feet and then back up to his father.

Kai Ta looked into his eldest son's eyes with a deep sadness. The weight of that emotion was almost unbearable for both of them.

"Where did I go wrong?" he thought to himself.

Somehow, there had to be an explanation for what had happened to Nai Pa. Though Kai Ta was not sure, this type of evil had an explanation, nor would it ever.

Crow again started to respond, but decided against it. He continued to stare at his father not saying a word. Finally, after a full minute of total silence, the eldest son broke his gaze and looked away.

Kai Ta gestured for the young boy to come over to him. He was aware the young child was probably terrified beyond imagination.

"Was Nai Pa terrified?"

He tried to push the thought out of his head, but was having difficulty distinguishing between Nai Pa and this young child.

David Dryver walked quietly towards the Indian who was gesturing for him to come to him. He took small steps unsure of what was going to happen next. Doubts and fears ran through his mind. He was deeply afraid he was going to be killed. He stopped in front of Kai Ta, who seemed to him like a giant.

Squatting down Kai Ta plopped down on his knees in front of the boy so they could look into each other's eyes. The tears had slowed, but still were evident on his cheeks. He looked at the frightened boy and imagined that to this child he looked withered and old.

The older Indian leaned in, wrapped his arms around David, and pulled him into a hug. He held him as he had done his youngest son so many times.

Crow glared at his father and at the young child. The anger flooded back into him, yet he sat silently waiting. He knew it would be more prudent to sit quietly and not interrupt.

"When I'm free, then I will find that little boy and cut his heart out," the warrior thought to himself. He hated his father and the young boy almost as much as he had hated his brother.

It was clear to the boy this man, the one who must be the Chief, regretted the slaughter of his family. He too had been wracked with sadness though David was not sure why.

His parents had been killed not this Indian's family. His brothers and sisters and his friend Tom had been slaughtered for no other reason than they had chosen to live in these woods. He was too saddened, though, and knew he had no reason to hate this man. He wrapped his arms around the man, leaned into his neck and sobbed into his shoulders.

After a few minutes, the Chief patted David on the back and let go of the boy. He stood placing his hands on the young boy's shoulders. Kai Ta looked at the others.

"Take him back east to the nearest settler village," the Chief instructed. "He's to get their alive and unharmed." He pointed to three warriors. All three mimicked their chief and leaned down towards the young boy. They gestured for him to follow them.

"Once he's there return to our village, do not return here."

Understanding what was being asked of him David nodded to the chief and began walking away from the Indians with the three warriors.

He stopped for a brief moment at the pile of bodies near the smoldering cabin. His mother and father lay there thrown into a pile as if they were rotting logs. Kai Ta was impressed the young man had stopped to show respect to his parents. He nodded to himself in approval.

Lowering his head little David Dryver said a prayer for his ma and pa, and for his siblings. Silently, without looking back, he walked into the forest with the three warriors of the tribe. The four of them would begin the long trek east.

Chief Ka Ta watched the little boy walk away and anguish washed over him. It flooded his body shaking him from head to toe. If only he had come a little earlier, he might have been able to prevent much. The slaying of his son. The slaughter of the settlers. So much pain. So much anger. So much sadness.

The emotions and feelings of guilt wrapped themselves around him like a blanket. After a few minutes, he pushed the emotions aside and decided it was time to deal with his eldest son.

As he watched the young settler walk into the forest with his warriors the Chief turned to face the bound warriors. The fathers of the seven other warriors had just now returned and each had taken a place directly behind his own son. Judgement had been made.

One of them spoke to the other warriors who were now standing nearby confused. All knew a judgement of some sort had been made. Now, waiting in the silence of the morning, they heard one of the seven fathers speak.

"Our son's, your fellow tribesmen, have broken the most sacred covenant of our tribe. They have killed one of their own." He paused a few seconds, waiting for the reality of what was being said to sink in.

All the standing warriors turned and looked into the woods realizing that Nai Pa was there. A few of them stepped away from those bound warriors fearing that even being near them would contaminate them.

The seven bound warriors sat quietly at the feet of their fathers. None looked up. All kept looking at their own feet awaiting a judgement they knew would surely come.

This was not the way it was supposed to have gone and now the warriors sat quietly. They were waiting for the judgement of their fathers. They realized Chief Kai Ta had given decision-making power to their fathers in this matter. Their kinsmen, not the chief, would decide their punishment. All of them continued to looking down dazed at the recent turn of events.

All except for Crow.

Crow sat stunned, realizing the magnitude of what had happened. It was apparent events were now pushing his fate, and the fate of his friends, into the hands of each of their fathers. He was sure nothing would happen. Each of his warriors had followed his orders, which the warriors of a tribe should always do. They should not be held accountable for decisions made by their leader. That meant they would not be held responsible for Nai Pa's death.

If anyone was to be banished from the tribe, it should be him. He held himself rigid waiting for each of the fathers to announce his judgement against his own son.

Looking up, trying to meet the eyes of his seven friends, Crow was hoping to show them to be brave. None of the seven would look up. They all continued to look towards their bound feet, awaiting the outcome. The judgement would come and they would meet it with courage.

As Kai Ta looked to each of his friends standing behind their own sons, he found it very difficult to guess as to what their judgement would be. He made sure to make eye contact with each father nodding to assure him he would accept his judgement. Each man returned his gaze not showing any emotion.

Almost as one, each father placed his hands upon his own son's head. Each gently leaned their son's body backward placing their backs up against their father's legs. Slowly, they tilted the heads so that each was looking upward into the eyes of his father. The other warriors who were standing were riveted to the moment. They looked from father to son waiting for the father's judgement.

The warrior who had spoken before said sternly as he looked into his son's eyes, "We are ashamed to have been your fathers. We are ashamed to have ever called you sons. We are ashamed you have ever been a part of the tribe."

Each of the bound warriors sat silently accepting their father's words.

Crow sat in disbelief. He was shocked about the words spoken aloud. *"Are they mad?"* he thought to himself.

These seven warriors were all that were good in this tribe. Without them, Crow reminded himself, the tribe would have made peace with these settlers.

"Fine." If they were to all be banished then they would start their own tribe. Within a few years, they would return and kill all of the warriors of the tribe. Any of those who stood now before them would pay with their lives. He held his anger in check not wanting his seven friends to lose hope.

"The least I can do is show them by example."

Slowly, with each son was staring into his father's eyes, the elder warriors removed their flint knife from their sheath. The seven bound warriors realized their fate. None of them fought against their fathers. They sat without moving waiting for the judgement to be issued and carried out.

Crow saw what was happening, but refused to believe it.

"Stopppp!!!!" he wanted to scream.

He leaned forward, but held his voice in check realizing his seven friends had accepted their fate and were not going to try to prevent it.

Leaning in slightly the seven fathers in unison reached down beneath the chins and cut their son's throats from the left ear to the right. The seven bound warriors never said a word, accepting the judgement of their fathers. In this, they were true warriors.

The razor sharp knives did their work quickly and all seven bodies slid to the ground. The blood and the life ran out of them quickly.

"NOoooooo!!!!" Crow screamed. He flung his body around rolling in anger towards the fathers of the seven warriors. *This could not be happening.* His anger quickly changed into fear when he realized if these seven warriors had been judged by their own fathers and sentenced to death he most likely had a similar fate before him.

He rolled onto his back and looked at each of the seven fathers. None of them showed any emotion about what they had just done. Crow lay there unmoving.

"Banishment! That's what the judgement should have been!" After a few seconds, Crow started to roll hoping to make it into the forest and hide.

Three of the standing warriors flung themselves on top of Crow pinning him to the ground.

They had thought he was trying to roll himself into his friends who lay dying beneath the feet of their fathers. They held him firmly until he stopped struggling. They sat up on their knees, keeping their hands on Crow's body. The three of them turned to look at Chief Kai Ta for orders.

Crow was panting from the exertion. Even with his strength and height, being bound was too much for him to continue to fight. He stopped aware all the warriors present were now looking to his father. They were waiting the judgement just as they had waited the judgement of the fathers of the now dead warriors.

Slowly, Crow turned his head and looked to Chief Kai Ta, his father. His judge.

Standing in the morning light Crow was reminded of the Great Father. Surely, this is what the Great Father would have looked like. The thought fled shortly as the anticipation flooded Crow's mind.

The Chief locked his eyes on those of his son Cha Kai Ta and held his gaze.

The next words sent chills up Crow's spine. The silence of the forest was broken by the words of his father.

"Stake him," Kai Ta said.

Even bound it took the strength of ten other warriors to pin Crow to the ground and slowly begin binding his arms and staking him to the ground.

He struggled, cursed, pleaded, bit, attempted to head-butt the other members of his tribe, but in the end, he was staked spread-eagle to the ground. The panting warriors, worn out by the exertion, stood in a circle around the former member of their tribe, waiting for the next command from their chief.

Kai Ta stood silently a few feet away from the warriors and the one tied to the ground. He would no longer think of Cha Kai Ta as his son. He was a nothing. A nobody. He was beneath the tribe, contemptible.

Kai Ta stood silently weighing his next decision over in his mind. He had already decided Cha Kai Ta's fate even before the seven fathers' had executed their own sons. The biggest decision would be who would witness it.

"They have seen too much bloodshed already," he thought to himself. Thinking of the other warriors, some of them friends of those who had been killed, Kai Ta knew he needed to send them back to the village.

Even worse, they had witnessed the judgement carried out by the fathers of their friends.

"Too much." he thought to himself again.

The anguish he had originally felt had been replaced by hatred. He yearned to exact vengeance for his youngest son. Even if it meant taking that vengeance out on his oldest son.

He had made the decision to think of Cha Kai Ta as a thing, not a person. He would not even recognize him as his own. This made the hatred and the anger purposeful and would allow him to do what must be done.

Turning to the other members of his tribe, Kai Ta spoke softly, but sternly.

"All of you must return to the village and prepare the tribe to move." A few of the warriors shuffled their feet confused. "This slaughter of these settlers will not go unnoticed."

Before he could finish his sentence a younger warrior blurted out, "Should we not have killed the young one then?"

He immediately regretted his statement as the other warriors, especially the chief, glared at him with contempt. He looked down quickly and decided he would remain silent.

"Soon, the white man and his soldiers will return. They will find this cabin burnt and will look for someone to blame. It should not fall on the shoulders of our tribe. Our tribe should not have to bear the burden of the sins of others. Yet if we stay they will surely do so." He looked down at Crow and spat at his feet.

"You seven, my comrades, my friends, I can't ask you to stay to bear witness to what must be done. Your hearts are already heavy enough. I leave it to you, but ask those that can stay."

The seven warriors stepped forward and one of them said, "Our chief, we will stay."

They turned to the other warriors and barked orders quickly explaining what would need to be done to prepare for another move. They wanted the tribe to be ready to move the moment they returned.

Kai Ta, Chief of the tribe, stepped forward to each warrior who was preparing to leave and clasped his hand on their forearms. "I thank you my brother, my friend, for being a part of my tribe." The warriors returned the compliment and the handshake.

A few were puzzled by the chief's remarks. Others, the more experienced warriors knew this would be the last time they spoke with their chief. Those few responded, "May the Great Father guide and protect you my chief."

Kai Ta nodded with approval and the warriors of the tribe headed off into the forest. Kai Ta waited silently for about fifteen minutes and turned to his friends.

"Please bring the body of my only son Nai Pa. Lay it here on the ground, next to this lump of flesh. Don't let it lay too close, though, I don't want it to contaminate Nai Pa's remains and thus contaminate his spirit."

Crow heard all his father had said and shuddered. The bindings were too tight to escape and the other warriors had covered his mouth with a leather strap. Just as he had done to Nai Pa.

"Father, please don't do this."

Crow's eyes burned with hatred as he glared at his father. Surely he knew what Crow had done had been for the good of the tribe. A small part of him played the events over and over in his head. Crow convinced himself he was still being tested.

"That's it, he's testing me. Yes, he's testing me and my punishment will be banishment."

In those few moments, as the warriors gingerly brought the body of Nai Pa and laid it next to the one who was no longer a human, Crow had decided he would show bravery, He would no longer struggle, he would no longer fight, and he would no longer plead.

His father surely would see how brave he was and would change his mind. He would punish Crow, but punishment would mean banishment.

Chief Ka Ta walked about fifteen steps away from Crow and motioned for the other warriors to follow.

"Do you see," Crow thought. *"He's already starting to realize that I am a true warrior. He will not kill me. I am his only son."*

Crow continued to watch silently waiting for the final judgement to come.

As the warriors gathered around Kai Ta, he once again thanked them for the years they had fought together.

"When this is done, return to the tribe and move to the north and to the west. Go across the Great River and far away from this place. I would like to be left by the mouth of the cave, remember, the one we spotted a little ways away from here."

The warriors nodded remembering seeing the mouth of the cave, which opened up, from the ground a mile or so behind them.

"I will guard Nai Pa, and hopefully, with the Great Father's help guide his spirit into the stars."

When he was sure the warriors understood his wishes Kai Ta once again embraced the seven of them. He patted them on the backs. Each of them did the same to him.

"You have been a good chief," many of them added, realizing after this moment the tribe would no longer be Kai Ta's to lead.

The eight warriors turned in unison and faced the thing, which was bound and staked to the ground. Walking over the first seven warriors encircled Crow in total silence. Each of them removed their flint knives and held it at their sides. Kai Ta finished the circle taking his place at the feet of his former son.

The heat of the mid-day sun began to beat down on the group of Indians as Kai Ta raised his knife and pointed it at Crow.

"You are no longer my son. You are no longer a member of our tribe. Your name will never be spoken again for you are no longer among the race of men. You are no longer human. I curse you and your very existence."

Crow watched in horror as his father stepped between his legs and stood over his torso. Kai Ta sat down on Crow's waist.

Leaning in, he silently cursed. Kai Ta placed the flint knife along the leather straps, which bound Crow's mouth shut. He sliced the edges of his mouth, opening the flesh all the way to the ear. Crow writhed in agony. His father placed his hands upon Crow's head and cut along the other side of his mouth, almost to his other ear.

He reached down with his left hand ripping open Crow's tunic. Leaning backwards, pointing at the sky, Kai Ta screamed, "I curse this evil thing that used to be a man...I curse him for eternity. May his soul burn forever, forbidden to join the Great Father in the stars."

Kai Ta raised his flint knife high above his head, paused, and drove it deep into Crow's chest. Pulling the knife out again, and again, he continued to do so until a big hole opened up in the chest of his former son. Reaching in Kai Ta quickly cut out the heart and raised it above his head.

"DO YOU HEAR ME GREAT FATHER. I, CHIEF KAI TA, FATHER OF NAI PA, YOUR DESCENDENT, CURSE THIS THING FOR ETERNITY."

Looking down at the dead body of his former son, Kai Ta tossed the heart in the opposite direction of Nai Pa.

"The wolves will eat heartily tonight," he said aloud.

He quickly cut the leather straps that had bound Crow. Kai Ta re-sheathed his knife and bent over Crow's body. Without any assistance, he pulled the body up and hoisted it over his shoulder.

Turning towards the direction of the cave, he said, "My friends please assist me by bringing the body of my only son, Nai Pa." The other warriors gently picked up the body of the younger man and followed their chief.

He raised his left hand and the nearest warrior placed his knife, which had been dropped, into Kai Ta's hands. The Chief nodded a thank you and turned away from his friends.

The group of warriors led by their Chief walked into the woods and eventually came to the edge of a clearing. The small mouth of a cave poked up from the ground. It was half-covered with dead branches, but clearly visible to the naked eyed.

Slowly, the burden of his former son on his shoulders, Kai Ta made his way to the cave. When he reached the mouth of the cave, he turned his body half way and without hesitation threw Crow's lifeless body down into the cave. A thumping sound returned a second later verifying the body had struck the floor of the cave.

A few feet away the Chief sat on his knees waiting for the body of Nai Pa. He wanted it placed next to him.

When it was done, Kai Ta leaned over and kissed his son's forehead. The tears returned staining his cheeks.

Kai Ta unsheathed his knife once again and reached out his left hand. Another warrior placed his own flint knife into Kai Ta's hands and nodded in approval.

The Chief turned the blades inwards towards himself. He looked to his friends one last time and nodded. They remained passive watching as Kai Ta raised the knives to his face and stabbed out his own eyes.

The blood ran down his face faster than his tears. His cheeks were covered in a scarlet liquid and the chief lay down near the body of his youngest son.

He extended his right arm and gently placed his hand up Nai Pa's shoulder. Gently, he began singing a lullaby, the one he had heard his wife sing to their children many times.

The warriors of the tribe, his seven friends, stood silently watching in admiration the bravery of their chief. Slowly they turned as one and walked away into the forest in the direction of their own son's bodies.

EIGHT

─── BIRTH OF THE WENDIGO ───

Gather around me children, for I have a tale to tell. A tale which must be learned and forever passed down from one generation to the next. This is the tale of evil, of hatred, of those parts of man which cause the shattering of all that is good in nature.

This is the tale of the first Wendigo. SHUDDER with fear at the name, for the Wendigo is a curse of nature and an evil plight upon the land and on our people.

The first Wendigo was once a proud warrior, strong of body, but weak of mind.

The first Wendigo committed the greatest act of heresy which can be committed by a member of a tribe.

The first Wendigo, in a fit of rage and jealously, slay his father and mother as they lay content in their teepee, both fast asleep.

The first Wendigo was a warrior whose heart had become so blackened by jealousy and hatred that his act of rage led to the greatest sin of all.

The Great Father who had been watching the warrior intently, as he did with all the members of the tribes, still refused to intervene believing that the warrior would come to his senses and drop the knife, far before he used it to murder his parents.

After witnessing the horrific act, the Great father appeared in person to the blood-stained warrior. The one whose heart had become so blackened that it appeared he had none. The Great Father in his rage shined like a burning sun in the teepee. He knelt above the two parents whose lives had already fled their bodies and tears dropped upon their already cold cheeks. Standing, the Great Father turned to the warrior. His melancholy demeanor didn't lessen the rage which burned in his heart from witnessing the murder of the two parents. Slowly he extended his hand and pointed his forefinger at the blackened warrior.

"I curse you for eternity," the Great Father said softly. Frozen with terror at the site of the Great Father the blackened warrior did not resist when the hand reached out towards him entered his torso and plucked out his heart.

In that moment, the Great Father transformed into an eagle and flew swiftly with the warrior's heart in his beak back to his teepee in the sky. And to this very day, that heart is nailed to a post in the middle of the Great Father's teepee, along with the other hearts of those who have been turned into the Wendigo for the sins they have committed.

After having his heart plucked out of his chest, the warrior fell to the ground screaming in agony. He was fully aware he had no heart. Rising, he looked one last time at his mother and father, exited the teepee, and walked alone into the forests. He was aware he would not be allowed a warriors death, but instead would be cursed to roam the lands. As he entered the forests all remembrance of anything before left him and he became the embodiment of evil, he became the first Wendigo.

Great Lakes Region Indian Tale of the First Wendigo

LOST HUMANITY

Deep in the darkness hidden among the thousands of crevices which pocketed the ceiling, walls, and floor of a cavern located deep underground, the centipede reversed its course and backed up its eight inch elongated body. It did so quickly hoping it had gone unnoticed by others within the cave as it had moved from crevice to crevice.

Having survived the perils of this cave, for this long, the centipede was well aware it was imperative not to leave itself exposed to attack. It searched for a crevice deep enough to house its entire body hoping to have enough protection to survive another day.

Day and night never came and went in this cave. The cycle of time, without light from above to mark its change, droned on and on. Without a clock to mark off seconds, minutes, days, weeks, months, or years life in the cave was one continual struggle for survival.

Hours before the centipede had ventured out of its hiding place driven by hunger and the need to feed. Hunger and survival were the only two reasons the inhabitants of the cave would leave the safety of shelter found within the many crevices. Many of these inhabitants had come to the cave accidently scurrying into the darkness that was the mouth, not realizing they would never return to the daylight far up above.

Others, like the centipede, had been born in the cave and never knew daylight even existed. Having been born inside the cave the centipede made up for its lack of eyesight, which had never been needed, by using its antennae. They were highly sensitive to microscopic changes within its ecosystem.

The decision to exit its crevice came when its antennae had picked up one of those very microscopic changes in the air molecules within the coolness of the cave. Something was stirring a few feet away silently along the wall. The decision to leave its crevice brought perils of its own, but the centipede had not fed in a few days and quickly the decision was made to go on the hunt.

The brown centipede, which had forty-five segments and eighty-three legs, moved quickly toward the cause of the disruption. It moved towards the organism, which had caused a change in the flow of the air molecules within the quietness of the cavern.

Many of its segments had one leg; some were even missing both legs. Some of the missing legs had fallen off from the day to day grind of life within the cave. Most though, had been bitten off by other cave-dwelling predators or had been lost as the centipede was locked in silent combat with one of its prey. It had lost many of its legs over its tiny lifespan.

Moving silently, almost gliding along the wall of the cave, the centipede slithered a few inches, stopped, slowly inched closer to its goal. Finally, there in the darkness of the cave, unheard and unseen, the centipede struck quickly and savagely, sinking its fangs into an unsuspecting cave cricket. The venom injected into its prey the centipede backed off for a few seconds, watching and listening with its probing antennae. The brown cave cricket writhed in agony. The poison worked quickly almost instantly paralyzing the cricket and preventing its attempt to escape.

Almost immediately the centipede scampered over the cricket, flipped it over, and began to feed. It began chewing the body of the cricket as quickly as possible draining the cricket of its life-giving juices. The centipede stopped, waved its antennae around, and began to feed again. It repeated this process quickly and quietly. It seemed to know instinctively the longer it remained exposed the greater the chances it would become the hunted.

In this cave every living thing was a predator. Whether it was the one of the small brown bats, or the larger rats, which lived near the mouth of the cave far above or whether it was the boundless number of insects, crickets, worms, centipedes, millipedes, or boundless bacteria in the cave, especially deep in the darkness, it was eat or be eaten. Everything was a predator which meant everything was also a potential prey.

Having finished its meal, the centipede moved to find another crevice, one which would house it in safety. Eventually it settled on an almost invisible crack in the wall of the cave. The centipede moved quickly, then slowly, then quickly, then slowly, as it wound its body backward into the crevice. It was hoping the crevice was deep enough to hide its entire body. Its rounded head flattened out into a pair of light brown antennae which it waved gently back and forth into the air.

The centipede had become a master predator detecting subtle changes which to most other organisms would have gone unnoticed. Life in the cave was dangerous.

The cave remained a cool fifty-eight degrees year-round. The blackness only seemed to grow deeper further within the cave. The cave dwellers closer to the entrance were bathed in a gentle light which made its way down ten or fifteen feet from the sloping mouth located twenty to thirty feet above. Beyond that depth the organisms below had never experiences sunlight and its life giving properties.

Slowly, the centipede continued its backward movement placing its entire body into the crevice. It became satisfied with both the shelter and the safety it would temporarily provide. It would be a few days before the centipede would need to leave the safety of this crevice. A few days before the need to feed would again drive the centipede to abandon the safety of this shelter.

The centipede stopped waving its antennae only after being assured other predators weren't nearby. The cavern, from top to bottom had an abundance of life, most of which would use the many crevices or small fissures of the cave to hide themselves from others.

Suddenly, subtle changes in the air molecules caught the centipede's attention. These changes, mainly coming from above, caused the centipede to wave its antennae. It probed the air trying to locate the causes of the changes.

The antennae stopped waving.

*Thump....*Something hit the floor of the cave. The loud thud echoed throughout the darkness as the centipede attempted to pull its antennae even further into its crevice.

Life in the cave succeeded only by avoiding others in the cave. The loud thump, something dropped from above, meant something new was now in the cave. New meant unknown. Unknown meant danger.

It was a good number of minutes before the centipede was convinced the cause of the disruption was done. Suddenly, though, the sound of more thumps echoed throughout the cave.

*Thump....Thump....Thump...*The quietness of the cave was lost in the repetitive thuds as more objects were tossed from above and began striking the floor of the cave.

Seven more times the silence was disturbed as unknown objects struck the cavern floor. The centipede and all the other occupants of the cave waited in complete silence unsure about what this change would mean for life inside the cave.

The silence within the cave returned after a full minute as the echoes died down. The long pause provided little comfort to creatures of the cave huddled within their crevices hoping to avoid notice. The centipede waited hidden inside its crevice for the cave to return to normal.

Pain.....Pain, utter agony.

How long he lay in the darkness he did not know.

Each moment was a mixture of physical and emotional pain which racked his body in utter torment. The pain was severe enough it caused him to lose consciousness. He would awaken in terror afraid of where he was only to have the waves of pain sweep over him again.

He could not remember who he was. He could not remember why he was there. Where he was, locked somewhere in complete darkness, escaped him as well. And just as he would begin to try to piece together what had happened to him the pain would return in agonizing waves.

*Drip....drip....drip...*Something was dripping in the darkness... Something...somewhere...

The pain gripped his body again rippling through his torso, up through his head, along his face, and flowing back down his body in gigantic waves. The excruciating pain was felt in his chest, in his shoulders, in his arms, in his face. Sharp, piercing, agonizing. He lay there motionless as fear swept over him, replaced by pain, only to be replaced by fear again.

Agony...pain...drip...darkness...pain...drip...drip...agony...

How long he lay there he did not know. He was pretty sure he was lying face down though. His face, bathed in the coolness of stone pressed against his flesh, was also bathed in agony. The complete darkness and coolness of the stone only seemed to magnify the trauma he felt.

Each time he passed out from the pain only to awaken later in complete confusion. He simply could not remember. It took a long while before he was able to determine he was lying face down. It took even longer to have that memory stick. Before that moment, each time he awoke a newborn, scared, dazed, and confused.

The darkness confounded him. Up. Down. Left. Right. These were not easily determined. Eventually, the feeling of the coldness of the stone on his face allowed him to realize he was lying face down. He passed out again as the agony wracked his figure.

Who am I?

Drip...Drip...Drip...

The torment returned like a jolt of lightning. His left eye, which he tried to open, was swollen almost completely shut. He forced it open a sliver, ever so slightly, aware something syrupy covered his face making it even more difficult to open that eye.

Not that it mattered. Even with the eye open slightly nothing could be discerned. He was lying face down in complete darkness. The stone cold floor felt soothing to his face. He was pretty sure the right side of his face had completely caved-in. The flatness of his cheek against the stone-cold floor assured him part of his face was broken, if not completely shattered into pieces.

His face ached, his cheeks burned with pain. A searing pain ripped through his body again causing him to pass out once more.

Drip…Drip…Drip…

How long he lay listening to the sounds of the dripping water he did not know. It had to be water. *What else would drip non-stop?*

Drip…Drip…Drip…

"*Where am I?*" The thought was fleeting when his body was afflicted with another wave of pain which passed along his torso, shot up through his shoulders, and settled somewhere along his face on either sides of his mouth.

"*Who am I?*"

The dripping water echoed throughout the room bouncing off the walls. He lay there listening to the sounds of the dripping water hoping the waves of pain would eventually go away. He tried unsuccessfully to force his left eye to open further.

Fear began creeping into his heart. The terror burned within his very essence while he lay in the total darkness of the room with the stone cold floor.

He wanted to stand, to shout, to scream, but he knew he would not be able to do so. Pain was shooting throughout his body, in orgasmic waves as it rippled through his limbs, through his torso, through his head, only to subside for a few moments and then to return again. He had lain there so long in the pitch dark. The pain was now an almost welcome sensation. At least that was something.

Drip…Drip…Drip…

He passed out once more.

The darkness once feared became less feared with each passing moment. The agony which still flowed along his body from top to bottom became less painful with each passing moment. How long he lay there he had no idea.

Days…weeks…months…years. He lost count on the number of times he had passed out from the pain.

Drip…Drip…Drip…

That sound continued. The sound of water came from somewhere within the cave. He had figured out he was lying face down somewhere in a cave. The cold floor pressed up against the right side of his face was less cold than it had been before.

His agony hadn't really subsided. He decided he had just grown more accustomed to it. It was almost a welcome sensation since he had not been able to move in a long while. The searing pain allowed him to realize when he was awake. There was a difficulty between knowing when he slept and when he was awake. The agony rippling through his body was the only proof he had he was not dreaming.

When the waves of pain rippled through him he would tense up each muscle, frozen until the agony subsided. Sometimes it would take a few minutes, sometimes he had been frozen in agony for hours. Sometimes, even days.

The darkness became more bearable. His fear was slowly being replaced.

As the pain and the fear mixed together, and became more tolerated, they began to be slowly merged into hatred. The hatred burned in his heart so intensely he often tried to focus on that while the waves of agony wracked his aching body.

Drip...Drip...Drip...

The dripping sound played out in his head over and over. He used the rhythmic sound to help create a mantra which he enjoyed. Instead of *drip...drip...drip...*it became *kill...kill...kill...*

It was easy to do...to replace the natural sound of the dripping water with what was playing out over and over in his head. He no longer questioned who he was or where he was or why he was there. He didn't care.

The anger and the pain combined with the fear of the unknown had produced a hatred and now a maddening sense of anger.

Lying face down, his body mangled and twisted as it was, he knew moving his right arm was going to be impossible. His right arm had been wedged beneath him from the shoulder to the tip of his fingers.

His left arm lay stretched out away from his body. His fingers ached when he tried to move them. His eye still covered with a sticky substance would still barely open. The sticky substance had hardened and was now caked across his face and eyes.

His chest ached, though the pain in it lessened and had become a dull, throbbing sensation. His mouth, on both sides, was still complete torture. Sharp and piercing, each side of his mouth felt as if they were on fire.

The darkness seemed less dark as time went on. Eventually he could make out vague shapes nearby. Whether they were boulders, or rocks, or something else he could not be sure. There were seven of them. It didn't matter. He couldn't move. This was going to prevent him from finding out.

Drip…Drip…Drip…kill…kill…kill

He tried once more to move his arm without success. The effort sent more waves of pain through him, even more intense than he had expected. He passed out once again.

The centipede crouched defensively within its crevice almost driven to the point of madness. It had refused to exit the safety of its shelter even as a ravenous hunger swept through its body.

Waving its antennae gently in the air the centipede had detected the presence of blood somewhere down on the floor of the cave. Frequently the bats overhead would die and fall to the cave floor. The spilled blood as these dead bats hit the floor would create an epic battle between the dwellers of the cave.

Many creatures would exit their crevices and completely ignore each other if only to have access to the life-giving blood. The sweet nectar was a maddening enticement to many occupants of the cave. Most though, including the centipede, fought the urge to leave safety based on an instinct to survive.

The loud echoes, which had occurred many days ago, if not weeks, had brought a change to the cave. The centipede still had the instinctual reaction of the unknown and was doing its utmost to avoid leaving the safety of the crevice.

The heavy thuds, coming in repetition so quickly had changed the normal race to consume, devour, and reap the bounties of the life-giving blood. Days had gone by since the quietness of the cave had been disrupted. The centipede had refused to move from its crevice.

After the passing of many days, the centipede had been driven almost to the point of madness by the smell of blood. Eventually the need to feed and the odor of blood was too much for the centipede. Slowly, the body exited one segment at a time, unsure about leaving the safety of its crevice.

It was prepared to jam its body back into the crevice. It was also prepared to fight to the death if needed. Slowly it moved until eventually its entire body exited the crevice. The smell on the air which was that of blood and decomposing bodies was almost too much to bear.

While the coolness in the cave slowed down the decomposition process things in the cave still decomposed. This only added to the enticement to leave the security of shelter.

The centipede hurriedly slithered down the wall moving its segmented body over cracks and fissures. The opportunity to feed on the blood replaced any fear it had about leaving the safety of its hideout. The centipede moved quickly toward whatever had died on the floor of the cave.

Drip...Drip...Drip...kill...kill...kill
The mantra had played over in his head so much as he lay motionless. He woke always hearing *kill...kill...kill* now instead of the dripping water.

He almost startled himself when he realized he had moaned, "Kill... kill...kill."

At some point he was awakened by a tingling sensation along his face. Slowly he opened his left eye a sliver. The sticky substance was still making it difficult, yet he was able to make out the outline of some multi-legged creature slithering along his face. Something was now crawling on his face. Its tiny legs tickled his forehead. It slowly made its way down to his cheeks.

A thousand tiny legs seemed to touch him during its journey along his face. It stopped for a few seconds in different places.

The tickling was agonizing especially since moving his arms and swatting whatever it was away was not an option. Slowly, the tiny thing which seemed to be slithering its way across his face, stopped at his mouth.

He remained frozen hoping it would enter his mouth. How long he had lain there he had no idea. How long he had gone without food wasn't a certainty, but if whatever it was on his face moved a little closer he was going to use every ounce of energy in his body to clamp his mouth shut. He could feel the drool pooling along the edges of his mouth.

The centipede seemed to be testing, probing his face, trying to determine its best course. It slowly slithered into his open mouth.

Pain wracked his jaws the moment he clamped shut his mouth.

He heard, no felt, the crunch as his broken teeth pierced the body of the centipede. The pain caused a level of agony he had not experienced since the first time he awakened, but he did not care. The juices of the centipede filled his mouth and oozed into the back of his throat. The thrashing bug tasted like nothing he had ever tasted before.

The legs of the centipede wriggled as the body died. His mouth exploded with pain as he slowly opened and closed his teeth. The crunch of the centipede grinding between his teeth continued as he instinctively swallowed the tiny creature.

The pain was too much and he passed out once again.

"Heee Heee Heeeha."

The noise of his elation surprised him. It was shocking.

He realized he had woken back up and had been remembering the sensation of the kill. He had been remembering the crunching sound his teeth had made the moment they had pierced the body of the insect.

It had caused him happiness to know the centipede had wriggled in an effort to break free only to have died being crushed and eaten. The sound of laughter burst forth from his lips. The pain was overridden by the elation. He continued to laugh.

The *drip…drip…drip…*replaced now by his laughter echoing off the walls of the cave.

More…I want more…

He laid face down waiting patiently for another victim to wonder haplessly across his face. He tried once again to move his left arm.

"Heee Heeeeeee," his laughter echoed throughout the cave as the fingers on his left hand twitched minutely. He could hear the bones crackle while they moved slightly.

He was sure the bones had been broken by fall to the cave floor. The thought brought a burning rage into his heart. He continued to try to move his fingers. Slowly, they moved, crackling in the dark as he closed his left hand and made a fist. The effort was mind numbing as another wave of pain shot up his arm and into his chest. He did not care; the pain was worth the effort.

Drip….Drip…Drip…kill…kill…kill

He closed his eye, not from pain, but from exhaustion and for the first time fell to sleep happy.

Laughter.

The laughter echoed off the cave walls, bouncing off the ceiling, then ricocheted back to him.

Lying motionless in the darkness he wasn't sure where the laughter was coming from and even worse from whom.

He wanted to lift his head, but that kind of quick movement was still beyond his capability. The energy provided by the insect he had eaten had given him the opportunity to lift and move his left arm closer to his body. He felt a thrill as he had done so and realized if he ate more he would be able to do more.

The second bug had crawled across his face after what seemed like an eternity. It followed the same path as the first bug and slowly entered his mouth only to fall prey to the same fate. His left eye glimmered with excitement as he crunched down and began eating the bug. The juices slithered down his throat as he swallowed convulsively.

"More. I need more," he thought to himself realizing he had dazed off and had ignored the laughter while caught up in his own thoughts.

The small, brown cave bat landed on his cheek so lightly that he almost did not feel it. It immediately leaned down and began to lick his cheek brushing its rough tongue up against his face quickly and quietly in the darkness.

It had been forced into leaving the safety of its spot on the cave ceiling out of necessity. On a normal day the bat would eat between twenty to thirty insects picking them off while they exited the crevices hunting for food themselves.

Lately, though, the number of available insects had declined, the cause of which did not matter to the cave bat. What mattered was being able to feed. That action had been altered forcing the bat to fly down to the floor of the cave.

It had been aware of the presence of blood, but the instinct to survive over-rode the bat's movement down from the precipice above. It could not wait any longer.

It flittered down, quietly; aware even bats could become the prey of other animals, which frequented the cave. Landing gently on the decomposing body, a body which had not moved in a long while the bat immediately began lapping at the dried blood.

It scurried over the face of the animal drawn by a larger pool of dried blood near the animal's mouth and by the left over saliva. A source of moisture within the cave was to always be explored.

The bat was completely unaware the animal had opened one eye a tiny sliver. It continued to lap at the dried blood gorging itself on the free meal.

The bat ignored the fresh drool which dripped from the mouth of the animal. It might have been an indication the animal was still alive, but the cave-bat was caught up in a moment of ecstasy driven by the buffet of blood.

Slowly, yet carefully the bat moved towards the mouth. The bat entered the dead animals open mouth, between the animal's teeth, drawn by the smell of even fresher blood located at the back. After a slight moment's hesitation the bat entered the tiny cave of the animal's mouth.

Death was instantaneous as the animal clenched its teeth shut. Bones crunched and the bat's blood squirted into the back of his throat. Slowly, the animal began to chew with a glimmer of elation spreading across its face.

A shrill of laughter mixed with a fit of hoarse coughing echoed throughout the cave.

He clenched, chomped, and tore the bat apart without ever opening his wide-gaping mouth. He slowly lifted his head, the first effort to do so since he had entered this cave, aware the pain was now a little more tolerable. Using his left hand he pressed gently against the floor of the cave and rolled over onto his back. His bones crunched like matchsticks as he rolled, the effort wearing him out. He lay in the darkness, on his back, staring up into the empty darkness.

"HaaaaaHeeeeeee," he laughed into the darkness.

The coolness of the cave felt a relief on his back.

"Kill…..kill….kill…" he screamed into the darkness. He closed his eyes and fell into a blissful sleep.

If he had ever been a human, he did not know. While the moments in the darkness grew into what seemed an eternity his touch on reality and sanity faded, lost somewhere in the darkness near the trickling water which still came from somewhere up above.

Dreams of a life in some distant past filtered into his mind replacing the physical agony which slowly began to fade. The dreams happened frequently at first, enveloping him with deep pangs of warmth only to be replaced by sadness when the memories sank and seemed to disappear forever into his mind.

Emotional agony grappled with physical pain hoping to wreak havoc on his body and mind. These dreams were eventually replaced slowly by nightmares which always bathed him in fear. This emotion was ultimately replaced by anger and hatred.

The emotional turmoil had won the fight and any sense of humanity slipped away into the darkness knowing it would never again return.

Slowly, as the dreams became more sporadic, he began to care less and less about what he had had been in his previous incarnation. He cared less about what was becoming of his lost humanity.

Laying in the darkness of the cave, the difference between being asleep and being awake were of little consequence. There were moments he felt he hadn't been asleep for months. There were also moments he felt he had been asleep for years. The two seemed the same as his thoughts and emotions settled on one agreed upon reality.

He had a hatred for all living things.

The first dreams of his past flitted into his consciousness; at least he had assumed they had been dreams of some past life. The dreams all started the same.

Deep in the woods, near a small creek, there were groups of teepees nestled together for warmth and protection.

In one teepee, a small Indian woman, kind and caring, bent over him, singing softly to him, hoping to help him get to sleep. Her voice was smooth and calming while he lay looking at her in the light by a warm fire. The smoothness of her skin brought memories of a warmth to him deep inside the darkness of the cave.

In his dreams she would caress his cheek picking him up and holding him closer to her face. It took him a long time and many dreams to realize he was just an infant in these dreams.

Her warm breath smelled of honey. Lovingly she sang her lullaby to him. The firelight cast flickering shadows along the walls, but he knew not to be afraid. As long as she was there holding him, humming to him, caressing him, he had nothing to fear.

Then, while he lay in her arms, the smiling eyes would lose their laughter and she looked at him with an intense hatred.

Her face melted in the wavering light and her skin changed her into an old man. The old man, also an Indian, glared at him with eyeless sockets which dripped thick drops of blood down leathery cheeks.

The old man, gray-haired and a face weathered by the ages, looked at him without eyes, without emotion, without sympathy. The man lifted a knife above his head, the serrated edges of the flint knife glimmered in the light.

The man's hand lifted, pausing for a few seconds, waiting until their eyes met. Then, without warning, the old plunged the knife deep into his heart. He screamed in agony trying to clutch his chest.

He was aware his arms would not move. They felt immobile, as if a weight had been placed on each of them. He lay frozen, in his dream, watching helplessly while the old man shoved a hand into his chest and ripped out his heart.

Nearby, a young boy, no more than eight years of age laughed. The boy pointed at him, staring at him with dark, piercing eyes, laughing while the old man held the heart above his own head, chanting some type of incantation.

He hated the boy, hated his laughter; hated everything about him.

"If I ever see him, I am going to kill him," he thought in his dream.

"I am going to kill him, and then..." in his sleep a smile spread across his face, *"I am going to eat his heart. I am going to devour all of him, every last piece."*

His wide-tooth smile showed an elation which was unwitnessed within the darkness of the cave.

As he lay asleep, dreaming about killing and eating the young boy, and possibly the old man, the hunger-pangs found their way into his stomach and he knew that it was time to feed. It had been a while since the small cave bat had landed on him and had been devoured. His smile continued remembering how it had felt to crunch the tiny bones with his teeth. The screech of the bat had been cut short in the darkness of the cave. His teeth had pierced its body, tearing, shredding, crunching, as he devoured it, elated at having killed.

The bat had provided him with enough energy to roll over and the energy to continue to live. He had decided it was no longer enough to wait for the other inhabitants of the cave to come to him. It was time he hunted, time he killed, time he fed.

The thought of hunting and killing something sent a thrill throughout his body. His body still ached. The broken bones still crunched as he moved. The sound of him rolling over reminded him of the crunch of twigs being broken in a forest.

He used every ounce of energy to roll back onto his belly. Slowly, he pulled himself up onto all fours, knowing he was going to make an effort to crawl and explore his surroundings.

Whether or not it was born of instinct, or the innateness of having witnessed other dwellers of the cave devoured as they exited their hiding places, the various insects, tiny brown bats, the blind flatworms, the poisonous centipedes, and the white, cave beetles all seemed to shrink further into their crevices hiding from the new predator which had dropped from the ceiling of the cave.

Having finally gathered enough strength, after what seemed an eternity of agony, he rolled over, the creaking of his bones echoing off the walls and breaking the ever present silence of the cave.

He lifted his arms no longer aware of the sharpness of the pain within his body, and pulled his hands closer to his face. His eyes had adjusted to the lack of light and he noticed that he could barely see the shape of his hands even within the darkness of the cave. Other shapes within the cave, memories of so long ago, when he had first awakened, returned to his thoughts.

Long-nails, resembling the claws of a mountain lion protruded from his hands.

His eyes had begun to adjust to his surrounding, though the darkness still prevented his seeing with complete clarity. Yet, he was happy to be able to see shapes in the darkness.

Slowly, he ran his hands along his face, feeling the dry, brittle hair at his scalp, the leathery forehead, wrinkled by age or the conditions in the cave.

His hands moved down his face stopping with fascination as they reached his mouth. His mouth seemed enormous. He realized the edge of his lips, the opening of his mouth, seemed to extend from one ear to the next. His fingers remained on his mouth for a long while the fascination and the sensation sank into his consciousness.

Opening his mouth, he felt his teeth, which were broken and sharp. The irregularity of the jagged edges shocked him for a few minutes.

Hunger pangs shot through his body. He ran his hands down his neck and along his torso. His fingers stopped at his chest when they found a gaping hole on the left side of his body. The tattered shirt was torn in a multitude of places, especially at his chest. He was mesmerized for a few moments, but did not stop too long to wonder what that actually meant.

Taking a few quick breaths he could hear the wheezing of his lungs in the darkness of the cave.

"*Why is there a hole?*" He didn't dwell on the thought.

Fear and anger coursed through his veins when he realized the hole was the size of his fist. He slowly inserted his fingers into the cavity almost afraid of what he was going to find.

His fingers searched, but found nothing. He removed his fingers from the gaping hole and continued down his torso. Unsure of what it meant to have a hole in his chest he stopped thinking about it realizing it didn't really matter. He was alive and his stomach was growling loud enough to break the silence of the cave.

"I'm hungry," he thought to himself, realizing not only was he hungry, he was ravenous.

It had been a long while since he last had eaten.

He rolled back onto his stomach, then pushed his hands flat against the floor of the cave, and lifted himself up on to all fours.

He inched forward slowly pushing one leg forward then the other. The scraping of his shins along the cave floor wasn't painful. In fact, he enjoyed the sensation. The sound reminded him of two pieces of tree bark being rubbed together.

He was unsure about whether or not he could sustain himself in this position since his body seemed to shake all over with the effort it required to move. There were a few moments when he felt he might collapse, but in those times he would stop, and wait for the steadiness to return.

His finger nails scraped along the stone floor as he moved. He enjoyed the sensation it caused and was slightly elated by the thought the cavern floor might be sharpening his nails into claws.

The gaping smile returned and an echoing laugh escaped him periodically bouncing off the cave walls and returning to him. A thrill of excitement ran through his body. He realized he enjoyed the sound of his laughter.

"Heeeehaaaaawww!"

The sound echoed through the cave forcing the remaining cave-dwellers to pull themselves even further into their crevices.

The movement required an immense amount of energy and effort. He inched ahead; his hand came into contact with something soft.

Nausea swept over him when the hunger pangs grew in intensity. It had been too long since he had last fed and his mind and body had both forced him to the conclusion it was time to eat. The thought of the blood of the bat caused his mouth to water as he slowly moved his fingers along the soft object on the cave floor.

"Heeeehhawww heee heee."

Booming laughter echoed off the walls.

He couldn't see himself, but he knew the wide-gaping smile had returned. His blood-shot eyes peered down at the object and excitement coursed through his veins as he realized he had found a body.

In his elation he passed out and collapsed.

He stared in through the teepee at the woman and the little eight year old boy who were snuggled together around the small fire. She smiled and hummed to the boy oblivious to his presence just outside.

The little boy looked into the fire obviously enjoying the warmth and his mother's arms wrapped around him. They were huddled under the blanket while giant snowflakes fell outside blanketing the ground in whiteness. The gentle sounds of the evening filtered in to the two as the singing of snow birds filled the air.

The flap of the teepee had been left open a sliver allowing him to observe unnoticed by the pair. The father had gone out earlier hoping to find some game for the family to enjoy in the waning light.

Evening would soon turn to dusk and the family would once again settle in for a long wintery evening. Leaning in slightly towards the woman the boy smiled as she pressed her cheek against his forehead and she gently kissed the top of his head.

Anger coursed through his body as he watched the pair.

Anger flooded into him. He was aware this woman, the woman who had been in so many dreams, the woman who had showered him with so much attention, was now giving that attention to someone else.

He could hear a baby crying somewhere in the tent. Both the mother and the boy seemed unaware of the crying or were choosing to ignore it.

His blood boiled and he took a step closer to the tent. The crying of the baby continued ignored completely by both mother and son who looked lovingly at each other.

She continued to hum. In his other dreams the humming of the woman filled him with joy. Now the humming hurt his ears. He hated the sound almost as much as he hated the little boy. The boy lifted his eyes from the fire and stared directly at him the moment his body filled the opening in the teepee.

The wail of the baby continued. The mother followed her son's eyes to the teepee opening and her gaze met with his.

They both started to laugh hysterically at him. They lifted their hands pointing in his direction.

His thoughts were flooded with hatred and anger. He took a step inside the teepee and moved silently towards the two. His hands flicked open and his inch long claws glistened in the light.

He walked around the fire reached down and grabbed the woman by the hair. She screeched with laughter as he picked her up and flung her across the teepee floor. The boy continued to taunt and laugh even when his hands wrapped around the little throat.

He lifted the boy raising him to eye level. All the while the little eight year old boy continued to laugh unafraid at what was about to happen. His long nails dug into the boy's neck and he leaned in and clamped his mouth down on the boys' neck.

Years of fury, anger, and frustration boiled over into this moment. Violently he tore into the young boy's body. The woman screamed savagely. He hadn't realized when her screams had replaced the laughter, but they did now that he had begun to feed.

She rushed at him madly with her arms outstretched, ready for combat. He turned and caught her by the neck with his left hand. His hands broke her neck instantly and she fell to the teepee floor.

He continued to feed, drops of saliva running down his mouth. He was completely unaware the father had returned and had entered the teepee. Looking up from his feeding their eyes locked onto one another. The father was an elderly man, white-haired, aged, and wrinkled.

"WHAT HAVE YOU DONE? WHAT HAVE YOU DONE MY SON?" the elderly Indian yelled into the teepee.

Tears of anguish ran down his cheeks. His eyes, coal black, burst open and blood trickled down the leathered face.

The old man moved forward pulling a knife from its sheath. It had been tied to the right side of his body. The stone knife glimmered in the firelight. Even without his eyes the elderly Indian walked over to him without hesitation.

He froze unable to feed any longer. He wanted to reach up to claw at the elderly Indian, but was unable to do so. His hatred was replaced by fear. The fear froze him instantly.

In the distance, somewhere far, far away, the baby continued to cry. The laughter of the little boy and the woman echoed off the walls of the teepee. The sounds mixed with the screaming of the elderly Indian man, who continued to yell screaming into his face.

"WHAT HAVE YOU DONE? WHAT HAVE YOU DONE, MY SON?"

He turned his head to look down at the remains of the eight year old boy. The head was turned towards him and the eyes were locked onto his. The lifeless mouth opened and the little boy, most of who had been devoured, began to laugh.

As the elderly Indian reached out, grabbed him by the throat and pulled him down to eye level. He was aware that his arms were frozen at his sides and he wasn't going to be able to put up a fight. His arms felt as if they were pinned by unseen hands. Pinned to his sides.

Even though he couldn't move his eyes looked down trying to figure out where the knife was. The knife sank into his heart, the pain seared through his body.

"WHAT HAVE YOU DONE? WHAT HAVE YOU DONE, MY SON?"

He awoke with a start in the cave grasping his aching chest. It took a few minutes for him to realize where he was, once again. The reality settled in, anger coursed back into him, and so did the hunger. He had collapsed into a pile across the cave floor onto something soft. He remembered now how he had found something inside the cave and the effort had caused him to collapse.

He lay on his belly and once again pulled himself up onto his knees and hands. Leaning in closely he realized he had found a body.

The elation swirled in his mind and his mouth began to moisten with saliva. He leaned in closer his eyes were able to make out the specific shape of a body. He looked around slowly. In the darkness, the outlines of seven shapes could be made out.

"Heeehawww."

The sound filled the chamber once again when he realized he would no longer be hungry.

Without hesitation he leaned forward grasping the first body by one of its ankles. He yanked off a leathery covering from the foot, pulled it up to his mouth and began to feed.

PART II
WHAT COMES AFTER

NINE

1918

LOCAL CHILD GOES MISSING

....stated the parents of little Jonathan Crause. The eight year old has been missing since June 1. It has been two nights since his mother tucked him in into his bed. Jonathan's mother reported tucking him in after saying the Lord's Prayer that evening.

Jonathan's parents reported they woke early on Saturday morning hoping to get the cow milking finished before the sun came up. His Pa had gone to Jonathan's room to wake him up, as he has done for many years, and Jonathan was gone. After frantically searching the house and the barn, both parents called on relatives and neighbors to help begin the searching. Local authorities are searching the nearby wooded areas along with volunteers from the surrounding communities.

Jonathan is the fourth child reported missing.

Anyone with any information regarding the little eight-year-old boy is encouraged to contact the local authorities immediately.

*Excerpts from an article in the **West Washington Gazette**, June 2nd, 1918*

MISSING

The spring of 1918 in southern Illinois began the way most springs always do in the early days of March. A brisk, cool, spring air early in the mornings would begin to warm by the afternoon to be bookended by an almost even cooler evening. After a brief few days of drenching rain, which caused rivers and creeks to expand well past their banks, the sun returned bringing much needed relief from the previous season's bleak winter cold.

Wild flowers bloomed all around, up in the tops of trees, in bushes, and sporadically along the myriad patches of wild prairie grass, which often grew almost to the height of a man. A bright mixture of purple, greens, yellows, and blues brought the nearby forests to life while a multitude of birds sang each morning to no one in particular.

About forty miles east of the bustling city of St. Louis, life meandered slowly along the Kaskaskia River in the same way the water flowed beyond its banks and then back into its original boundaries.

Cabins made of wood, and thatch, were routinely built, but the wooded areas and fields were not very densely populated. Each family worked diligently to get their fields ready for the planting. Every farm family along the river knew they were planting for the survival of their family and the survival of their neighbors. Excess crops meant the opportunity to barter for other crops and other staples.

It was in the early morning of March the first tremor hit, a slow rumbling along the New Madrid fault and seemed to spread out like the waves of an ocean. The water in some of the rivers and creeks flowed backwards in some spots while the earth rose and fell like an undulating caterpillar.

The farmers in the fields felt their feet move beneath them.

The second tremor was stronger than the first and it became evident to all that an earthquake was hitting the area.

The women, who had been busy helping their husbands ready the fields, prayed to the heavens. Many fell to the earth and lay prostrate on the dirt hoping the upheaval was about to end.

What was unnoticed, since it was located miles away from any nearby houses or cabins, located deep in the woods out along the winding river was the second tremor shook the ground, but also caused the collapse of some timbers, which had fallen across the mouth of a cave. Those same timbers fell partially to the floor of the cave and became wedged in a pile from top to bottom. Sunlight, which had not done so in many a year poured down into the deep crevice.

After a few moments of silence an animalistic screech, something akin to laughter, echoed up from the base of the cave. The forests fell into an ominous silence. The birds and animals waited for the source of the screeching to emerge from the depths of the cave.

The Reverend Sims looked out at his Congregation, a mixture of the young, the middle-aged, and elderly, well aware his next words would need to be soothing enough to calm the fears apparent on many of their faces. A few babes were being rocked silently in the arms of mothers, sisters, aunts, or friends.

As he looked out from his podium, the Reverend Sims slowly pulled a red kerchief out of his pocket and used it to dab the beads of sweat, which had already begun to form on his forehead and neck.

Many in the congregation fanned themselves hoping to provide a brief respite from the warmth in the church. The late morning service was ending and he did not feel like he had done what he needed to comfort those in attendance.

He was aware they were now past the noon hour, but still dreaded allowing the others to leave. The evenings had become a nightmare for many families. At least four eight-year-old boys had disappeared, all taken from their homes in the dead of night. Some of those children had even been asleep on the bedroom floors near their parents. Ever since the earthquake, which occurred at least two months ago, it seemed a curse had settled on their little Southern Illinois community.

The summer heat, although already a month into the season, was really just starting to begin.

The waves of heat rode across the fields in an almost blistering fashion. Most of his flock, farmers by nature, would rather have sat in the shade on this warm Sunday afternoon hoping to gain one more day's rest before a hard week of work in the fields.

May would soon turn into June and the crops would need tending, having to nurture them in the way a mother nurtures a baby in her care. These were God-fearing, hard-working people. The crops needed tending even with the events, which had struck fear into everyone's hearts.

"What do I say to them?" he thought to himself.

"Four children. Four gone in the last few weeks,"

Doubts assailed him. *"Has it been weeks? Months? Years? Days?"*

The stress of thinking about the evil, which had come to their community, made it difficult to concentrate. Sims sighed heavily; aware many in the congregation would correctly read the stress and worry about how he was feeling. He wondered whether he were up to the task of assuring his congregation.

"My friends, our hearts have been made heavy. The love we have for one another and the love we have for all of God's children...." he paused as if to clear his throat and continued, "that love will live for eternity. As we leave today keep your neighbors in your prayers. Offer support to one another in this time of need. This time of loss."

A few of the women, sitting in the front pew, began to cry. Each leaned towards each other holding hands and offering silent prayers for the safe return of their sons. The nearby men, the fathers of the missing boys, each placed their hands protectively on the shoulders of their wives.

Reverend Sims left the podium and walked down. He kneeled down, grasped two of the women by the hands, and said quietly, "Let us pray."

Everyone in the church bowed their heads and prayed in unison. "Our Father, who art in Heaven, Hallowed be Thy Name; Thy Kingdom come, Thy will be done, On Earth as it is in Heaven. Give us this day our daily bread, and forgive us our trespasses, as we forgive those who trespass against us; and lead us not into temptation, but deliver us from evil. Amen."

The Reverend stood and said, "Thank you. Would the gentleman in the Congregation be willing to stay for a quick meeting?"

Many of the men, those who were already standing hoping to make a quick exit from the church with their wives and children, slowly sat back down. The grief on some of their faces was obvious. It had been an exhaustive day knowing many of their friends and neighbors were here in the church grieving for their sons, all who had gone missing and had not been found.

The fathers of other eight-year-old boys, there were four or five who still had sons that age, instinctively looked towards their wives who nodded acknowledging they would be vigilant and watch their sons closely.

After the doors to the church shut, blocking out the sunlight, Reverend Sims looked to Sheriff Jones and asked the question many of the Congregation had wanted to ask. "Mr. Jones, do we have any leads?"

Sheriff Jones, who was only a part-time Sheriff, cleared his throat aware everyone in the room was looking to him to provide an answer.

Jones stood, turned to the other men, and responded, "None, yet Reverend. But, we're hoping for some leads, something which will lead us to the children." He sat back down knowing his presence was resented by some of the men. Especially without an answer as to who was responsible.

"I'm needed when I'm needed," he thought.

The rest of the time, he was just another local farmer trying to make ends meet. His shoulders sagged wishing he had something to help with the situation.

"I have an answer!" a loud, booming voice came from the back of the church.

All of the men, including the Reverend, turned to see which of the congregation members had made the statement.

It was Tom Jackson, the local town drunk. "I have an answer," he repeated, a little more softly. The Reverend's stern look helped Jackson recognize he had spoken too loudly.

"Tom?" the Reverend said. His first instinct was to ask Tom to leave, but he fought against the urge hoping Tom had something, anything that would help.

"Look. I know what you all think about me." Tom stated, matter-of-factly.

"It taint' no secret. Hell. I probably deserve all of it. Nevertheless, I have to admit, that I have been really bothered by all these kids being taken. I know Farmer Jones, there even suspected me at first as many of you proly did too." Tom paused, waiting for his words to sink in.

The Reverend felt he could almost read Tom Jackson's mind. *"He wishes he had a flask of whiskey with him."* Clearly though, Sims knew Jackson would have had an even more difficult time being listened to if he were drinking. *"Which, he usually is."*

"Well, after the second little boy was taken, I decided to do some searching myself. I took my ol' bird dog Blue and started sleeping in the day,"

Many of the men chuckled since he mostly slept off his nightly drunk the next morning. Jackson continued either not hearing the chuckling or refusing to notice it. Sims was not sure which.

"And then standing guard in town late at night."

A few of the men perked up, turning to look at Tom Jackson, intrigued about where this was going.

"Well, we stuck mostly to town, unless Blue got whiff of something. We...right before the last little kid was taken, Timmy, I believe."

Jackson paused and looked straight at Timmy's father, "I'm sorry, sir." Timmy's father nodded as he fought back tears.

"Well, your family lives relatively close to town." Tom Jackson licked his lips. The Reverend Sims was aware that everyone in the church was looking at him trying to judge whether he was drunk or just an idiot.

"Anyway, Blue began to whine a little and pointed out to the south of town. I grabbed my shotgun and put Blue on a leash. We began working our way to whatever it was that was grabbing his attention."

It was clear he now had everyone's attention. Their eyes bore into him expecting a revelation, which would help find the missing children.

"We were almost to your cabin when someone came running past us. He was tall. Very tall. Blue began to bark at him."

Tom leaned up dreading what he was about to say, but hoping anyone there would believe him. "The very tall man stopped and glared at us though he was too far away for me to make out who he was or what he was carrying. He had something cradled in his arms."

Timmy's father leaned forward and yelled, "Why didn't you tell us any of this?"

Tom Jackson paused knowing there were going to be many angry people when he finished his story.

"Well, to be honest, I didn't think any of you would believe me. And you know what, it's not because I'm the town drunk, it's because of who it is that I thought I saw."

Some of the men stood turning to face Tom Jackson. Others turned away, shaking their heads in disbelief, frustrated.

Reverend Sims stood up and said, "Gentlemen, at this stage, I think it's worth listening to anything which might help." Those who had turned away turned back to Tom.

"Go ahead," Tom the Reverend said.

Tom Jackson stood up clearly uncomfortable and continued. "Blue was scared and I ain't seen him scared much. When I squinted, I have to admit I thought I was looking at a Scarecrow."

Tom paused, realizing how it was going to sound. "After glaring at Blue and I for a few seconds, he… it… it turned and then began to run away into the woods."

"We ran up to the edge of the woods, but Blue wasn't having none of it. He wouldn't go any further." Tom reached into his pocket and held something up high. It was a patch of clothing.

"I found this torn piece of clothing and think it came from whoever was holding Timmy."

The men exploded into a fit of cursing, cussing, laughing, pointing, anger, and frustration. Some stood. Those standing sat back down.

"Listen to me!!!!" Tom Jackson's voice boomed loudly in the small church.

"I know what I saw. Does anyone have anything else to say that helps?" Tom lowered his hand rubbing the patch of clothing between his thumb and forefinger.

Reverend Sims realizing many men were on the verge of leaving, even with his presence, stood and raised his hands for silence.

"Gentlemen. Men. Please. Let him finish." He looked towards Tom hoping the man would finish quickly.

Tom began again, "Well, the way I see it, I'd like us to form a posse, and use our hunting dogs to track this man, this man in a scarecrow outfit, to where he's hiding out. I ain't going at night, now that I see how Blue reacted. But I think we should track him in the daytime."

Tom said, matter-of-factly, "What the hell do you have to lose? If I am wrong, I'm still the town drunk. If I'm right, we can catch this maniac and hopefully find some of the kids. Hopefully…all of them."

Tom knew the fourth kid had disappeared just a few days ago. It had been a few weeks since he had spied on the Scarecrow man who must have been holding little Timmy. He had been afraid to tell anyone what he had seen.

When the fourth kid disappeared Wednesday evening, he had made the decision to fess up and let the town know what he had seen.

The entire group of men quieted down many contemplating the logic of what Tom Jackson had just said to them. Each knew it was the only lead they had, so far, and whether or not they thought he was crazy it would not hurt to follow up on it.

The Reverend stood and said, "Okay Tom. We will meet you in town tomorrow morning."

The next morning, a few minutes after sunrise, Reverend Sims and twelve other men met Tom Jackson in the front of the church. Some of the men from the previous day had failed to show, but that did not bother him. He was actually surprised to see fourteen men in total, including himself and the Reverend, in attendance. Three or four of the men had brought their hunting dogs and he had Blue, his prized bird dog.

"Let's get started." Reverend Sims said.

The men nodded in agreement. Many had brought their shotguns and a few had pistols.

Tom Jackson kneeled down and took out the patch of clothing. He calmed Blue down. The dog whined for a few. After sniffing the patch Blue moved a step backwards. The other dogs, many of whom were trackers like Blue, nipped and pushed through each other to get a whiff of the patch of clothing.

The dogs began whining hoping to get away from the men and track the scent they had smelled on the patch of torn clothing. Three men mounted their horses and looked to the Reverend.

"You three try to stay as close to the dogs as you can. We'll catch up soon enough by following the barking."

The dogs were released and each broke into a fast run hoping to be the first to track the patch of clothing to its owner.

Tom Jackson, Reverend Sims, and the others began following on foot. The horse riders galloped on ahead across the fields towards the nearby trees.

The yelping dogs led the riders on horseback to the south of town almost to the exact spot Tom Jackson had mentioned when speaking to the other men. This was where he said he had spotted the Scarecrow man. The dogs ran in a pack.

They neared the woods, changed their direction, and began running east towards the Kaskaskia River. The horses galloped at a steady pace easily keeping up with the dogs who continued to seek out the scent, which had been on the patch of clothing.

Reverend Sims and Tom Jackson walked together in a brisk pace, walking with the other men silently, but with an avowed purpose. The Reverend was shocked to see the dogs end up almost in the exact location Tom had claimed he had been in his story. He began to suspect that maybe Tom was not drunk after all.

He prayed Tom's patch of clothing would help lead to the culprit and the children.

After about forty-five minutes of tracking, Blue and the other hunting dogs came to a dead stop in the middle of the woods. Slowly, they exited the trees and walked for about five minutes stopping about a hundred yards away from the opening of a cave.

The darkness of the mouth of the cave seemed to swallow up the light. It opened up from the flattened ground, clearly in a patch of open land between two stands of trees. The darkness inside hid the depth of the cave.

It was obvious the cave mouth had been partially covered by the trunks of some trees. These, though, had collapsed and had fallen down into the cave.

The horses, ridden by men, stopped near the dogs and refused to go any further. The three men pulled their shotguns and dismounted tying their horses to the branches of nearby trees. All of them looked uneasy. It was apparent the dogs and the horses were afraid to go any further.

The three men agreed they would wait for the group of men who were following on foot. An hour later those on foot caught up to the group on horseback. The men waited to explain the animals, both dog and horse alike, were afraid to go any further.

Reverend Sims spoke, "Well gentlemen we've come this far. Let's stick together and see what we can make of this."

He moved forward, his shotgun placed in front of him ready to fire, if needed. The other men fanned out in a line and walked with the Reverend towards the mouth of the cave.

Tom Jackson's skin crawled as the goosebumps rose on the nape of his neck. He looked to the other men who clearly were as nervous as he was. As a group, they all made it to within a few feet of the cave when they froze in their tracks.

"Heeeeeheeeeeehaaaawwwww!!!!!!"

The sinister laugh emanated from down in the cave. The men all froze terrified.

The laugh was not loud, almost barely audible, but clearly, someone was down in the cave.

"Timmy!!! Billy!!! Johnny!!!" One of the men yelled loud enough hoping to hear a response from one of the missing children. Suddenly, something was thrown out of the cave, landing with a thud, and rolling a few feet from the men.

Reverend Sims moved over to the object and using his foot rolled it over. He backed away, making the sign of the cross. It was little Timmy's head.

A few of them men bent over dry heaving. One of them threw up. The others cursed, asking God for help.

The soft sinister laugh trickled up from the cave again, "Heeehaaaaww!"

The men all retreated a few steps afraid to look down in the cave.

The Reverend Sims knowing an evil had come to their community looked to the men who had arrived on horseback.

"You two. Ride to town quickly. Bring saws, wagons, and as many other men as you can gather. We will stand guard here until you return."

He whispered the directions hoping whomever, whatever was in the cave would not hear him.

The two men were happy to be away from the cave. They jumped up and rode their horses away. The dogs all barked and turned in unison following the men.

Tom Jackson, the Reverend Sims, and the other men kept their guns at the ready. They backed away from the cave a few hundred feet.

"What's our plan, Reverend?" Tom asked quietly. He also, did not want whoever was down in the cave to hear what they were discussing.

He wished he had a shot of whiskey to calm his nerves. He had almost wished he had been wrong and none of the others would have believed him. Yet someone was down in that cave.

That person had killed little Timmy and most likely the other kids. Tom Jackson kept his eye on the mouth of the cave half expecting the Scarecrow man to poke his head out and laugh at them. If he did, Tom planned to blow it off with his shotgun.

About two hours later most of the men in the community arrived in their wagons bringing tools and other guns. The men of the town gathered around in a circle while most kept a watchful eye on the cave.

The Reverend Sims spoke.

"We believe whoever, whatever has been taking our sons is down in that cave. We either can go in and get him or seal him up burying him alive as a punishment for his sins against God and our community."

Some of the men started to clamor they should go in and get the murdering bastard.

Tom Jackson asked what was on everyone's minds.

"Who's going to go down there and get him?" Not one of the men spoke up. Those who had seen little Timmy's head were still visibly terrified.

Silently, without speaking, the men agreed the best course was to cut down some large trees and seal up the mouth of the cave. They would quickly cover the cave and place heavy boulders, too heavy for one man to lift, over the timbers.

Reverend Sims pointed to some trees about a fourth of a mile away, "We need to cut down large trunks. Then we will drag them over and cover the mouth of the cave. The trees are heavy enough that it would take twenty men to move them. The scoundrel will be locked in there and will die a slow death."

Tom Jackson nodded in agreement.

"You five," the Reverend continued, pointing to Tom and a few others. "You five keep an eye on the mouth of that cave. If he comes out shoot him."

Five large trees were cut down and stripped of their branches. Each was cut about twenty-feet long and then dragged over to the cave. The men had all gathered around most with their guns drawn in case the Scarecrow man should try to escape. The horses had to be controlled by three men to keep them from bolting away from the mouth of the cave.

Each log was rolled into place, one next to the other very quickly. Eventually the mouth of the cave was completely covered. To finish off the covering of the cave, the men had used their wagons to gather large stones from the nearby riverbed. Stones were laid across the logs, weighting them down into place.

There were no more children abducted during that summer. Eventually the Scarecrow man, the one seen by Tom Jackson carrying little Timmy into the woods became just a story passed down from father to son until it disappeared into history.

TEN

1988

EARTHQUAKE TREMOR FELT IN WASHINGTON COUNTY

On March 17th, St. Patrick's Day, which is supposed to be a day of good luck, local authorities received many calls about houses and barns shaking in the Washington County area. Authorities did their best to calm the fears of residents by explaining the earthquake tremor was mild in nature. The tremor, which was felt from Nashville to Okawville, from Ashley to Lively Grove, was mild and did little damage.

It did not register even a one on the Richter-Sale. No major structural damage was reported to any buildings or houses. The tremor had been felt in Washington, Marion, and Clinton counties on the 17th at approximately 8:00 am. In the neighboring counties, no structural damage was reported, either.

Students at Kaskaskia College, most of who were in classes at that time, reported feeling the floor shaking beneath their feet for a few seconds. Okawville-native David Dryver, who is eighteen years old and a freshmen at the college, observed, "It was over and done pretty quickly, but it does make a person realize that up against Mother-Nature our man-made structures don't stand a chance." Dryver is attending college with the hopes of becoming a teacher.

Scientists explained these counties are stacked together on top of the New-Madrid fault line and are prone to tremors and small earthquakes from time to time. Most often these tremors are mild and do not cause much damage.

One local resident, Tim Reynolds of Nashville, IL, a ninety-year old farmer and Veteran of World War II, reminded people of the earthquake that struck the area in 1918. He was barely seven years old that year.

In 1918, the earthquake was strong enough to shake some buildings off their foundations. Extensive work had to be done to repair the damage. While no deaths related to the earthquake were reported, the residents of Washington County reported seeing the Kaskaskia River flow backwards in some areas.

Topographic maps indicate an the New Madrid fault covers an area along the Mid-west extending down to the southernmost part of the United States.

*Article from the **West Washington Gazette** March 19th, 1988*

THE GIRL I AM GONNA MARRY

"What was that?" the sleepy-eyed eighteen-year-old college student sat up at her desk, almost in a frenzy, a look of terror sweeping across her face. She had fallen asleep in her desk during her 8:00 am College Algebra class.

David Dryver, and the rest of the class all would have laughed at her antics except every single one of them had frozen, also.

For a few seconds, the room had rumbled, seemed to lift, and then dropped back into place. The classroom shook so much the Professor had stopped in mid-sentence, tilting his head to the left, looking like he was listening for something on that side of the room.

David watched the professor's features, looking to his reactions before determining how he should respond. The man had remained calm which helped alleviate the fears of the rest of the class. All fourteen of them watched the professor intently.

David scanned the room looking at his other classmates to see which of them would be hysterical. Usually, there was at least one in every group. So far, none of them had become overly distraught. Like him, most were caught up in waiting to see what the professor thought they should do.

David had signed up for this 'early bird' College Algebra class on the advice of his academic advisor. She had called him last week proclaiming Kaskaskia College was going to offer a class which would start an hour before most other classes.

Initially, David had fought the urge to agree; well aware it would mean he would need to get up an hour earlier than he had been used to. He knew his mom would insist he jump at the chance to get one of his classes done a few hours earlier than normal. Still, he enjoyed the extra hour of sleep his later classes provided.

The final selling point had been the advisor's positive statements about the professor. He was a strong math teacher and made sure his students understood the material completely before moving on.

David had struggled in high school math. He had not had what he would call a strong math teacher and realized quickly if he were going to make it through College Algebra; he would need to have a dynamic professor. David had to admit his advisor had been right. The professor was the best teacher he had ever had.

"That's going to be me someday," he thought.

David had been jotting down notes about the professor's style from the moment he entered his classroom. So far his notebook had the following notes scribbled into the pages: *greet every student with enthusiasm, don't judge your students, have a good sense of humor, be organized, and be confident.*

As far as he could tell that was a pretty good list for a freshman in college. Hell, it was a pretty good list for anyone hoping to become a teacher.

David looked at the girl, who was still clearly startled. *"Yep, that's the girl I'm gonna marry,"* he thought to himself.

Of course, if his girlfriend knew he thought the same thing about every cute girl in all of his classes, he probably wouldn't end up married. Castrated maybe, but not married.

The professor did not waste any time. He directed the students to leave the building as quickly as possible.

"Let's meet up in the courtyard away from the buildings and trees." As the students got up to leave he added, "I'll take attendance when we get there."

A few students sighed and the girl, the one who had been startled, complained, "Can't we just go home."

"Yep, that's the girl I'm gonna marry," David mumbled to himself, chuckling.

He was half attempted to go ask her if she wanted to catch a movie, if they were released from class for the day. *Police Academy 5* was coming out and what better way was there to hook up with a girl from the class than a comedy.

David decided against it, realizing he was already in love and would marry, if all things went well his childhood sweetheart. *"Now that's the girl I AM going to marry!"*

The class met in the courtyard along with the other faculty and quite a few students who were already on campus. After waiting about fifteen minutes, the professor made the decision to let his students go home. It was going to be a moot point to keep them when no one, especially the sleepy-eyed girl, would be able to concentrate.

None of the students put up a fight, even when the professor joked, "I don't want any of you to feel like I am cheating you out of a quality education."

David responded, "You are forgiven." The professor smiled while a few of the other students laughed.

Walking in a group towards the parking lot David noticed a familiar van pulling up onto the campus.

The logo for the *West Washington Gazette* was printed on its side. The driver pulled into a spot, grabbed a notepad and camera, and stepped out of the van. She started to walk towards the students, most of whom were more worried about leaving than talking with a reporter.

"Why not?" David thought to himself. Walking over he waited for the reporter, a woman from his hometown, to close the distance to him.

ELEVEN

2018

EARTHQUAKE TREMOR FELT IN WASHINGTON COUNTY

…On the morning of March 22, 2018, at approximately 8:37am, the county of Washington, IL was rocked by an earthquake tremor. Local authorities reported the tremor caused widespread damage to many homes, bridges and highways. The tremor registered a six on the Richter scale, which is used by scientists to determine the power of an earthquake.

Insurance companies put the estimate of the damage in the millions. Many local residents are worried more tremors could be on the way.

The last earthquake, felt in this area, occurred in 1988. Prior to that researchers had to go all the way back to 1918 for information about a local earthquake.

*Excerpts from an article in **West Washington Gazette** March 23rd, 2018.*

TREMOR

Thomas Dryver met his father David at the door clearly excited about today's events. He had called David earlier in the day, leaving a message, but David had been too busy to respond.

"Did you feel the earthquake?"

David had to admit to his son that he had only felt bits of the tremor over in the Belleville Area. There had barely been any ground shaking further away to the west.

"Dad, we were in Algebra getting ready to start a quiz." The fourteen year old continued his story without taking a breath. David listened intently aware he would have been this excited at Thomas' age.

The excitement reminded him of his own experience with a tremor. Where had that been? Oh, yeah. It was at Kaskaskia College.

"When I was going to college, at Kaskaskia," David responded, "We felt a tremor, but nothing as nearly powerful as this one. He thought to himself for a few minutes remembering the interview he had given to the local Okawville paper. "I was even interviewed by the WWG."

Thomas looked fascinated by what his dad had told him. "I wish they would have interviewed me," he blurted out.

David smiled at his son appreciating his enthusiasm and excitement. The fourteen year old was still thrilled to have witnessed an earthquake.

"What would you have told them?" David asked.

Thomas thought for a few minutes and said, "I think I would have said you better go ask my father. He's the expert on earthquakes around here."

David and Thomas stared at each other for a few seconds before they both burst out into laughter. David reached up and patted Thomas on the head, absolutely loving one of those father and son moments. Thomas shrugged, not minding that David was messing up his hair.

He and Thomas talked for a minute longer before Thomas said, "I'm going up to my room. Uncle Shorty sent me some more arrow heads and a couple of flint-knives."

David's brother Shorty had been and avid arrow head hunter for as long as he could remember. Shorty had spent many years looking around Carlyle Lake and other locations for the native-American artifacts.

David had never taken to the arrowhead hunting, but Shorty had passed on that passion to his nephew Thomas, David's son. David nodded, acknowledging what Thomas had said.

Shorty had already given Thomas about fourteen arrowheads and three flint knives, the most recent one just a few weeks before. It had been found a few miles away.

He had called David, describing his finds and asking if Thomas was around. David had passed off the phone to Thomas, who had been waiting rather impatiently. The two rolled their eyes at each other during the brief exchange.

"Hey Uncle Shorty," Thomas said quickly. David had walked away and had not heard the rest of the exchange. That was a few weeks ago.

David was proud his son had taken to the hobby knowing how much joy it brought to his older brother. He watched Thomas leave the room.

David had looked around the home, both the walls and the foundation, and had not found any cracks. He breathed a sigh of relief since he had not found any damage to his home.

After the brief search, he picked up the phone to call his wife.

TWELVE

SCARECROW MAN

CHILD ABDUCTED FROM HOME

Eight year old Brandon Colden, a third grader, was reported missing by his parents on Thursday, May 31st. Local police have been conducting an extensive search with volunteers of the nearby woods.

Okawville Chief of Police James Watson has begun an investigation.

Excerpts from an article in the **West Washington Gazette**, May 31st, 2018.

THE MAN IN THE SCARECROW COSTUME

David Dryver sat in his family room watching *Fox News* on another slow Saturday night. It was almost mid-night and his wife and three children had already gone to bed, exhausted from playing another marathon game of *Monopoly*.

He chuckled to himself reliving the moment he realized the four of them had made a pact to defeat him at all cost. He had been the wheelbarrow, his favorite *Monopoly* character for as long as he could remember. He had also been undefeated in *Monopoly* with his family for as long as he could remember. It was not about winning or losing, of course. He smiled to himself.

"Especially since I won," David thought to himself.

It was just the opportunity to sit down and play a game with his children. David had grown up in a large family, but his father had been a drunk and an abusive husband and father.

Sitting in his chair, David privately winced thinking about the many beatings his father had had dished out. Having been one of the younger ones, his were severe, but fewer in number.

David had always sympathized with his two oldest brothers, especially his oldest Martin. Martin always seemed to bear the brunt of the beatings. His father took out all of his anger and resentment on Martin.

David always seemed to remember one in particular. His dad had come home drunk, as usual, and had decided the five boys needed to be taught another lesson about being a man.

David was sure his father could not actually provide a logical explanation about why five children needed to be taught a lesson. The drunkard would never be able to give a reasonable explanation. It had taken David years to realize his father was just a little man inside, deep inside. A scared little man who had his own issues. The beatings he had dished out were a mask for his own shortcomings both as a father and a man.

David remembered his father forcing the five of them to sit on the couch. He was sure all five of them had thought about running, but that would have only made it worse.

If they ran, they would have run to their mother who was asleep in her bedroom. David's dad would have then taken the beating out on his mother, which he always did when she tried to intervene.

His dad had screamed at all of them demanding they deal with their punishment like men. All five of the boys had grown used to this and none of them had cried that evening. David's sisters were excluded from the beatings, but that didn't leave them immune from the abuse. It would be years later before David would find out what his sisters had gone through.

Leaving the room for a few minutes, David's father had returned from the kitchen with a broom. He walked along the couch back and forth in front of the boys ranting about how they were disrespectful brats.

David's father waved the broomstick back and forth in front of their faces daring any of them to argue back. They knew better and all five looked straight ahead knowing not to make eye contact. His father stopped in front of his youngest son, Preston, David's younger brother. David was the second to the youngest. Both had been through it enough to know not to cry.

Smack!!!!! Smack!!!

David's father brought the handle down across Preston's legs twice. Preston winced from the pain, bringing a smile to his father's lips. The drunk pointed to the other side of the room and Preston quickly got up and moved. David's father moved on to David, repeating what he had just done to Preston.

He always started with the youngest one and worked his way up to the oldest. David remembered vividly his father being angry none of them were crying.

Even though he had demanded they be men, he really had wished they would cry and beg him to stop.

The five boys had seen this game too many times and the ending was always the same. Coming to the oldest of the boys his father lifted the broom handle high above his head and brought it crashing down onto David's oldest brother's lap. His father did so repeatedly until the broom handle broke.

"*Five, six, seven times.*" David couldn't remember.

David remembered Martin sitting quietly on the couch trying not to give his father the satisfaction of seeing him cry. How he did that David had no idea.

He had grown up promising himself he would never be that kind of a dad. David had made a commitment to be a father whose own children would look back at their childhood with fondness.

It was eleven o'clock on a Saturday evening and the April chill was in the air. David's wife had patted him on the arm before she took the children up to bed.

"If I fall asleep in one of their beds make sure I come down to our room," she said. She leaned in and gave him a peck on the lips.

"I love you," she said pausing and then said, "Oh, and by the way, you suck." David smiled knowing that she had been referring to the *Monopoly* game.

David had been down to two-thousand eighty-three dollars and only had four properties. The others had refused to barter any of their properties and it was clear he had no chance of winning unless a miracle happened.

And happen it did. His oldest daughter, his twelve year old, had shown pity on her old man and had taken his two-thousand dollars and given him Marvin Gardens.

He had had to give up a railroad, which left him with three properties. They were *Marvin Gardens, Ventnor Avenue, and Atlantic Avenue.* That gave him a chance. The others had howled and protested and David remembered his daughter's defense of the trade.

"He's done." She declared pointing at David's stack of eighty-three dollars.

Miracles do happen, though, even in *Monopoly*. David had relished in what he called the greatest comeback in *Monopoly* history.

Slowly, he had turned things around and had won the game. Everyone in the family had laughed as they realized Dad, dear old Dad, had come back and won again.

As his wife gave him the light kiss on the lips David smiled watching her walk the kids up to their rooms.

"I am a lucky man," he thought.

He again laughed thinking about the *Monopoly* game and his family. He had nodded to his wife, stood up, and went back into the family room to watch some television.

As he slouched down on his favorite leather chair David grabbed the remote off the arm of the chair and flipped on the television. He turned it to *Fox News* and settled in hoping to catch up with today's events.

David had watched television for about an hour when he realized he was ready to fall asleep. He had toyed with the idea of sleeping where he was, but knew his wife would want to come down to their own bed. David walked down the hallway to the front door in the darkness, turned left and went up the stairs to get his wife. She had dozed off in their nine year old daughter's bed and it took a few minutes to get her to wake up.

At the top of the stairs, David turned on the light so she could watch her step down the stairs. He walked behind her down the stairs and waited until she opened the door to their bedroom. David made it to the bottom of the stairs and then reached up and turned off the hallway light.

He turned to go into his bedroom, not noticing the man standing in front of his house.

David sat up in complete darkness panting heavily. He looked around quickly realizing he was in his bedroom and his wife was still sleeping soundly next to him.

He had gotten used to the little nightmares which came to him on a frequent basis. David had chalked them up to his childhood experiences and his wife had come to accept them also.

David uncovered his legs and sat up, draping his feet over the edge of his bed. He stood up and decided he would go get a drink of water. David had once told his wife he had not slept a single night through without waking up once or twice. Early in their marriage she had smiled and patted him on the arm.

Fifteen years in, she had accepted, as a matter of course he would wake up once or twice a night, go check on the children, and look around the house.

David looked at the clock on his night stand. *"One-thirty,"* he thought.

Opening the door to their bedroom David quietly went up the stairs to check on their three children. All were fast asleep so David walked down the stairs in the darkness. He had originally planned on turning right to go down the hallway to his kitchen. He had planned on getting a drink, checking the back door and going back to bed. As he turned, something caught the corner of his eye. Something was standing in his front yard.

In the darkness, David leaned in pressing his face up against the pane of glass of his front door. On the edge of the road, standing on the edge of his yard, stood a man.

David froze as a shiver of fear ran up the back of his neck into his head. He could feel the goosebumps rising on his forearms. The very tall man, who seemed to be dressed in some type of Scarecrow costume, stood unmoving staring at David's house.

"What the hell?" David thought. He knew he should grab his phone and call the police, but he couldn't move.

David lifted his right hand, reaching out hoping to turn on his front porch light. He was startled a second time.

He had been so focused on the man in the Scarecrow outfit he had not noticed the elderly Indian man who had been standing next to him in his hallway. David didn't jump. He didn't yell. He had been startled, for sure, but he felt no fear at the presence of the man in the hallway.

Turning his head, David looked at the elderly Indian, quietly standing next to him. The man had streaks of what must have been dried blood running down his cheeks. Locking his eyes on the Indian's face David lowered his right hand back to his side.

"He's afraid of you." the elderly Indian said.

The elderly Indian was standing with his back to David's front porch looking past David's shoulder, down David's hallway. His face was leathery brown and had a mixture of dried blood and tears on his cheeks. It took David a few seconds to process that the man had no eyes.

David turned back to the man in front of his house. The man was a giant, obviously taller than most men David had ever encountered. He looked from the elderly Indian back to the man in the Scarecrow costume.

David whispered, "What?"

The elderly Indian repeated himself, "He's afraid of you."

He stared over David's shoulder, refusing to make eye contact. His eyeless sockets seemed to stare off into the distance as if he were looking miles away.

David was not quite sure why the giant of a man, the one who was not too afraid to walk around in a Scarecrow outfit, would be afraid of him. Clearly, though, something was keeping him from coming any closer to the house.

"Maybe he thinks I have a gun." David was sure the man saw David standing at his front door.

"Heeehawwwwweeeee!!!!" The man in the road leaned his head back and laughed sadistically into the night. He laughed so loudly David knew his neighbors, his wife, somebody else should have heard it.

The man in the costume raised his right hand, extending his index finger and pointed directly a David. He lifted his left foot as if he planned on taking a step into David's yard.

"He's afraid of you," the elderly Indian repeated.

David had not even turned to look anymore at the man standing in his house. He felt safe with this man who had come into his house uninvited.

The man in the yard, though, David felt uneasy about him. He was sure this man meant to do him harm and to harm his family.

As David reached up with his right hand again, intending to turn on the porch light, the man in the Scarecrow outfit shifted to his left on his right foot. He took off running south along Front Street.

David watched in amazement. The man took long strides which carried him further away and out of sight. He turned, planning on asking the elderly Indian who the man was and why he was afraid of David. He was alone in the hallway.

David shuddered in the darkness. Waiting a few minutes David turned and went into his bedroom.

"It must have been a dream," he thought to himself.

THIRTEEN
THIS IS THE APOCALYPSE

FOUR CHILDREN NOW MISSING

....Chief Watson reported. The Okawville Chief has accepted an offer from the Nashville Police Department and the County Sheriff's office to help with the investigation. Reports indicate that officials have also been in contact with the FBI.

The disappearances of the four children seem to have occurred in a similar manner. All of the parents reported putting their eight year old sons do bed. In the morning they were gone. There were no signs of forced entry though two sets of parents indicated the front doors, which had been locked the night before, were both found unlocked.

Excerpts from an article in the **West Washington Gazette**, June 25th, 2018.

SNOWFLAKES

"Mr. Dryver?" the female voice called over the radio.

David was sitting at his desk working with two computer monitors, doing his best to match up the number of special education students in the IEP system with the number in the school's Student Information System. Summer school was in full-swing and he had been doing is utmost to keep up with the demands of both.

It wasn't going to be an easy task, but five years into his position as Department Chair for Special Education at Belleville West High School he had come to realize the only way to eat an elephant was one bite at a time.

He had learned that phrase on his first year on the job after calling his Director swamped. He felt like he was hyper-ventilating when he had explained he felt like he was falling further and further behind.

Mr. Carpier had answered his call almost as if he had been expecting it.

"How do you eat an elephant?" he had asked David. David had asked the necessary, "How?"

"One bite at a time." Mr. Carpier responded. He had even chuckled when he said it.

He had had David's job at the sister campus, which was Belleville East, years before and definitely knew it was a difficult, if not almost impossible task.

"Mr. Dryver???" the voice asked again, bringing David out of his reverie about Mr. Carpier, who had since retired.

David leaned up grabbed his radio pushed the button and responded, "Yes."

The walkie talkie then beeped.

"Damn it!" he thought to himself.

These were new digital radios the school district had recently purchased. "Piece of shit," he whispered to himself.

It was taking a little while to get used to the idea when a button was pushed the operator had to wait a second until it beeped. The beep indicated the person could then talk.

He pushed the button waited for the beep, and said, "This is Mr. Dryver."

"Mr. Dryver...Conner's in the library again." the voice on the other end stated matter-of-factly.

Conner was the pudgy little ninth grader who had come over to Belleville West at the beginning of the summer school year, which was three weeks ago. He was a Spectrum student, a student with Autism, and had been a handful. Conner's transition to high school had been difficult to say the least.

He had gone to eighth grade in a very small school. The size of Belleville West and the expectations being placed on him in high school had almost been too much for Conner to handle.

"And don't forget medication." David thought to himself as he responded, "I'm on my way."

Conner was prescribed medication, but it clearly wasn't having any positive effect on his ability to deal with the rigors of high school. Since he had come to West, he was spending almost as much time hiding in the library, as we was time in the building. Conner had definitely begun to test the patience of the teachers.

David hoped if they were all patient enough Conner would acclimate and there would be a decrease in his outbursts.

David opened the door to his office and said to the school psychologists, "Mr. A...I'm heading to the library. Conner's down there again."

Mr. Attler gave a thumb's up and said, "I'll let Ms. Cambridge know when she comes back."

Ms. Cambridge was the Speech and Language teacher for the district and the resident guru on working with students with Autism. She was out of the office. Turning to leave for the library, the only thing David could think of was, *I hope she gets back soon."*

Walking down the hallway he turned left and headed towards the library at a brisk pace. Conner had not done anything dangerous to staff, as of yet, but a person could not help but get the feeling that a violent reaction was pretty close at hand. David clipped the radio on his belt and turned in to the library.

He scanned the room. There were about fifteen students in the library. Some were working quietly on computers, others reading, a few even playing chess over in the corner.

Looking around he did not see Conner who recently had taken to either lying on a couch with his shoes off or lying under the tables singing loudly.

"*Good,*" David thought. He's not around the other students and disrupting. He looked the other direction and saw the para-educator sitting on a chair around the corner away from the tutoring rooms.

"He's in tutoring room A," she said quietly not wanting to draw too much attention their way. "He's been in there about five minutes, without permission, of course." She was fresh out of college recently hired, but David had found her priceless.

Tania Espers was a petite blonde who had recently graduated from Southern Illinois University with a major in Special Education. She had not been able to get a teaching job this year and had agreed to take a job in District as a para-educator. It was a great district and she was hoping eventually to turn it into a full-time teaching job.

David and the others had been very impressed with her resume and the interview. She was young, enthusiastic, and had the "it" factor when it came to working with high school students, especially high school students with special education needs.

"Good," David responded turning to Tania to ask what had happened.

"He was given a writing assignment in English, "she responded before the question was even posed.

"From there it was downhill. At first I thought he was coming to your office."

B122 was the safety zone for all students, especially those who needed a quiet place to go to regroup. They had been working diligently with him to go to B122 instead of the library, but he was having none of it.

They had offered rewards, threats of consequences, kind words, everything they could think of. Yet, when he left he immediately ran to the library.

"Well, at least he's in a tutoring room," David smiled. Tania smiled back in agreement.

"Right now, he's not disrupting the library like he did last time."

Conner had sung so loudly the last time the staff had evacuated all of the students. It had taken calling his parents to finally get him to quiet down and leave peacefully.

David was tempted to go that route this time, but since Conner had gone into the tutoring room, maybe it won't be necessary.

"Maybe."

David was getting ready to say let's check on him when something bumped harshly against the nearby wall from the inside of the room. A few books on the outside shelf fell to the floor.

He and Ms. Espers ran to the door of the tutoring room to see what Conner was doing.

"This is the Apocalypse!!!!" Conner shouted.

He was standing in the tutoring room with a heavy wooden table pressed over his head. Conner's face was flushed red and it was clear the exertion of lifting the table was having an effect on him.

Conner screamed, "This is the Apocalypse!!!" again and pressed the table above his head lifting it up and down as if he were a weightlifter.

"You can't make this up." David thought to himself.

He had often told his wife that someday he would write a book about all of the things he and the other teachers had witnessed over the years.

Whether it was the mad pooper on the third floor or the kid who wrote another student's name in feces on a bathroom stall, no one would ever believe teachers had to deal with these kinds of things at school.

David looked back and saw a worried look on the librarian's face. He slowly opened the door, only partially, to speak with Conner.

David grabbed the handle with his left hand, opened the door about twelve inches, and put his foot in front of the door. He wanted to prevent Conner from being throw the table at him, but did start to worry Conner might chuck the table through the window.

David kept his foot there to prevent the door from being slammed back shut. Years of experience, some training, and a lot of luck had prevented him from receiving any serious injuries. He hoped to keep it that way.

Ms. Espers stood a few inches behind him. They both peered through the space created by the opening in the door. Conner turned and looked at them a look of rage clearly on his face.

"Conner," David said, in a calm voice.

Conner turned, growled, and leaned back with the table clearly intending on throwing it across the room and at David. Luckily, the table was too solid and quite heavy. The weight of the table won the battle and Conner had two choices release the table or fall to the floor backwards on top of it. The table crashed to the floor.

"*Whew!*" David thought. He didn't have much time to congratulate himself as Conner rushed the door with clenched fists.

The pudgy ninth grader grabbed the door with both hands and tried to yank it open. David had a pretty solid grip on the door handle and prevented it from being pulled open.

"Conner, calm down," Ms. Espers said calmly, doing her best to de-escalate him.

Conner growled and tried to push the door shut with both hands. David's foot prevented that from happening, too. Clearly frustrated, Conner turned his body sideways and tried to lean through the narrow opening. It was clear he was not coming out through that small space and apparent the door was not opening, either.

Ms. Espers continued to try to talk with him calmly, but Conner was not hearing any of it. He reached out with his right hand and tried to punch David.

On the second attempt, the first only missed because David had leaned back, David reached up with his right hand and grabbed Conner's wrist.

"Grab his other hand!" David said quickly.

Espers ducked in and grabbed Conner's left hand. The student's arms were crossed and he was wedged between the door and the frame.

"*Good.*" David thought. This would keep them all safe until the others had arrived. Everything had seemed to be moving in slow motion, but in reality only a few seconds had gone by during the whole incident.

Conner opened his mouth and leaned his head towards David's chest. His lips curled back and it was clear he intended to bite David on the chest.

"Oh, no you don't," David whispered, knowing his words would not prevent Conner from trying to sink his teeth into his chest.

David slowly leaned backward trying to maintain his grip on the door, while holding Conner's right wrist, and trying to keep his foot wedged in front of the door. Conner became frustrated when he realized biting Mr. Dryver on the chest was not going to happen. He slowly leaned back and began pulling backward with his right arm.

"*Damn, he's as strong as an ox.*" David thought. He realized his hold on Conner's wrist was loosening. Slowly, David's right arm moved inward, closer to Conner.

The wrist, slippery with perspiration began to slide through David's grip. When both of their hands had breached the opening in the door Conner leaned in slowly, opened his mouth, and bit down on top of David's right index finger.

Later on, David would find out from Ms. Espers that she did not even know Conner had bitten him. David had done his best not to show Conner what he was doing was causing him any pain.

As Conner's teeth clamped down harder and harder on the finger, Conner looked at David out of the top of his eyes. It was clear he was hoping the bite would cause David to let go of Conner's wrist, the door, or both.

Conner was having difficulty breathing through his nose while biting down on David's finger. Or, the exertion from the battle at the door had finally taken its toll. Either way, after what seemed like an eternity, the pudgy little Autistic ninth grader released his bite on David's finger.

The brief respite was all that David needed. He slowly opened the door and before Conner could burst into another fit of rage he and Ms. Espers moved in quickly and safely took him to the ground.

They were holding him down afraid he might once again try to attack them, but it became clear that even Conner had had enough. As David and Ms. Espers talked to Conner, the ninth grader slowly stretched out one of his hands reaching for a pillow which was sitting on the cushioned chair in the tutoring room. David grabbed the pillow and gave it to Conner who immediately put it under his head.

As the Assistant Principals arrived, along with the School Resource Officer, David was physically exhausted. He quickly switched out with the ninth grade Assistant Principal who assured him Conner's mom had been called and was on her way.

"Your finger's bleeding," one of the Assistant Principals said. David looked down. Conner had done a number on his finger, but thank goodness had not taken off any chunk of skin. He had, though, broken the skin.

"I've already had all the shots I need." he thought to himself.

"I'll go see the nurse." He said.

"I'll send you an incident report. Let mom know that it's time we have a meeting," David said to Ms. Espers and the Administrators.

He walked out of the library and headed for the nurse.

The nurse's office was not too far away from the library and luckily, there were not any students waiting to see either of the school nurses. David walked in and asked the student worker to let one of the nurses know Mr. Dryver was here to see them.

Mrs. Thomas came quickly to the door and saw David's finger was bleeding. She took David into the office cleaned it up and was offering some advice when Mrs. Juno burst into the nurse's office.

Mrs. Juno was the school social worker and also worked in B122. She was breathing heavily and said to David, when she saw him. "I heard what happened, are you okay."

"I'm fine." David responded. "What's going on?"

Mrs. Juno said, "You have to come and see the television." She waved at David hurriedly and left the nurse's office without turning to see if he was following.

David left the office and turned left heading towards the counseling office. They had a television set up which ran CNN all day long. As he entered the office David was shocked to see all the counselors and about fifteen students standing around the television.

"What's going on?" David asked, clearly intrigued about what they were so excited about.

The television reporter was standing on the outskirts of Okawville, wearing a parka. Heavy snowflakes, the kind which arrived in a blizzard, were pelting him as he talked about the *El Nino*.

David stared blankly at the screen shocked into silence. *"It doesn't snow in summer."* He couldn't believe it. Snow in August. In Okawville. His hometown.

Mrs. Juno said excitedly, "The snow isn't the weird part David." He turned to look at her, not quite sure what she was saying.

"What?" was all he could manage in a response.

"It's not that it's snowing, it's where it's snowing." She turned and stared at him.

"It's only snowing in Okawville. There is a heavy blizzard, already two inches on the ground." It was clear that she was not joking.

David looked back at the screen. He thought first about the children who had gone missing.

"We're up to six now," he thought to himself. *Five eight year olds and one baby have been abducted. Six missing children and now, it's snowing. A blizzard in August?*

David's sanity felt like it was moving to the edge of a cliff. His nightly dreams about the Scarecrow, the missing children, his incident with Conner, and now this, a blizzard in August.

Mrs. Juno, obviously concerned about him asked, "What's going on?"

He walked over to the door of the counselor's office intending on leaving, turned back to face the students, the counselors, Mrs. Juno, and the television screen.

He lifted his right finger, recently bandaged from the bite from a pudgy little Autistic student and said, "This…this is the Apocalypse."

FOURTEEN

FIVE & SIX

INTO THE HOUSE

"But why?" Eli started to ask his mother, who was tucking him into his bed.

The little eight year old boy was still trying to question his mother about why his little brother, barely two months old, needed to sleep in the same room. Eli didn't need his little brother over there making noises, keeping him awake.

"That's enough," his mom whispered.

She had already explained, probably a hundred times, the two families had decided the children should bunk together in their house.

Eli's little brother had been moved into his room for a few days, his mom had explained, so his neighbor's kids, his friends, could sleep in the baby's room. The parents of both decided siblings should stay in the same room. Otherwise the children would be up all night giggling to each other.

After the abduction of the other four children, many in Okawville had begun to panic. Families had decided, mainly out of fear of the unknown, to combine houses when sleeping, hoping having more adults to guard their children would help better protect them.

Nancy Jones, mother of two, had been relieved when their neighbors had asked if they would be willing to combine houses and sleep over. Nancy had been very happy. Her neighbors' son was seven years old, but she was sure they were just as nervous.

All four parents had agreed readily to the arrangement.

The kids, on the other hand, were not so enthusiastic. Eli had argued about having to bunk with his baby brother. The neighbors kids, Charlie, a seven year old, and his sister Emma, who was five, argued as much as Eli.

The kids clearly had not come to grasp the seriousness of the abductions.

"How could they?" Nancy thought to herself as she looked at Eli.

She patted him on the head, leaned in and gave him a kiss. "I love you," she said.

Nancy stood up and looked a few more seconds at Eli. Mad, he rolled over and tried to ignore his mom's gestures. She shrugged, looked at the baby, little Ben, who was still sound asleep in his crib.

Nancy met her neighbor Cherie coming out of the other bedroom.

"How are they?" she asked. Cherie shrugged her shoulders realizing they both had had the same discussion with their kids. The two women walked down stairs to talk with their husbands. It was 8:00pm.

The man in the Scarecrow outfit leaned silently up against the wall near the front door. He listened intently to the two women as they walked down the stairs chattering about their fears.

The smile, which stretched from one side of his face to the next, returned. Blood red eyes gleamed with excitement. Both women were completely unaware of his presence, separated by a locked screen door.

"You coming?" Cherie asked, turning to walk down the hallway.

Nancy had paused at the front door. She leaned in and pressed her face on the glass looking out. It was quiet outside and nothing was stirring. Snowflakes trickled down out of the starry night.

Nancy reached down with her right hand and made sure the door was locked. She turned to walk down the hallway, completely unaware of the Scarecrow man who now stood in the window.

He looked down and reached up with his left hand. The lock clicked, the latch sliding to the unlocked position. He had already entered the house before Nancy had made it to the end of the hallway.

Silently, the Scarecrow man glided up the stairs. The four adults, sitting towards the back of the house in the kitchen, were unaware he had even entered the house.

The Scarecrow man's fangs glistened in the darkness as he stood over Eli's bed.

Drops of saliva oozed out of his mouth and dropped onto the carpeted floor. Gently, he reached down, sliding his hands beneath the sleeping little boy. Eli shifted in his sleep and the Scarecrow man paused for a few seconds. Silently he finished the movement, lifting the eight year old boy into his arms. Turning to leave, the Scarecrow man was briefly startled by the movement coming from another bed.

The Scarecrow man moved slowly over to the other bed. Leaning over, the ear to ear smile returned as he looked down at the sleeping baby boy.

The Scarecrow man glided down the stairs silently with Eli in his arms and the baby Ben nestled in his mouth. Reaching the door, he flicked his fingers causing the door to pop open. He stepped through before the screen could slam shut. He walked down the porch steps, turned to the left and started running away from the house.

Nancy was startled to hear the screen door open and shut.

"Was that the door?" She asked. A look of fear swept across her face as she turned towards the others. The four adults ran to the front of the house and peered out the window. The streets and yard were empty. The silence of the night greeted them. The snowflakes continued to fall.

"I thought you locked the door," Nancy's husband stated. He reached down and pushed open the door. "I did Nancy responded."

Nancy, a look of fear in her eyes, responded again with a quick "I did."

The four of them bounded up the stairs to check on their children.

FIFTEEN

THE WOLVES THAT WOULD NOT HOWL

MORE CHILDREN GO MISSING

Near panic has set in in the town of Okawville as another child has gone missing. The children, all eight-year-old boys, were believed to have been abducted in the middle of the night from an as yet unnamed person. The lone exception is the abduction of a baby, the brother of one of the missing children. The baby and his eight-year-old brother happened to be sleeping in the same room. The mother of the boy reported that she had put the two to bed. Her neighbors, who happened to be staying in the same house, also reported that the front screen door was locked. There was no forced entry. Authorities are expanding their investigations and are now looking at any felons, recently released, who may have had convictions related to children.

...in one case, the boy's father was sleeping in the same room on the boy's floor.

*Excerpts from an article in the **West Washington Gazette**, July 17th, 2018.*

FBI, STATE LAW ENFORCEMENT IN OKAWVILLE

...including the presence of the FBI. Chief Watson was pleased to report that the FBI's famed missing person task force has arrived and has begun assisting in the investigation. There are now six missing children, five boys all eight years old and a baby.

"We appreciate any help that the FBI and State Police are willing to provide," Chief Watson stated.

Residents in Okawville have begun sleeping with their lights on. Many parents are now having their children sleep in their bedrooms until the culprit is apprehended.

*Excerpts from an article in the **West Washington Gazette**, July 18th, 2018.*

THE ALPHA FEMALE

Silently, the Alpha female lay at the mouth of the den staring out into the coming night. Another sleepless night was ahead and the exhaustion she felt had to be suppressed for the good of the pack.

The den was a temporary shelter, one of many in the last few weeks. She had recently moved her pack, what remained of them, hoping to keep them one-step ahead of the beast and certain destruction.

The Alpha had been doing everything possible to avoid meeting the Beast, a predator that had recently come to these woods. It had entered the forests and had begun feasting on deer, squirrel, coyote, and wolf alike. The Beast had not distinguished between predator and prey and all the inhabitants of the forests were feeling the effects.

Her pack, in particular, had felt the repercussions brought by this new super predator. No longer the dominant predator she had considered taking the rest of the pack and fleeing further to the south. She had been resisting the urge, mainly because this was the home of her ancestors.

Years ago, in lands further to the west across the great river, her ancestors had made the decision to flee their hunting grounds. Rival packs had made the day-to-day struggle for resources a matter of life or death. Thus, forced out of their ancestral hunting grounds, the pack had traveled in the dead of the night, seeking refuge in the woods of Southern Illinois.

She was the seventh in a line of Alpha females, descendent of those who had led the wolves originally into this area. Her ancestors had been diligent in their efforts to survive undetected by man. They had done so by hiding and gliding through the night unseen, and would oftentimes avoid taking prey if there was even a remote possibility they would be discovered by man.

They had also gone undetected, by not doing that which most wolves in North America were known to do. This pack of wolves, following their great migration east, had decided long ago to survive in the modern age of man, specifically in the woods of Southern Illinois that they would no longer howl. It had taken years of training and years of discipline for this trait to become innate and almost a part of their DNA.

By now, it was instinctual in nature having been taught from wolf to wolf from generation to generation. The suppression of this innate trait had allowed their pack to grow and flourish and had allowed them to become the dominant predator in the woods. Their numbers, prior to the beast, rivaled the many packs of coyotes, which also inhabited these very forests.

By not howling, by suppressing the urge to be a wolf, the wolves were able to hunt and forage in relative safety. Many of their prey, including the dogs at nearby farmhouses, were thought to have been taken by the large number of coyotes, which frequented these woods and were often spotted by man. If it was not the coyotes, there were more than a few mountain lions, though these were fewer in number and not as well known. No one ever suspected there were wolves nearby. If the Alpha had her way, that would continue.

The Alpha fought against the urge to abandon the home of her ancestors. She was still hoping to remain in these hunting grounds. Recently, she had begun moving the pack on an almost nightly basis. Hoping to keep the Beast from finding them, the strategy, so far, seemed to be working. It had been a few days since the Beast had caught any of them, unaware.

The Alpha female wolf lifted her head off her front paws and stared out of the den into the waning light. She knew in a few minutes the time of the Beast would begin again and this Beast would once again be on the prowl. She watched as the snowflakes began to gather near the mouth of the den.

She also knew they had stayed in this den for two days and nights and soon they would have to find a new den. Hopefully, a new den could be located by tomorrow tonight.

While she wanted to avoid going out into the coming darkness, knowing it usually brought the Beast, the Alpha knew she did not have a choice. The darkness would also help hide her movements. She needed speed and stealth hoping both would make her movements harder to detect.

She stood and looked back over her shoulders. The Alpha nipped at one of the other wolves letting him know she would no longer be on guard at the mouth of the cave when the first light of day made its appearance.

Her message was clear as the remaining wolves moved away from the mouth of the den and further back into the cave. The wolf maintained her place ready to sacrifice her own life in defense of the pack. She needed to wait at least one more day before moving them.

A meeting had been agreed upon and would occur in the morning. After that meeting, the pack would be on the move hoping to find another place of safety. The meeting, which would take place in a clearing, on the edge of a forests a few miles away, was necessary. She would meet the dominant buck of these woods hoping to form an alliance, which had never been formed before.

Silently, she lowered her head back to her paws hoping the pack would survive one more night. They could move in the morning, if an agreement could be reached. They would have the strength and numbers and move to a place of protection.

The last light of the day disappeared for good and the mouth of the cave was covered in darkness. A few stars winked at the Alpha female as she lay facing the oncoming night. She closed her eyes for a few minutes hoping to rest and gather enough strength for tomorrow's meeting.

SIXTEEN

A SUMMER'S SNOW

DUSK TIL DAWN CURFEW ORDERED

Local authorities, along with the FBI, State Police, and activated National Guard units have ordered a "Dusk till Dawn," curfew for Okawville. The only exceptions will need to be emergency or work-related matters. Check-points have been set up on every road leading into the town.

"I feel strongly this is necessary," Chief Watson of the Okawville police Department stated. The law-enforcement agencies recently have made changes with the hopes of preventing more child abductions. The agencies are also working long hours looking for clues which will lead them both to the children and the person behind the abductions.

Additionally, National Guard soldiers will patrol the streets of Okawville after dark. The hope is the presence of these troops, along with the manned-checkpoints, is enough to deter the man behind the abductions.

*Excerpts from an article in the **West Washington Gazette** July 18th, 2018*

EATING AN ELEPHANT

On the third day of snow it became apparent the weather had settled into a peculiar pattern. Heavy snow in the evening would accumulate all through the night only to dissipate into a light snow flurry in the day time. Most of the snow would melt in the coming summer sun. And then, the process would start all over again.

It was with the arrival of morning, as the snow was tapering off, the wolves and the deer quietly entered the town of Okawville.

Since it was early August, the snow which accumulated over-night would melt by the end of each day, only to begin the process all over again that evening.

The second night of snow was much heavier than the first and the third heavier than the third. All three nights of snow had been enough to envelope the ground in a white blanket.

Meteorologists from across the nation were immediately dispatched to study the phenomenon hoping to offer some type of plausible scientific explanation.

The snow which had begun the first day, only in Okawville now encompassed almost the entirety of Washington County. Most of the meteorologists as well as some of the locals were placing the blame on an El Nino pattern, but nothing definitive could be found to explain the cause of the summer snow.

Many in the community, both residents and visitors were left scratching their heads in disbelief at the sight of the snow. This event, paired with the disappearance of the children, and the term *Once in a Lifetime* event could be heard nightly on the news. The carnival atmosphere would have been a festive one if there were not missing children.

The remaining members of the wolf pack walked single-file along Highway 177 entering Okawville from the south.

They passed un-noticed by the workers at the tractor dealership on the south end of town, hardly noticing the giant green tractors lined like sentries along the side of the road to their right. Ripening corn fields, most of which had begun to seemingly melt under the onslaught of the snow, guarded their left and seemed to be kneeling to the animals as they silently glided into town.

Led by a female wolf, the Alpha, the pack included a smaller, younger female, barely a year old, three males, and three pups. The previous eight weeks had seen most of them hunted down and devoured by the Beast or killed in the defense of each other.

Either way, the survival of the wolf pack was going to be decided by an act of desperation. Entering a town, especially when wolves were not even known to inhabit Southern Illinois, brought an abundance of dangers.

The wolves though were in agreement with the deer the best chance of survival now rested at a location inside the town.

Silently they moved down the center of the street, the wolves flanked by a large herd of deer, twenty-three, which were themselves led by a large fourteen-point buck. One of the pups ran around the buck's hooves nipping playfully, only to be called back by the Alpha with a quick bark.

Ignoring the pup the large buck, which had scars on its left-side from a recent encounter with the beast, continued its march into the town. On-coming cars, there were a few on the streets at that hour honked, then slowed as the drivers gaped in astonishment at what they were witnessing.

The Alpha female wolf head held high walked on, oblivious to the stares of the occupants of the vehicles. A few men, those who lived on Front Street, came out onto their porches to see what all the fuss was about. Some cursed and a few ran back in to their houses to retrieve their guns. They came back on to their porches though none raised their rifles.

They wondered in confusion about why wolves and deer would come into Okawville. And why, would they come in together.

Recent events in Okawville, the missing children, the summer snow, and now these animals caused a few to make the sign of the cross and pray to the heavens for some protection from the evil curse which had gripped their town.

The animals, both predator and prey, continued their journey down the street, as flurries of snowflakes whipped around them caught up by a gently blowing wind. It was clear they were not about to be deterred from their purpose. They never wavered even in the face of a few oncoming tractors and cars.

July had blended into August. Deer and wolf alike strolled gently with a purpose walking past the city park ignoring the men and women of Okawville. Cell phones replaced rifles and occupants of the homes soon began recording the events which had never been seen before and would most likely never be seen again.

Some residents, on a normal day, might have been completely shocked. Some, though, didn't react with much surprise. Some called their friends, some called 911 to report what they were seeing.

As the animals continued their trek moving into Okawville almost three city blocks north on Front Street, they came upon the house they were looking for.

As the deer and the wolves neared the house the local and State Police arrived on the scene parking their cars in the middle of the road about a block away. A few members of the National Guard, those who had been patrolling the streets of Okawville the night before exited the Circle K and walked over to the police cars hoping to see what the excitement was all about. One man, a Sergeant, dropped his coffee as he stared in disbelief at the oncoming wolf pack and herd of deer.

He immediately began to call someone on his cell phone as he stared in disbelief.

Turning left the animals walked in unison along a house with an asphalt driveway. The deer and wolves walked in silence past the two-story Victorian home down the driveway. They moved quickly and quietly past the asphalt and continued along the concrete driveway into the back.

They quietly crossed over the gravel parking spaces into the backyard. There, the wolves settled in a group in the center and the deer, all twenty-three, made a protective circle around the wolves.

Almost on cue, all of the animals lay down in the melting snow and waited patiently for the occupant of the home to return.

The owners of the residence had already gone for the day. Both parents were at work and the children had gone on to school.

It didn't matter to the animals, both predator and prey. Something had led them to this spot, to this sanctuary. Instinct had driven them here to this location. They knew this was a place where even the Beast feared to go.

David Dryver sat at his desk on an early Friday morning preparing the forms for the upcoming IEP meetings. The Summer school had come to an end so it was time to begin anew. His goal, now, was to prep ahead as far as possible. In doing so, he would alleviate the hectic pace of those first few school days.

"Just eating an elephant one bite at a time."

He sat leaning forward over his desk, though he periodically lost focus thinking about the children of Okawville who had gone missing.

Tears welled up in his eyes. He empathized with what the parents must be going through. Dark circles had formed under the very eyes which had been standing sentinel all through the night staring out his front door. Each night he watched as patrol cars and National Guard Humvees silently moved down the streets through Okawville. The headlights cutting through the whipping snow had not made him feel any safer.

The National Guard had been sent in to Okawville by the Governor, and a dusk to dawn curfew had been put in place. That protection, and that curfew, hadn't prevented another of the abductions from occurring a few days ago. This one had occurred in another nearby community. Though, Addieville, whose children attended the Okawville school district, had always seemed a part of the community.

Yet even on that night the Scarecrow had been there, staring at his house, a silent vigil whose presence only meant danger to his family.

"And the eyeless Indian, he was there, too."

State militia and the State Police used dogs to scour the town of Addieville for any sign of where the last abducted kid had gone. There weren't any noticeable tracks to follow as many thought there might have been given the snow fall.

Many residents began to wonder if it was time to flee Okawville, at least temporarily. Others, like David and his family, had chosen to stick it out. Many families had hunkered down and even a few had decided to spend the evenings with one another. In the churches on Sunday mornings a few preachers had even begun to question whether Okawville was cursed.

Most parents, including David and his wife, had begun sleeping in shifts, while gathering all of their family members to sleep in one room.

The elderly Indian was still entering his dreams, speaking to him frequently, offering the same cryptic, "He's afraid of you."

He clearly was referring to the Scarecrow who continued to appear nightly in his dreams. That bothered David the most. The eyeless sockets of the Indian, stained with tears of blood, had almost become a welcome relief when David would look out his front door.

A few times, when the Scarecrow would lift a foot almost as if it were going to take another step towards the house, the eyeless Indian, who never looked at David, but continued to look over David's shoulder as he talked continued with his admonition, "He's afraid of you."

David sat at his desk staring at the computer stone-faced; he remembered the conversation he'd had with two friends last night at his dining room table. He had called both of them and asked them to stop by for a beer.

Tom Smith was a Sergeant in the Illinois National Guard and was a part of the unit activated by the Governor to help provide protection and support to the town of Okawville. He lived in Nashville, Illinois, a neighboring town, but had many friends who lived in Okawville. For him, the missing children were something he took personal and he gladly patrolled the streets in the evenings as the residents of Okawville slept.

The part he never admitted is that as the snow spread throughout Washington County and the abductions moved to another town, he had a growing fear that Nashville, and its children might be next.

Tom had been in the Guard for about twelve years. He had stopped by David's house with another friend, the Chief of Police of Okawville Joe Watson to check on David and have that ice cold beer. David's wife had already gone to bed, their three children sleeping on their parents' bedroom floor, as the three men sat at his dining room table talking about the missing children. They stared out the window as the dusk began to settle and the heavy snow fall began to increase.

"I just don't get it," Tom was saying. "We've had the best tracking dogs in the state trying to pick up their scent. Five children and a baby just don't disappear without a trace. Especially, over the course of four weeks. And now, god-damned snow in summer time."

David sat quietly, at his table, sipping his beer, wondering if he should mention his dreams. This wasn't a time to freak out or to cause chaos, and the last thing he wanted to do was to make two friends of his think he was going crazy, but he was sure the dream maybe was not a dream and the Scarecrow in his front yard might have something to do with the missing children.

"They have to be related."

"But why the elderly Indian? Why tears of blood and why eyeless sockets?"

There were just too many unanswered variables for David to be comfortable saying they weren't anything other than dreams.

"How long have we all known each other?" he asked.

The two men looked at each other and then back to David.

"Why?" Chief Watson asked.

"How long?"

"Hell, David, I'd say going on twenty-five years, at least." Tom replied. "What's that have to do with what's going on here with these missing kids?"

David leaned back tipped his beer and took a long drink. He swallowed and looked from Tom to the Chief.

"In all the years we've known each other, have either of you ever known me to tell tall tales, or to embellish about anything?" He waited for their response, but only received shakes of the head from both.

"Well, I have to say, initially, I thought that the missing children had to be the work of a serial killer. A sexual predator? That was when the first one went missing. Then when the second and third disappeared on the same night eight days later, I knew deep down the town was in trouble."

The Chief and the Sergeant looked at David, waiting patiently for him to finish his thoughts. They both knew the FBI profilers had been taking a look at whether or not the perpetrator had a fascination with the number eight. Five children, all eight years old, all disappearing eight days apart. Some in the same evening. And the baby?

"Now here we are on the seventh day, and tomorrow is the eight day." David stopped, almost as if he had changed his mind about opening up to his friends. The silence in the room was almost more than all three of them could bear.

"Well?" Chief Watson asked. "Where are you going with this?"

"Do you believe in dreams?" David asked the two men, knowing this would take the conversation into a realm of make-believe. He wasn't sure what their response would be.

"I guess I do, David," said Tom. Tom looked from David to the Chief and then back to David. "Just tell us what you want to say."

David decided his best course of action was to just tell them about his dreams. He explained the first dream, which had occurred on the same night as the first abduction. David described the Scarecrow man in every detail possible, the leathery brown skin, and a large, gaping smile, which stretched from one ear to the next, blood red eyes which seemed to glow in the dark.

David did his best to pass on the sense of fear he had felt when he would look in his front yard and see the Scarecrow staring back at him. The Elder Indian who would appear suddenly, standing behind him, looking away from the Scarecrow and past David, with the eyeless sockets and the tears of blood streaking down his face.

David's friends listened attentively as he continued to describe the words of the Indian. Tom and the Chief listened in silence holding their judgement until he was finished.

"So, what do you think it all means?" the Chief asked, wondering if his friend had begun to lose his sanity.

"I know you think I'm crazy, but I feel like the Scarecrow is behind the abductions. I feel like he's been in front of my house staring at me and for some reason he fears me." Now that it was out in the open David felt both a relief and a foreboding. Waiting for his friends to respond was almost more than he could bear.

Tom decided to take a more positive approach. "Do you think it's possible that you are feeling guilty because your son hasn't been taken?" He wasn't a psychologist, but guilt could cause many a sleepless night. David shook his head as he sat in silence.

David sighed, knowing his friends weren't convinced it was anything but a dream. "I know, it sounds crazy. But we have seen some crazy shit, wouldn't you agree. The kids. The snow. Strange things are happening and there has to be a reason...a cause." David tipped his head towards the window as if challenging his friends to explain away the billowing snowflakes in August.

The Chief leaned forward and said, "There sure is a reason. Some crazy bastard is abducting eight year old kids and now a baby. For what reason, we don't know yet. But, he will make a mistake, I can guarantee you that. And when he does, we will catch him. Hopefully, the kids are still alive. If not, well, maybe I will be able to dish out some justice before we take him in." The chief stood up finished his beer and left.

Tom remained seated and was a little more sympathetic to David. He stood, patted David on the shoulder and said, "Thanks for the beer Dave. Stay safe tonight."

David was brought out of his reverie by a knock at his door. It was Mrs. Juno, the Social Worker. He nodded to her through the window of the door and she entered.

"Did you get any sleep last night?" she asked knowing he hadn't. David shook his head and reached up to rub the sleep out of his eyes. He looked tired and knew the other people who worked with him were deeply worried.

"Well," Mrs. Juno said, "if I didn't shock you when I showed you the news report a couple of days ago, I think I might have it topped." He looked at her with a puzzled look on her face.

"Didn't you tell me you live at 607 South Front in Okawville? The house with the asphalt driveway?" She stared at David with an obvious mixture of excitement and sympathy.

He nodded almost holding his breath in fear of what she was going to say next. His cell phone, which he had placed on his desk, began to vibrate. It was Tom, but David was too engrossed in his conversation with Mrs. Juno to answer it.

"You really need to come see the news, again."

They both exited his office and headed towards the counselor's office again. David had a déjà vu moment when he realized almost the exact staff, minus a few students, was watching the television screen as had done so before.

"What's going on?" he said. Everyone in the room, in unison, turned to look at him. Their faces all turned back to the television.

A news reporter was standing in front of his yard with a number of police officers. Cameras were focusing in on something in his back yard.

"Why the hell are television reporters at my house?" His heart felt as if it had leapt into his throat.

"Residents of Okawville, as if they haven't had enough to worry about, woke up this morning to find wild animals roaming through the town."

The reporter was gesticulating excitedly as he described the wolves and deer who had taken up residence in the backyard of this Okawville home.

"The police initially were going to put down the animals, but animal control officers have talked them out of it until the owner of the home can be contacted. The situation is too unique to respond without getting some type of logical explanation." The reporter continued excitedly.

David was watching the report when the counselling secretary's phone rang. She picked it up and responded.

"Counseling office this is Mary." She listened and then handed the phone to David.

"Hello," David said. It was Chief Watson on the other end.

"Dave. You need to come home."

Tom Smith sat in the driver's seat of his Humvee listening to David's voice-mail message for the third time. The Humvee was still parked on the side of the road facing David's house, less than a block away from where the animals had trotted onto David's property.

"Damn it." Tom muttered to himself. He sipped his coffee and frustrated shoved the phone back into his pocket. This day was definitely turning into a nightmare. He was beginning to wonder whether or not they weren't all a part of some governmental scientific experiment. He could not explain all he had heard and seen and definitely felt like Okawville itself was becoming completely unhinged.

Tom noticed Chief Watson whose squad car had pulled up near the other cars blocking off Front Street. The police had set up squad cars in a two-block radius to keep traffic out of the area. Only residents of homes within the perimeter would be allowed in or out.

"Chief Watson!" Tom called out from the open door of his Humvee. Chief Watson held up a hand to let him know he would be there in a minute. Tom continued to sip his coffee patiently knowing the Chief currently had a lot on his hands. It included moving the reporters back outside of the perimeter. Every time he would move one another would slip in and begin filming from in front of David's house.

After a few minutes of establishing what needed to happen, Chief Watson walked over. "Hey Smitty." he said. Tom responded in kind. "Chief."

"How was the patrol last night?" the chief asked. Knowing it probably was the same as before.

"Well," Tom started not really knowing how to say what he was about to say. He knew the Chief had not been too excited with David's story telling last night. Tom started to explain where they had patrolled and that nothing other than heavy snowflakes were spotted.

"But, we rounded the corner down on the other end of town about a half-mile down the street. I noticed something standing what I thought was in front of David's yard." Tom waited for the chief to respond.

"You noticed something, what do you mean you noticed something?" The Chief looked at his friend ignoring the Private who was sitting in the passenger seat.

"Yeah, about three o'clock this morning the Private and I were making another pass along Front Street when we noticed a man standing in front of David's yard." He looked at the Private who nodded in agreement. The Chief looked back to Tom.

"It was hard to see at first, with the heavy snow, but as we pulled closer whatever it was, whoever it was, turned away and began running along the street, towards the south."

The Chief opened his mouth to respond seemed to think better of it and listened attentively.

Tom swallowed a sip of coffee stared into the dash of the Humvee and continued.

"From what I could tell, it was a man. Tall, very tall. Long legs. By the time we made it to David's house the man had made it past the railroad tracks." Tom paused again. "I've never seen anyone ever run that fast."

David's story played over again in Tom's head as he explained to Chief Watson there was someone, something standing outside David's house last night. If he hadn't seen it for his own eyes he never would have believed it.

The Chief looked again at both men and said, "Keep this to yourself for now." He turned and pointed at David's house. "I've called David and he's on his way home." The Chief looked at Tom and fear swept over the faces as both men as they said in unison.

"Today is the 8th day."

SEVENTEEN

THE HUNT

EL NINO' HITS WASHINGTON COUNTY

....which was not completely unexpected. Scientists re-iterated to an already jittery population that the snowfall in Washington County in the summer is not completely knew. Snow also was recorded in the area in 1918.

"It's the effects of El Nino," Sam Cretian, a meteorologists from Channel 7 news stated. He went on to explain that the 'turning over' of the water in the Pacific Ocean has otherworldly effects on the weather globally.

"Rain in the desert. Snow in the Mid-west." He said. "Of course, with all the other things going on in this part of Illinois, it's easy to see why some would be afraid."

*Excerpts from an article in the **West Washington Gazette** August 2nd, 2018.*

THE PLAN

As the evening in Okawville began to settle in for another night of abnormally cold weather both the wind and the flurries of snow seemed to pick up steam. Gusts of wind whipped through the little town causing the residents, those who had decided to stay, another round of fear.

Snow had already begun to accumulate, again, and it seemed the biggest blizzard to hit Washington County was on its way. It would not have been a surprise to anyone except this blizzard was hitting in the summertime.

David Dryver sat at his dining room table looking at his computer. He had decided to pass the time, as he waited for the others to arrive, by doing some research. He had already Googled Native American legends and the best he could come up with was the thing that had been staring at his house was a Wendigo.

Why it had chosen his home, *him,* as its target was beyond anything he could reason. David had not been one to believe in ghosts and certainly did not believe in something as far-fetched as a Wendigo, though he was well on his way to changing those beliefs.

"I am fucking crazy," he thought to himself as he continued to read the descriptions. It was becoming clear whatever it was was not going to stop, unless someone stopped it.

"Is that even possible?

The abduction of the children, probably the murder of the children, the extreme blizzard-like conditions, they were all connected. How his house and how he played into this he could not even imagine, yet there was a connection he was certain.

David looked up from the computer and glanced at the *walking stick* leaning up against a wall in the corner of his dining room. He had hunted around in his garage for about fifteen minutes before finding the stick stacked away with the others on a top shelf.

Years ago, when he had been driving through Arizona, David had stopped to buy a souvenir for Thomas. He remembered being told the stick had magical properties, which were designed to protect its owner from evil spirits. He remembered chuckling to himself, but bought it anyway. He knew his son would love it since he collected arrowheads and other items of Native American origin. The stick intrigued him.

"Maybe that's why it hasn't come any closer," he mumbled to himself.

Uncertainty about the events of this summer plagued his mind. The elderly Indian had visited him again, in his dreams. He could not convince himself he was dreaming any longer.

"Maybe, I've been awake each time." He thought. *"If that were the case David then the man in the Scarecrow outfit, or the Wendigo itself were real."* The taking of the children was real. So was this crazy weather. As far as he was concerned, anything was possible. Doubts assailed him, though he could not argue with what was happening.

David lost himself in his thoughts again, remembering those eyeless sockets looking over his shoulder past David, as he stood at his front door staring out the window.

The bloodstained tears streaking down the leathery cheeks had never ceased to make him cringe, no matter how many times the elderly Indian stood in his hallway. The quiet streets being covered with a blanket of snow, in the middle of summer, only added to his confusion. The Indian's blood stained cheeks were etched into David's mind.

Each time his heart had been beating so loudly he was surprised it was not loud enough to wake up his wife.

David jumped as his phone rang. He picked it up immediately so it would not disturb his wife and kids.

"Yeah," he said quietly. Chief Watson responded, "You okay, Dave?" David nodded in the affirmative. He then realized the Chief was on the phone and would not be able to see his answer. "Yes."

"Good. We will be there around 10:00 pm."

Before he could acknowledge what the Chief had said the Chief hung up. David pushed himself away from his laptop and stood up. He stretched his aching limbs and went to the kitchen. He looked around for a few minutes, found the cup he was looking for and poured himself some coffee.

"I'm going to need a lot of these," he mumbled again, almost dreading the plan the three men had come up with earlier this morning. David smiled at his wife who sat watching television with their children. She smiled back and snuggled under the blankets.

She had not argued when David had told her their plan. Deep down his wife knew something had to done. Something radical or more children were going to disappear. Something *HAD* to be done to protect the children of Okawville. She had made the decision she and the kids would bed down in the family room tonight. David was glad, since it meant he could see the three of them.

"So what do we do now?" Tom Smith almost whispered.

The four men sat together at the dining room table. They had spread out a map of Washington County. Tom Smith had brought the private, the one who had witnessed the scarecrow-like man standing in David's yard the night before. The private remained quiet, letting his Sergeant do all the talking for him.

Chief Watson leaned in and looked over the map. He knew he had no idea how to respond, but did not want to look like he did not have a plan in place. Staring at the map seemed to be the best thing to do.

David was the first one to speak. "Well, it looks like we need to wait. If anyone needs to get any sleep, it should be done in pairs. Two of us need to be awake at all time."

The four men nodded knowing none of them would actually get any sleep tonight.

The private leaned in and finally spoke. "Well, the way I see this it's going to be very difficult to keep up with this man, especially if he cuts through alleys, behind houses, and through the woods." The others nodded, encouraging him to go on.

The private leaned over and picked a box up off the floor. He had brought it with him from the Humvee.

"I think our best option is to use this," he opened the box and pulled out a drone. "We can track him, from above, to find out where he's going. Once we locate his hideout, then the four of us can follow and capture him."

"The three of us," Sergeant Smith said. "Remember, private, this isn't an authorized mission. I cannot have you with us. Besides, I'd like someone here to protect the house in case this maniac returns while we are gone." David breathed a sigh of relief knowing someone would be here while he was gone. The private thought about arguing his case, but only nodded in agreement after seeing the look of desperation on David's face.

"Do you think you can use that in these conditions?" Chief Watson asked. The private nodded in the affirmative. He went on to explain the military-grade cameras were designed to pick up movements even at night and could be used effectively even in total darkness.

"It actually uses military technology and uses night-time vision similar to what the Special Forces use in the active duty services. Not as good, but for our purposes, it should do the job."

The private, who had already run his idea past Sergeant Smith, finished explaining he could stay in the Humvee in the drive-way and would be able to follow the man hovering a few hundred feet above. He went on to explain he could give the men immediate feedback on direction and location of the lunatic. "The Scarecrow Man should be easy to track, if he shows himself."

"The Scarecrow Man?" Smith responded. The private nodded and the four men left it at that.

Once the plan was set, David walked quietly into the family room to check on his wife and kids. The kids were fast asleep on his floor. His wife turned on the lamp, leaned up and asked him how it was going. He reviewed the plan, seeing the relief on her face knowing someone would be in the driveway looking out for them while David was gone. He leaned down and kissed her. As he left, David turned back and looked at his children. They were all fast asleep, oblivious to what was about to happen. David did not notice Thomas had been wide-awake the whole time.

The Scarecrow Man stood in the front yard of David's house inching slowly closer to the front porch. Gusts of wind tore at its tattered clothing causing the fringes to flap back and forth. Snow flurries seemed to circle around his legs enveloping him in a blanket of bone-cold flakes. It was unimaginable anyone could stand in this weather without being chilled. He did not seem to mind the cold and was oblivious to the gusts of wind.

David, who had fallen asleep sometime after midnight, stood up quietly and walked slowly to the front door. He froze in his tracks when he realized the scarecrow was standing directly in front of him on his front porch.

The two of them leaned closer to the windows of the front doors. Their eyes, only separated by a few inches, met and each of them froze their movement.

The grotesque mask covering the thing's face widened with elation as it realized David's fear, which was written across his face, was real. David's heart raced. He questioned what would cause the scarecrow to come this close. *"It's never come onto our porch,"* he said to himself.

David was glad the door was locked, but realized the thin pane of glass was of little protection should it decided to come in uninvited. He wondered why the elderly Indian man had not appeared.

He also wondered if he should yell for his friends. *"Maybe, this time, I am dreaming."*

Slowly, the scarecrow lifted his right hand up to the door and placed it on the windowpane. Long, sharp nails extended out from the skeleton thin fingers.

A shiver of fear passed through David as he realized the scarecrow, at least for now, did not seem to be frightened of him any longer. The scarecrow's leathery brown skin, shriveled with age, pressed against the window. Slowly, very slowly, the scarecrow leaned in, it's eyes still locked on David's. David backed away slowly from the door a few inches. His heart was racing and he wanted to scream for help.

The scarecrow lifted its left hand, while the right was still pressed on the windowpane. It grabbed the handle of the screen door and turned the handle. As it began to open the screen, David panicked, realizing the screen had not been locked.

"No!!!" he thought. David quickly moved forward to lock the screen.

It was too late. The Scarecrow pulled open the screen, pushed open the other door and stepped into David's house.

"Nooooo!!!!!!" David screamed. He sat up in the dining room aware he had been startled out of a nightmare.

"David, you okay?" Chief Watson, who had been awake with Sergeant Smith, asked. Both men had been startled by David's scream. They had been sitting with David who had fallen asleep at the dining room table.

"What time is it?" David asked.

"One a.m." one of the two men responded.

David was so caught up in his dream he could not have said which one told him the time. He rubbed the sleep out of his eyes and went to get a cup of coffee.

David looked down the hallway towards the front door and noticed someone standing in his front yard. He froze.

"What's wrong?" the private, who had just woken up, asked, after noticing David stopping in the doorway.

Without turning towards the others, David replied, "It's here."

The four men stood at David's front door looking out at the tall figure standing in the front yard. He was at least seven feet tall.

The Sergeant had been the first to comment on the man's height. The figure with the leathery face widened his smile, if it were possible, showing sharpened fangs, which seemed to cover his face from ear to ear.

A young boy, probably eight years old lay draped across the tall man's arms, held firmly against his chest. The child was asleep, or dead, they could not tell which. The group looked closely hoping to identify who it was. Slowly, David opened the wooden front door to his home. His screen door, primarily made of glass, remained shut.

"David!" Chief Watson whispered. David ignored him stepping closer to the screen door.

The scarecrow-like figure seemed amused to see the four of them looking at him. Bravely, he took a step closer to them. He moved into David's yard.

The child, nestled in the arms of the scarecrow man mumbled something and rolled inward, unconsciously seeking warmth from the blustering cold wind. The scarecrow looked down and its wide-toothed mouth opened in a mocking smile. Blood-red eyes lifted again and locked onto David's.

Chief Watson reached down slowly un-holstering his gun. The man in the scarecrow outfit seemed to pay him no heed, unafraid of the weapon.

"Careful, chief," Smith whispered.

"I can drop him!" the Chief whispered. "We may not get another chance."

"If you drop him," the Sergeant argued, "we may never find the other children, if they are even still alive." The chief's shoulders sagged as he remembered the other missing children.

The odds were all of them were dead, but he could not be sure. Moreover, if they were not, Sergeant Smith was correct. They needed this to play out just a little bit more.

"Private." Smith continued. "You know what you need to do." The private quietly backed away from the men at the door and went to retrieve the drone. They had agreed he would exit the back door and launch the drone, hoping to find their man from two-hundred feet above.

The three men continued to stare at the giant scarecrow standing unafraid in the front yard. The figure was taller than most men they had ever met.

"Dad?"

David turned to see his son Thomas's startled face. Thomas was puzzled to see the three of them standing at the front door. David looked quickly at his son and back to the scarecrow figure. A look of fear spread across its features and it immediately turned and fled south towards the railroad tracks. Its long gangly legs made it look like a giant grasshopper running into the night.

"Thomas, go back to bed," David said hurriedly. He locked the doors and ran back to the dining room.

Thomas Dryver looked out his front door and noticed the tall scarecrow running down South Front Street carrying what he thought was a little boy in his arms. The running scarecrow left a wake of snow flurries whipping around his feet as he ran.

David grabbed the walking stick from the corner of his dining room as Chief Watson and Sergeant Smith grabbed the map and the flashlights. Each man put on his coat. They walked out the back door. David reached up making sure the doors were locked and asked, "Now what?"

Sergeant Smith said, "Follow me." They walked around the northern part of the house and down along the asphalt driveway towards the Humvee. The private was inside, already. The three men opened the doors and got in.

"Should we follow him?" David asked, aware the private was focused on guiding the drone through the thick snow falling from the clouds.

"That's a negative." the private responded. Sergeant Smith looked back to David and Chief Watson. "Correct. We need to let the private and the drone do their part. For all we know, this chase could go on for five minutes or for an hour."

"Can you see him?" the Sergeant asked. The private nodded, showing the men the video that was projected onto his screen from the drone. The drone was flying a few hundred feet overhead and clearly could see the outline of the large man running southeast along the railroad tracks.

"He's fast," the private said, closely following the man in the scarecrow outfit's movements.

The video from the drone bounced up and down and weaved back and forth, as the private fought the wind and the snow. The scarecrow man ran for about ten minutes and then circled towards the north of Okawville before heading out into the farm fields away from the houses.

"He's definitely heading north, almost northeast." Smith said, watching the private work.

David and Chief Watson sat quietly, not wanting to disrupt the private from guiding the drone. Everything rested now on following the man in the scarecrow outfit to his hiding location.

"There are a lot of old farm houses and barns to the northeast of the town," Chief Watson whispered. "Maybe that's where he's heading."

Suddenly, without warning, the man in the scarecrow outfit stopped, his ears tilted up towards the sky, as if he were listening for something.

"What's he up to?" the private asked. The four men leaned closer to the screen, hoping to discern what had made the man stop.

"I think he hears the drone." Sergeant Smith said. "That's impossible, though. The wind and the snow at that altitude would make it impossible to hear those plastic rotors."

The man in the scarecrow outfit balanced the sleeping eight-year-old boy in one arm, lifted his other and pointed directly at the drone flying above. The video on the drone began rapidly bouncing as if the drone were caught in a major amount of wind turbulence.

"It's going down," the private yelled. The video sent back by the drone concurred as it flipped over back and forth and landed with a thud. The video, though upside down, showed the man in the scarecrow outfit walking towards the drone.

The man picked up the drone and pulled it closer to his face. The leathery scarecrow mask widened, stretching its mouth open, and the drone was shoved inside. The video clipped off as the scarecrow bit down harshly on the drone.

The four men sat in silence, stunned the drone had crashed. They were stunned the scarecrow man had pointed a finger and had brought the drone down. It seemed impossible, but the wind seemed to pick up speed at the command from the scarecrow as it had raised its hand.

Now, as the reality of the situation sank in, Chief Watson screamed at the other three. "That's why I wanted to take the shot. Now do you understand?" He opened the door and stepped out.

The three other men stepped out, snow whirling around their feet as the gusts of wind ebbed and flowed like waves on an ocean. David stood silently, ignoring the curses coming from the other three. Slowly, he turned and began walking down the driveway.

"Where are you going?" Smith asked. He seemed stunned that David was getting ready to walk away.

"I don't know," David responded. "But I do know he, it, they, were last seen by the drone on the Northeastern part of town. Maybe there are some clues there. I'm going to find the drone."

The Chief, the Private, and the Sergeant stared at David in disbelief. Did he actually believe he could find the drone in this weather? Did he actually believe he was going to find this man?

The four of them were startled by a sound from behind them and quickly turned around. Thomas Dryver was walking down the driveway from the back of the house. He was walking between the Alpha Female wolf and the large fourteen-point buck.

David stood silently, watching his son answer the rapid onslaught of questions being posed by the other four men.

"What do you think you're doing? Why are you here? Shouldn't you be in the house? Why are you with these two animals? Does your mom know you are out here?"

"That's enough," David said. The three other men quit their bombardment of his son with questions he did not seem to be answering anyway.

"Thomas, what's going on?" David asked.

Thomas smiled at his dad and said, "It's the elderly Indian dad," he woke me up when the four of you were standing at the front door earlier.

"What do you mean the elderly Indian?" Chief Watson asked. He was aware of the dreams David had been having, but had been assured by David no one other than the four of them knew.

Thomas looked knowingly at the Chief and said, "The elderly Indian. The one with the eyeless sockets. He has been waking me up for a while now and asking me to stand behind my dad at the front door. That way the scarecrow man wouldn't come into our house. I think the scarecrow would like to kill my dad. He hates you dad."

Thomas reached up and patted David on the shoulder. Almost in a protective manner.

David looked stunned at Thomas. The realization the elderly Indian had not been saying to him, "He's afraid of you," sank in.

He had always wondered why the man never looked directly at him. David nodded in agreement as his thoughts, almost random in nature now locked together as if a puzzle whose pieces finally made a wonderful picture.

Thomas went on to explain the dreams, which he had come to realize maybe were not dreams, but were a warning. Something bad was about to happened to Okawville. Why it happened, he did not know. He could not explain why the children, other than the baby, were all eight years old.

He could not explain what had happened to start it and he could not explain what needed to be done to stop it.

"When I came out the back door these two were waiting for me." Thomas said, gesturing toward the wolf and the buck.

He turned and pointed towards the others in the back yard, all still huddled together for warmth.

"Something tells me they know where we need to go." The wolf, almost as if understanding what he said, whined in agreement. The buck slapped his hoof against the asphalt driveway snorting loudly into the chilly night air.

"That's fine," David said. "But you aren't going."

Thomas started to protest, but David gave him the look which said, "Shut the hell up and do as you're told." Thomas stood silently knowing better than to argue with his father.

David looked at the animals and said, "Fine. Go ahead, lead on." The two animals stood silently not moving. The Private, the Chief, and the Sergeant all attempted to get the animals moving by getting behind them and gently kicking them in their backsides. They were wary of pushing the wild animals too far, though.

"They aren't going to budge," the Chief said. He turned towards the others and asked, "Any ideas?"

Thomas, who had stood silently watching with amusement as the adults did their best to get the animals moving reached out and quietly stroked the animals on their heads. "All right," he said. "Let's go."

The animals both began to walk with Thomas to the end of the driveway. The four men turned towards the vehicle and started to get in.

"Sorry," Thomas said. "But I don't think that's allowed. It has to be on foot."

"Are you kidding?" the Private responded, already regretting his decision to help. The four men turned and began to follow Thomas, the wolf, and the buck down Front street.

The seven moved silently through the desolate streets of Okawville, winding their way between houses, avoiding the National Guard patrols and those of the State Police. The wind continued whipping up the snow as the flakes whirled around their feet.

Sergeant Smith, at the encouragement of Thomas, had made the decision it was best to avoid any of his comrades, who would be driving around Okawville, hoping to prevent another abduction.

It would be difficult to explain why the five of them were outside at this time of night and would be even more difficult to explain why they were following a wolf and a deer.

As they finally exited Okawville, on the northeastern part of the city, the group picked up their pace. They began walking across the open farm fields. The wolf and the deer both seemed to be in their element and pranced and trotted with excitement. It was clear the wolf was using the scent of the scarecrow to track it. Thomas remained almost in the middle of both as he picked up his pace hoping to keep up with the two animals.

The four men, as a result, were forced to pick up their pace as well. The group wound along to the northeast and after about a mile and a half ran into the winding Kaskaskia River. Turning east, they followed the river for about another two miles staying in the fields and away from the trees. They were close enough they could almost see the wide ditch that was the river as it wound its way through the darkened forests.

Suddenly, the wolf wined softly and slowed down to almost a complete stop. The deer stopped in its tracks as the group looked ahead. It took a few minutes, but at the base of a group of trees and brambles, they saw the opening of a cave.

PRIVATE

The Private walked in silence listening to the wind, which blew harshly through the trees and across the snow blown fields. Walking behind Sergeant Smith, he began thinking back to when he had joined the National Guard.

"*How the hell did I get involved with this?*" he thought to himself.

His right foot caught up in a hole in the field almost caused him to fall flat on his face. He lunged forward, barely righting himself. He realized Sergeant Smith had not noticed and was still following the others.

The Private had joined the National Guard hoping to use the opportunity to help pay for his tuition at Kaskaskia College. He had been flown to Fort Benning, Georgia to spend the first part of his summer in Basic Training. Initially, the Private had yearned for home, missing his parents and his brother and sister. When he had left, his mom and dad having dropped him off at the Scott Air Force Base National Guard Recruitment station, he had no idea how difficult the next fourteen weeks were going to be.

The physicality of the boot camp was not too terrible. They were up at 4:00 am most days and in bed by 9:00 pm. Push-ups. Sit-ups. Running. He had whipped himself into shape in the months before he left, knowing it would be half the battle.

As the nights wore on though, he began to be homesick. His letters home to his parents and his brother and sister included his acknowledgement of how much he missed everybody.

The private remembered every evening sitting in the circle of guys as the Drill Sergeant called out the names of those receiving mail that night. He was sure every other guy felt the way he did and was always brought to tears when they handed him a letter.

The second part of his Basic Training went quickly, but since he was training in his MOS, it went even more smoothly. He was the first and only member of his unit to be trained in the newly created MOS involving the use of drone technology. Every unit, regular army through National Guard and Reserve was going to have one soldier trained in piloting drones. The private was thoroughly excited when his ASVAB scores put him in the category of getting to choose his MOS. His recruiter explained what he would be trained in and he was immediately hooked.

Only a year-and-a-half back, the Private was disappointed to find out he was being activated to help guard the city of Okawville.

Sergeant Smith, his platoon leader, intervened and convinced his Lieutenant and the First Sergeant into allowing him to go to school in the daytime and then to serve his time on active duty in the evenings. While it made for long days and nights, he appreciated his education not having been put on hold.

When Sergeant Smith assigned him to work alongside Smith in the evenings, the Private was happy. He and the 'old man' as he liked to call Smith got along well.

He had not actually believed they would ever catch the lunatic behind these kidnappings, but when he and Smith had witnessed the man in the scarecrow outfit outside the Dryver home, the Private was both thrilled and afraid.

He agreed readily to help track the Scarecrow Man with his drone. The way he saw it, if they caught the guy they would be de-activated and his life could go back to normal.

He did not realize the group would make the decision to hunt the Scarecrow Man on foot. And when the drone went down the way it did, the Private swore ice cycles had been dripping down his back when the hair on his back stood up.

He had walked in silence, coming along only because he did not want it to be known he was afraid to go. As the group had meandered its way between the houses, across the snow-blown fields, and along the edges of the trees, the private secretly regretted his decision to come along.

"This is crazy. I need to just let them know, right now that I've gone as far as I'm going."

But, each time he started to speak up, the wind would howl a little louder and the snow seemed to blow a little harder. The Private realized, too, if he stopped, he would have to go back on his own. The three men and even the teenager seemed intent on following the trail all the way to its fruition. The Private reached down and patted his pistol, holstered at his side. It provided a little comfort to know the four adults were armed.

The wind picked up speed and the feeling of ice cycles cascading down his back shot through the private again.

"I can't do this, he thought."

Just about the time he had decided he had had enough, the wolf wined to the group and the seven of them came to a halt.

"Oh shit!" the Private thought.

The private stood in the darkness next to his sergeant doing his best not to show the fear he was now feeling. Up ahead in the darkness, the clear outline of the mouth of a cave jutted up out of the ground.

CHIEF

Chief Watson had realized he had bitten off more than he could chew. He was forty-five years old and only a few years away from retirement.

He now deeply regretted the decision to follow the lunatic to his hiding place. It was evident, as the group of seven had walked out of the town into the frost covered fields they were placing themselves into an unknown situation and possibly playing right into the hands of a killer.

Gusts of wind whipped around his coat. He tried to tuck his head down further inside the collar for warmth. As the leader of this group of seven, at least that is how he saw himself; the Chief realized they should have passed on their plan to others.

"The FBI, the State Police, anyone," he thought to himself.

He continued to walk in the lead, having had some experience tracking fugitives, in the past. The Chief did not turn back, not wanting his two friends, the Private, and the kid to see he clearly was wrestling with what to do next.

Chief Watson cursed himself silently. *"Watson, you're an idiot."*

He began hoping the choice to follow the Scarecrow Man, the name given to the killer by the Private, would come up empty-handed.

Not that he did not want to save the kids, he did. He just wanted to make sure they had enough support to deal with this lunatic.

The Chief had not wanted to admit to this to the others, but figured if they walked around for a couple of hours he would simply throw his hands up and declare this trip a waste of time. He would be happy to get back to town and into a warm cup of coffee.

The Chief continued to walk, leading the group further and further away from the houses, which were now far off into the distance. Whenever he would get off track, the wolf and buck would force them to change directions.

He began to wonder if he were actually leading the group.

The wind howled through the nearby trees, startling him so much he felt like he had jumped a foot and a half off the ground. Not looking back, to see if the others had seen, Watson continued walking through the snow-blown field.

The Chief cursed himself, realizing he been daydreaming.

"Now is not the time to go on auto-pilot," he thought to himself.

The Chief realized it, even if the others did not, but what they were doing was very dangerous. If they managed to find someone, which he still hoped they did not, all of their lives were in jeopardy.

They had walked for about another half an hour in the darkness. Slowing his pace, the Chief started to turn to tell the others it was time to head back, when everyone in the group stopped.

Turning he looked in the distance towards the spot those behind him were looking and realized if he had kept day dreaming and walking he would have fallen into the mouth of a cave.

The Chief was startled a little, as the wolf began whining into the night. Both the wolf and the deer seemed very much on edge. They peered into the darkness at the hole in the ground.

Looking down at the darkness, which was the mouth of a cave, the chief cursed again to himself and almost pissed his pants.

SERGEANT

Sergeant Smith was an E-7 in the Illinois National Guard. He was proud he had joined the military and even prouder to serve his country.

Walking behind Chief Watson, Smith would periodically check with his right thumb to make sure that his M-4's safety was engaged.

Fully armed, both with a loaded M-4 and a pistol, Smith was sure whenever they found this lunatic they would have to kill the man. That did not bother him at all and he hoped he would be the one to get to do it.

Smith had served a year and a half in Afghanistan in the regular army and had recently switched into the National Guard. His wife had wanted him to quit, but Smith could not do that. The army life was for him. While the Guard was not the army, it allowed him to play soldier once a month and a few weeks in the summer.

His wife, after thoroughly arguing her case, had given up and accepted her husband would continue to be involved with the military. Smith was happy to be stationed in the West Frankfort unit, Bravo Company of the 2nd battalion. His experience overseas and his leadership ability meant that Smith was put in charge of his own platoon.

Many younger guys, most who had joined for the educational benefits, seemed to idolize Smith and responded well to his no nonsense style. He had to admit they had grown on him, too. The private reminded Smith of his own son who had overdosed on heroin a few years earlier.

"I can't think of him now." Smith thought.

It was hard though, when he looked at the private not to think of Ethan, his only son.

"My biggest regret, not being here for him," He thought to himself as the group continued to walk through the open-fields.

That guilt and the pressure brought by his wife were not enough to keep him from thinking about going back in full-time. Smith's thought of joining back up and going back overseas quieted down when he realized he would be able to see some of his high school friends. Both the Chief and David Dryver were as excited as he was to get him back.

Walking behind the Chief, Smith did his best to stay alert, though the snow flurries and the wind seemed to dull his thoughts. He continued to find his mind roaming.

The Sergeant knew full well, having been in combat situations, they were putting themselves in danger. He also knew, though, if they did not follow this maniac to his hideout more kids were going to die.

Seeing the Scarecrow of a man standing in David's front yard had brought the hairs on his neck on end.

"He's just a man," Smith reminded himself as he continued to scan the darkness ahead.

Watching the Chief, Smith noticed he had stopped and was just turning to say something when the wolf began to whine. He looked past his friend, into the darkness, half expecting to see a Scarecrow standing there. Instead, he saw nothing.

He waited, as his eyes continued to scan the nearby trees when he noticed something on the ground up ahead. A darkness, which stood out with the white snow around its edges, lay up ahead.

"Christ," the Sergeant mumbled to himself. Up ahead, peering up out of the ground was a cave.

EIGHTEEN

THE CAVE

RESIDENTS FLEE, RESIDENTS STAY, OKAWVILLE SETTLES IN FOR ANOTHER LONG NIGHT

Headline of an article in the **West Washington Gazette***, August 1ˢᵗ, 2018.*

DESCENT

Other than cursing themselves under their breath the four men and the one boy along with the wolf and deer, stood in total silence. The wolf had stopped whining aware the noise might notify whoever was inside the cave of their presence. The seven stood in the middle of the field staring into the darkness hoping nothing would leap out of the mouth of the cave.

Chief Watson gestured silently for the group to move away from the cave opening. Slowly and silently they backed off. The wolf and the deer moved with them, but both kept their eyes on the hole in the ground. They too were expecting the Beast to jump out from the opening into the field.

Once they were further away he felt a little safer. The Chief huddled them all together for a quick conversation.

"Listen," he started, aware he was not one-hundred percent sure his suggestion was the best course of action.

"We need to go down into that cave, but we're going to have to do it the same way we would clear a building." He looked at the others to see if any of them would acknowledge his suggestion.

Part of him was wishing one of the others would poke a hole in his plan and suggest they wait and call for some back-up. That would require, of course, someone to head back to David's house. None of the other men did anything, but nod in approval.

"There are five of us..." he paused realizing Thomas should not be included in the plan.

David had started to protest, but realized the Chief had spotted the error in his plan and held his tongue. He was acutely aware that out of the four men, he was the only one who had no experience with weapons. He also was pretty sure he was the only one ready to crap his pants at a moment's notice.

"In law enforcement, and Smith and the Private know this from their military experience," he paused again, "when we clear a room we take three to four guys and everyone covers a direction. We also stay in a compact group." Both Sergeant Smith and the Private nodded in agreement. David Dryer, who had watched plenty of cop shows, nodded he understood.

The Chief continued to explain using his fingers to show how each of them should bunch up when they were down in the cave.

"We need to get in and clear the cave as far back as we can," Watson continued.

Even though he was whispering he glanced over to the mouth of the cave which was still a good distance away. It was still too close as far as he was concerned. He knew all too well how much sound carried in a forest in the night. Luckily, the wind and the snow were covering his whisper enough for them to go undetected. The others had to lean in closely to pick up on everything he was trying to say.

David felt he had missed half of it, but nodded in agreement, not wanting to look too much like he was not picking up on what the Chief was saying.

"We don't know how far back the cave goes, but if we find any of the kids, we can't stop until we are sure the suspect is down..." he paused, "or not in the cave. Got it!" The four men and Thomas nodded silently in agreement. "We will either put the kids in the middle of us, or just tell them to stay put."

Thomas, who had been listening intently, leaned in and whispered to the men. "I think I need to go with you."

David turned to him and gently placed his hands on Thomas' shoulders. "Son, listen, I realize we needed you to come along and I'm proud of you for doing so." David was looking into his son's eyes, but with the wind, the darkness, and the snow, he was having a difficult time seeing Thomas' reaction.

He continued, "We....I need you to stay up here, out of harm's way. If you come down into that cave I'm going to be more worried about you and it might impact us helping those kids. Do you understand?" He waited for Thomas to offer up an argument.

Thomas nodded. He had understood no matter what he might say at this moment the four men, especially his father were against it. They were going to be adamant he would be more of a distraction than a help.

While he felt strongly he needed to be included, and he couldn't explain why he felt this way, he continued to nod in agreement, even after David had finished whispering.

"Besides," David continued, "I think you will be in good hands with these two," David gestured towards the wolf and the buck. The two animals stared back at them in silence. They were waiting for the men to get moving. The two had stood motionless for a few minutes, like silent statues in the middle of a forest waiting patiently for the discussion to end.

After a few minutes when the Chief had finished explaining what each man should do the four men turned and began moving towards the cave.

They walked as silently as they could, the howling wind providing cover for any sounds their steps were making.

Sergeant Smith carried his M4 carbine, a machine gun with a thirty-round clip. An additional thirty-round clip was at his side, though he couldn't imagine he would need it. Smith also had his Glock 19M pistol still holstered at his side. He had been happy to carry the Glock knowing the FBI typically had their own agents use this very weapon as a 'conceal and carry pistol.'

The Private had left his M4 carbine loaded with a thirty-round clip with Thomas. He had taken the safety off and put it back on, explaining to Thomas as silently as possible how to shoot and fire.

The Private was glad to unburden himself from his M4 since he had decided to go down into the cave with his pistol. He too carried a Glock 19m. He carried two additional clips, fully—loaded at his side.

The Chief carried his own Smith & Wesson M&P9 pistol in both hands which he was trained to do when clearing a room. The Chief had removed his gloves realizing at this moment they were a burden with what he needed to do next. His Matte Black Smith & Wesson felt warm in his hands since he had been carrying it when his fingers were gloved.

David, who didn't own a gun, carried a pistol which had been loaned to him by Chief Watson. It was also a Smith & Wesson M&P9.

When he had removed his gloves, copying the chief, the pistol had originally felt icy cold to the touch. It had been holstered at the Chief's side when the four men stood in his driveway.

All four men had tactical flashlights. The Private and Smith had brought their Army issued flashlights which could be turned into lanterns. The flashlights when twisted and separated would flood any area for 100 feet in all directions with very bright light. These lanterns, Smith hoped, would provide as much light as needed once they were down in the cave. A small part of him though, didn't think there would ever be enough light where they were getting ready to go.

The four men had agreed when they entered the cave they would do so in total silence. The Chief had explained sounds, movement, anything would echo in the cave notifying whoever was down there to their presence. He had still secretly hoped they would come up empty-handed. His heart was beating heavily now. He looked quickly at the animals and back to the cave. The Chief had the feeling both knew how scared he was.

The movement to the cave seemed to take an eternity as each man battled his own fear about what they were preparing to do.

In all actuality, they made it to the cave, from Thomas' location, in about two minutes. Looking back at Thomas, David tried to swallow, but realized he couldn't. His mouth had dried up and his throat seemed to be constricting. His breathing was coming shallow and quick.

"I'm scared to death." he thought, not wanting to voice these concerns and seem to the others to be a coward.

Reaching the mouth of the cave, Chief Watson turned towards the other three and gestured into the cave. He shined his flashlight at the opening and each man was able to see the pile of debris, old trees, and rotting timbers which at some point must have covered the mouth of the cave.

Some of them looked man-made and all had fallen down into the cave. The pile of debris was staggered so much, crisscrossing each other back and forth; it would be a relatively easy climb down into the cave.

The Chief looked back at the other three and mouthed, "Ready?"

The other three nodded back.

What each man was thinking at the time the Chief could only guess. He put the thought out of his mind and turned toward the first log. The

Chief began his decent into the cave; slowly picking his way down, hoping his movement through the logs would go undetected by anyone in the cave. The other three men shined their flashlights down into the cave hoping to provide him enough light to see his way down.

The Chief had holstered his pistol. He had been reluctant to do so, but he realized quickly he would need both hands for the climb down. The light provided by the other three was enough. Everyone was aware this was a very dangerous moment. If the Scarecrow man was at the bottom waiting for the Chief he was most likely going to die. Un-armed, he would be unable to put up any fight if he were surprised from the darkness of the cave. All the Scarecrow man had to do was wait and then he could pounce on the Chief.

Once he was about halfway down Sergeant Smith began his descent. The Private and David Dryver shined their lights hoping it would be enough to give Smith the opportunity to climb down safely. Smith kept his M4 pointed downward as he began going down into the cave. He had decided not to shoulder the weapon and would rely on only one hand. He wanted a weapon at the ready should either the Chief or he be attacked.

The two men picked their way back and forth amongst the logs, trying to find sturdy footing as they went. The snow from above had accumulated on some of the logs and while the going was quicker than they thought, the logs were slippery. Neither man, though, had too much difficulty.

Chief Watson, while Smith was about halfway down, made it to the floor of the cave. He immediately opened up the tactical flashlight Smith had given him to carry and turned it into a lantern. Light flooded the nearby cave.

Watson removed his pistol from his holster and took the safety off. He turned and scanned the entire cavern around him, half-expecting the Scarecrow Man to come charging out of the darkness.

The cave was empty.

He continued looking around while Smith continued to make his way to the bottom of the cave. The lantern, in addition to providing enough light for Chief Watson, helped Smith see better and made his movements a lot easier. When he was more than halfway down, Smith flashed his light upwards towards the mouth of the cave. He clicked the light on and off twice signaling for the Private to begin to climb down.

The Private started after Smith leaving David alone at the mouth of the cave. The Private didn't need to shine his light any longer since Smith had opened up his tactical light. The entire cave was flooded with light from floor to ceiling.

By the time the Private was half-way down, David turned towards his son and waived. Thomas waived back and David dropped from Thomas' sight down into the cave.

It took a few minutes longer than his friends, but eventually all four men were on the cave floor. The cave was now illuminated by the light of the lanterns. The four men waited in silence for David to gather his breath. He looked at them realizing they were trying to give him time to compose himself. He gave a thumbs-up and gestured for them to move ahead.

Once David had made it to the bottom and given his thumbs up, the Chief gestured to the three men with his right hand. He gestured down with his the palm of his hand and then held up one, two, three fingers. The Chief then put his right hand to his ear for them to listen.

He wanted them to know they would wait about three minutes to let their eyes adjust to the light in the cave. That would also allow them time to listen to the natural sounds of the cave.

The sound of trickling water was coming from somewhere up ahead and the Chief wanted every advantage they could have down in this cave. He scanned around the cave and realized up ahead to the left, about sixty feet away, the cave curved left.

Darkness from that area gave him a sense of foreboding. There was nothing in the main portion of the cave. This momentarily had caused the Chief to breathe a sigh of relief. He had been happy to find the man in the Scarecrow outfit hadn't been waiting for them at the bottom. Particularly since he would have been the first target of the lunatic. He had half-expected to be shot or stabbed when he dropped to the floor of the cave.

With that said, he now realized they would have to search the cave, exploring every nook and cranny, until they found the kids, the Scarecrow man, or came up empty-handed.

"I'm terrified," he thought to himself.

He knew the others were probably feeling the same way, but had decided to put on a brave face on. It was now up to him to get them into and out of this damned cave.

The Chief nodded to the others pointing with his right index finger towards the darkness around the bend. The three men nodded back and the four of them began the slow movement towards the darkness at the back of the cave.

Smith tapped the Chief on the shoulder and the group stopped. Looking back, Smith reached into his pouch on his pants and pulled out a chemo-light. He snapped the chemo-light, breaking the internal seal. The chemo-light immediately turned a bright blue-green fluorescent color.

The light mixed with the yellow light of the lanterns, but was so bright it could easily be seen. Smith threw one, pulled out another, and did the same. There were two glowing chemo-light sticks near the mouth of the cave.

Smith explained quietly he planned on dropping a few every so often. This would help the group find their way back quickly should they need to do so.

The Chief nodded in agreement. He had not thought about having to come back without their lights. If the lights went out, for whatever reason, and the back-up flashlights failed, they would need something to help them find their way back to the mouth of the cave. Otherwise, they could be lost there forever.

He quickly clipped the lantern around his belt-loop and moved out in the lead. The Private and Sergeant Smith each took up a position near the Chief's shoulders, the Private to his right, Smith to his left. They scanned ahead and to the Chief's sides.

Frequently they turned back and forth, their weapons pointing into the darkness at every direction in which they turned.

David brought up the rear. He had a lantern strapped to his belt-loop also, mimicking the Chief. He had been instructed by Smith to pay close attention to the three others, but to also scan behind them to make sure someone didn't sneak up on the group as they passed. Smith had been clear to David, when they were up top and whispering the plan to each other.

"Just remember, don't fall back too far from the group. The glance behind you needs to be quick enough that you don't get separated. But, don't run into us if we happen to make a quick stop. Understand?" David did, not sure if he would be able to do this without messing up.

Now that he was in the cave, moving as a group, he remembered Smith's words and silently cursed himself as he glanced backward. He had already noticed himself lagging behind. Smith had called it the accordion-effect. David had heard it explained by Smith before a few years earlier. Smith had explained the accordion-effect happened all the time when he and his friends rode their Harley's together. What would always start out as a tight-knitted group would eventually stretch back for miles. Stretching and condensing as the group rode down the highway.

Once, in an effort to catch up, he had bumped into the three of them. They stopped, looking back to see if he was okay. He was more embarrassed than okay, but gave the thumbs up. The group began moving again. The cave was completely silent except for the trickling of the water. It seemed to come from every direction.

They turned left around the corner of the main cavern and the light bounced along the walls of the cave up ahead. The main walls of the cave were pocked with tiny and mid-sized crevices. Some were tiny and some were large enough almost to be their own caves.

The four men gave their eyes time to adjust and then began to move again. They had walked for about three minutes moving further and further into the back of the cave when Chief gestured for them to halt. They did so and stood silently.

The other three peered into the darkness wandering what had caused them to stop. The Chief knelt down and stood up holding something in his right hand. The tiny red jacket the size of a toddler was covered with the muck and grime of the cave.

The Chief's face twisted into sadness as a few tears began to trickle out of his eyes. He grimaced and then, there, in the darkness of the cave, the three other men saw something out of him they had not seen in a while.

Anger swept across the Chief's face as he realized the lunatic was here somewhere in this cave. The jacket, since it was not on the missing baby, meant the baby was probably dead.

It was at that moment the fear of the unknown melted away and Chief Watson's anger took over. Without saying a word he turned and began moving further into the cave. He had decided no matter what they found the lunatic wasn't going to leave this cave alive.

The group began to move again. Each man looked ahead, to the side, and to the rear. The Chief's anger became infectious and each of the other men seemed to forget their fears. They allowed their anger to take over as the Chief had done. No longer were there four scared men in the cave. Now there were four angry men. Four men who had decided to avenge the children of Okawville.

They moved silently, but with a stronger sense of purpose.

Moving further into the cave, the Chief turned to his friends and gestured up ahead. The cave twisted again back to the left. They continued their march forward. They turned to the left again and immediately all four of the men stopped in their tracks.

This part of the cave was definitely inhabited by someone. There were piles of clothing along the wall to the left. The men scanned this part of the cave back and forth. The Private tapped the Chief on the right shoulder. He pointed to a natural ledge on the wall of the cave.

The Chief's eyes followed the Private's fingers catching sight of what had caught the Private's attention. Both the Chief and the Private raised their guns, pointing them at the Scarecrow costume which was propped up along the wall of the cave.

The leathery face of the scarecrow hung limply with its chin resting upon its chest. The long, stringy arms were crossed and resting on the equally long and stringy legs. The right leg dangled loosely over the edge on which the costume had been propped. The left leg bent at a ninety-degree angle and tucked neatly underneath the right.

Moccasins were tied to the pants, dangling over the ledge loosely. The size of the Moccasins meant the owner was a very large-sized man. The men waited staring closely at the chest to see if there were any rising and falling. The lifeless costume did not show any signs of movement which meant the owner had to be somewhere further into the depths of the cave. Once it was clear whoever had worn it was not still in the costume the Chief gestured for them all to move closer. He wanted to get a better look at this costume.

They began to walk forward, still in the tight group. The Private accidentally kicked something with his right boot. The clanking of the item echoed throughout the cave, its sound bouncing off the walls. The Private cursed himself realizing he should have been looking down periodically. It wouldn't do to trip on an item and lose his footing. He looked down quickly to see what he had kicked.

The hairs on the back of his neck stood on end as looked down at his feet. A small human skull the size of an eight year old child lay near his right boot. The Private knelt down, picked up the skull and turned it over for the others to see.

It was at that moment, as all four men looked down at the skull their anger once again was quickly replaced by a bone chilling fear. David quickly looked behind them expecting someone to jump out of the shadows of the cave. Even in the coldness of the cave beads of sweat gathered on his forehead.

The men realized this person, although probably a man had lost all of sense of humanity. The rescue mission, which had become a recovery mission, now had become a survival mission.

What type of man could do something like this to a kid?

The trickling water echoed through the cave. Each of the men played over in their heads what the skull meant. If one of the children had been killed the odds were the killer had murdered all of them.

"But why the skull?" the Chief thought scanning the cave around them. Surely, they would have found bodies, not bones. The hairs on his neck were still standing on end.

David had started to turn back, to look behind them, when the silent laughter began.

Startled, the four men looked around to see where it was coming from. Their guns waved back and forth frantically searching every nook and cranny their eyes could find.

Every one of those held a shadow which only worked to swallow up the light. Every crevice potentially held the killer who was waiting to pounce on them.

"Heeee....heee...hee....eeeiyahhhhhh."

The laughing grew louder in intensity. It was very difficult to pinpoint the direction from which it came. The four men turned in a circle back and forth their weapons pointed outward. Their backs were pressed up against each other as they subconsciously sought the security and safety of the physical presence of their friends.

David was sure the beating of his heart could be heard over the laughter. He did not know how to calm himself and struggled to suck in enough oxygen.

Gasping for air, he was surprised to find he was whispering to himself, "Stay calm," he said. "Stay calm." It didn't' seem to help.

A scraping noise brought the four of them around back to the scarecrow costume which was still propped up against the wall on the ledge.

The Scarecrow's chin was no longer propped against its chest. The face had been lifted by some unseen force and was staring at the four of them.

The large eyes, infused with bloody veins were open and full of life. They were also full of hatred as they glared unblinking at the trespassers. Slowly, as the Private pissed in his pants and the smell of urine filled the cave, the mouth widened and the Scarecrow man smiled.

NINETEEN

A BROTHER'S PEACE

Freeze

"FREEZE!!!!" Chief Watson bellowed, the sound of his voice echoing outward all along the walls of the cave and then back to the four men.

"Freeze, Freeze, Freeze," came back his voice at them from all directions. They broke their circle with the Private and Smith both moving to place themselves in a line with Chief Watson.

David moved around to the Private's side and all four men pointed their weapons in the direction of the man in the Scarecrow costume.

The man continued to laugh hysterically which also continued to echo through the cave almost drowning out the Chief's orders.

"Your hands! Show me your hands, you son of a bitch!" Watson screamed. The laughter continued unabated and the images of all of those missing children flooded into his head.

The Scarecrow man's shoulders bounced up and down while he continued his maniacal laughing. Chief Watson's demands and the guns pointed at him didn't seem to bother him at all.

David continually glanced behind them, as did Smith, to make sure there weren't others in the cave.

The Chief's right hand went to his belt and his shaking hand fumbled for his handcuffs. He dropped them once, cursed and bent to pick them up. The Chief had already decided once cuffed the four men would have to have a major discussion about what to do with this killer of children.

He had made plans in his head, without voicing them, about what to do with the man in the costume. He had been hoping to convince his friends this lunatic, this child killer, not be allowed to leave this cave alive.

"We'll tell people he fought and it couldn't be avoided." This killer wanted to hide in a cave. *"Let it be his coffin as well."*

Abruptly, the man in the scarecrow outfit stopped laughing as if a remote switch had been turned off somewhere.

Immediately the cave fell back into silence.

David's heart was beating so quickly he could no longer even hear the sound of the trickling water. It bothered him though he did his best to keep focusing on what was going on.

Looking over his shoulder he once again looked back to the wide-gapped smile of the man in the Scarecrow outfit. The fangs of the mask were yellow-stained. David looked at them, imagining they were also covered in blood.

The man's chin, or at least the mask, definitely was blood stained. It looked like fresh blood. David remembered the child the man had carried with him earlier.

"*Where is that kid?*" he thought to himself. They should have found something. Clothing. Shoes. Something.

"Put your hands above your head!" Watson said, lowering his voice.

Instinctively he had lowered his voice to keep the echoes from bouncing back at them and adding to the confusion of the moment. He too had been startled to his hear own voice echoing back at him. He imagined his voice running away further into the cave and then running back.

That wide-toothed smiled disappeared. The Scarecrow Man put both of his hands on the ledge at his sides. His palms were flat against the rock ledge, but his eyes never left the four men in front of him. Gently, he pushed down on the ledge lifting his body a few inches off the ledge.

Quickly, almost cat-like, the Scarecrow Man jumped down from the ledge and stood up to his full height. He had not taken his eyes off the men. His eyes bore into each of them with hatred and fury.

Towering above the others, the Scarecrow Man looked down at the four men in the eerie yellow light cast by the lanterns. His leathery hands hung limply down at his sides, the light reflecting off his finger nails. Light caused his fingernails to shine in the darkness of the cave. David's eyes slowly lowered to those fingers. The nails were long and sharpened almost into the point of talons.

The man in the costume gingerly took a step forward smiling sadistically at the four men who had their weapons trained on him.

"Freeze!" the Chief yelled again.

The Scarecrow Man walked forward another step, opening his hands palms up spreading his arms away from his body. The Chief opened fire.

Blam! Blam! Blam!

The sounds of the three gunshots echoed loudly around the cavern, down through the tunnels in both directions. David's ears screamed at him in agony, but it was clear the Chief's gunfire struck the Scarecrow man. Once, Twice. Three times.

The Scarecrow Man fell to the ground lifeless. It had happened so quickly the four of them were left stunned.

"It's over," David thought.

He breathed a sigh of relief. He could still feel his beating heart. Sounds in the cave seemed muffled, but David knew this would only be temporary. He had not been prepared for the loudness of the Chief's gun.

The four men continued to stand motionless waiting to see if the shots had found their target. They looked closely at the Scarecrow Man with Smith shining one of his flashlights at the man in the Scarecrow mask.

There were no signs of breathing. But, there hadn't been before. Each man doubted their senses since they had betrayed them once before.

"Jesus." David thought.

He had never been so afraid in his life. The Chief, Sergeant Smith, and the Private had all been trained for this kind of moment at some point.

David scanned around the cave. He was pretty sure there weren't any other 'bad guys.' Standing silently he still held his pistol out in front of him, cupped in both hands. He still had it pointed at the Scarecrow Man. David waited for one of the men to tell him what to do next.

The Chief looked to Smith and then back to the Scarecrow Man. It took a few seconds for him to gather his thoughts.

"Smith, go scout around the cave for the kids." Smith looked to the Private and nodded.

The Private turned and handed David his flashlight and then gestured for David to unclip his lantern and give it to him. David did so.

"Dave," the Chief started. "You stay here. Let's keep an eye on this pile of trash." The Chief wasn't convinced the man in the Scarecrow outfit was dead. He felt confident that his shot's had hit the man. He had watched as the man had dropped after being shot. But, there were too many strange things that had happened already.

For one, how had they not realized he was in the costume?

"That costume was lifeless a few minutes before."

Maybe the darkness of the cave had fooled their eyes and made them think it was an empty costume. *"That had to have been it,"* the Chief thought.

Silently he cursed himself for not being more observant. The Chief had decided he would not take any more chances, especially now that the four of them had split up. He and David would watch the man closely, until Smith and the Private returned.

Sergeant Smith and the Private turned and followed the cave around another bend and deeper underground. The cavern sloped gently downward into the earth.

Weapons up the two men scanned the unexplored part of the cave moving back and forth in a zig-zag from wall to wall. Both men looked up, then down, then left, then right. They walked shoulder-to-shoulder.

"Wait." Smith whispered. The two men stopped.

Smith's flashlight shone on a pile of clothing piled up against a nearby wall. Walking over together the two men were horrified to find the clothing of the missing children.

"Look," Smith said, pointing his flashlight to another pile a few feet away. There was another pile near the clothing along the same wall. Small bones were stacked against one of the walls of the cave. The Private turned away from Sergeant Smith and vomited.

He was embarrassed he had thrown up in front of his mentor, but Smith waited patiently understanding what the private was going through. When he had served in Afghanistan Smith had witnessed some battle wounds which had caused him to lose his lunch more than a few times.

Smith leaned in and elbowed the Private, as if to ask, *"You okay?"* The Private stood up and nodded. The two men continued and explored the remaining part of the cave. After a few minutes, after they were sure there were no surviving children in the cave, both men turned and walked back to the Chief and David.

After what seemed like hours, though had been no more than fifteen minutes, Sergeant Smith and the Private made their way back to the Chief and to David Dryver.

The Chief still had his gun drawn and pointed at the lifeless man in the Scarecrow Costume. *"Surely, if there were going to have been any signs of life they would have seen them by now."* Smith thought.

David turned to Smith with the intention of asking if they had found anything. The look from both men made him think differently.

He looked sternly at the dead man lying nearby and asked himself, *"How? How could you do that to children?"*

"Listen," Sergeant Smith said softly. "I think we need to talk about what to do next."

"What do you mean?" David asked.

He was puzzled when it was obvious they needed to bring help to carry the bodies of these kids out of the cave.

"That's the least we could do considering these kids were taken away from their parents, brought down into this cave and murdered." His eyes began to tear. He thought about Thomas, waiting for them somewhere outside this hell-hole. *"What if that were him?"*

"Dave. I understand that point, trust me, I do. But, there aren't any bodies."

Chief Watson inhaled loudly enough for the other three to hear. "None?" he asked sharply.

The Private shook his head acknowledging there were no bodies to be recovered.

"How is that possible?" David asked. He paused a few seconds trying to gather his thoughts. "Are you sure? Did you check the entire cave?" He looked from Smith's face to the Privates and realized the two were still in shock from what they had found. He looked around the two men into the darkness.

"My God...what did they find?"

Chief Watson broke the silence which had followed by asking, "What do you think we should do?"

He looked quickly from Smith to the Private, but immediately brought his gaze back to the Scarecrow man. He still half expected the dead man to jump up and charge them. It had been more than thirty minutes since he had shot the man. He should be dead. Still...

Sergeant Smith cleared his throat, nervous about what he was getting ready to say. He paused and said, "I think we should go back to town and forget any of this has happened."

David looked at Smith, a man who had been one of his dearest friends for a lifetime. He was shocked at what Smith was suggesting. He shook his head back and forth, expressing his disagreement by shaking it back and forth more quickly.

"Smith, these kids have to be taken back to their parents. Their parents need closure. It's the right thing to do."

The Private spoke up. "I would agree if there were bodies back there in the back of the cave." He waited and then continued, "But there aren't. There are only the bones."

The four men turned and looked at the lifeless body of the killer.

Chief Watson broke the silence by sobbing, tears flowing down his cheeks. "This bastard," he stammered, pointing to the Scarecrow Man. "What has he done?" The Chief started to ask the question, but David beat him to it.

"What happened to them, if there are no bodies?" The Private was the first one to speak up, expressing what most of them were now thinking.

"He ate them."

The four men turned in unison and looked over at the body of the man in the costume.

They stood silently for a minute or two, David and the Chief confused about what the Private had just told them. The utter shock each of them now felt pulsated between revulsion, anger, sadness, and hate.

The Chief had holstered his pistol now convinced the man was dead. Smith had thrown his M4 over his shoulder glad to be able to rest his arms. He had been so jacked up on adrenaline he hadn't noticed how fatigued his arms had become.

The Private looked at David, shrugged, and holstered his own pistol. Only David remained armed and he had decided he would stay that way until they were completely out of the cave. The comfort the pistol provided was minute, but was better than none.

"So it's agreed, then?" Sergeant Smith asked.

The four men had come to an agreement to let this be the final resting place of the missing children and the missing baby. They would return to town knowing the killer was dead. There would not be any reports of having found any of the missing children. They would not even report having found the killer.

The Chief explained if a report were filed they would have to explain where they had found him and how he had died. The State Police and the FBI would launch an extensive search of the cave and then would find the bones of the children.

David was not a fan of this decision, but he admitted the children's parents deserved much more than the explanation they had.

"How could they explain to those parents the children were eaten by some mad man in a scarecrow costume." That would be a burden too much for any parent to deal with and keep their sanity.

Smith looked to the other three men seeking for them to acknowledge his question in the affirmative. Chief Watson was the first to do so, followed by the Private. David waited a few seconds and agreed. They turned to leave when the Private asked the other three a question.

"Who do you think he is?" He gestured backward over his shoulder with his thumb.

Chief Watson had not thought about it, but it would be good to know if the man in the Scarecrow costume were a local or a transient.

He turned towards the lunatic and started walking over to him. Looking at the Private the Chief said, "Come over and remove his mask. I will snap a picture with my cell phone and run it through our database when we get back."

The Private paused almost wishing he hadn't asked the question. He followed the Chief's directions and moved over to the dead man in the scarecrow costume.

A shrill of fear crept back into him as he moved around the chief and placed himself beside the man. Chief Watson pulled out his cell phone clipped at his belt and began thumbing through buttons to get the camera to turn on. The Private was tempted to tell the old man all he had to do was push a button on the side and the camera would automatically appear. He decided against it and knelt down to remove the man's mask.

Leaning in, he reached down to grab the mask underneath the chin. He just happened to look into the Scarecrow Man's eyes. They raged with fury as they glared back at him.

The mouth slowly spread back into a smile causing the Private to jerk his hand back away from the fangs.

The Private, without turning had started to say, "He's ali…" He didn't get to finish the sentence.

The Scarecrow Man's left hand shot up quickly grabbing the Private by the throat. Long, talon-like fingernails dug into his throat cutting off the rest of his statement.

The Scarecrow Man leaped to his feet, his left hand still clutching the Private by the throat. A demoniac laugh echoed throughout the cave. The Scarecrow Man spun and threw the Private up against the wall of the cave.

The Private crashed into the wall striking his head in the process. He lay motionless on the rocky floor. The Chief, who had been fumbling with his phone, was caught off-guard; barely catching the Private's warning before being grabbed by both hands and lifted a foot off the ground.

"Eeeiihhaaaaaaa,"

The Scarecrow laughed hysterically fully aware he had fooled the four men into thinking he was dead.

His murderous laughter echoed throughout the cave. He realized he now had the upper hand and the lives of the four men were his for the taking. Quickly spinning he released the Chief and flung him harshly up against the cave-wall.

The Chief's body twisted into an awkward angle and he struck the cave-wall on his right side. The wind was knocked out of his body and his head too struck the cave wall. Not knocked unconscious the Chief fell limply at the Private's side. He struggled to breathe, a sharp pain shooting through his back.

Sergeant Smith and David had turned to each other to speak softly when the Private and the Chief walked over to the body.

"Dave, I know it's not a decision you are comfortable w…" He had been interrupted by the laughter echoing throughout the cave. Both men turned simultaneously towards the Chief and the Private.

Both were completely startled to see the Scarecrow Man leap to his feet and throw the Private up against the wall. They were startled again when the Chief was lifted and flung in the direction of the Private leaving only the two of them to deal with this mad man.

It was at this moment everything seemed to move in slow motion for David. He didn't know if it was his heightened sense of fear or an extra adrenaline rush.

It had only taken a few seconds for both the Private and the Chief to be taken out. He hoped the Private wasn't dead as his lifeless body lay prostrate near the Chief. After flinging the Chief up against the wall the Scarecrow Man laughed again with glee and bounded over to the Sergeant and David.

Smith had reacted by reaching around with his right arm to quickly unshoulder the weapon. He had been moving to bring it up into a firing position when he was struck full force with a backhand from the giant man who towered at least a foot above them.

Smith's M4 was knocked from his hands and landed a few feet away from them. Staggering from the blow he turned back to see and feel the Scarecrow Man's fist mashing up against the side of his face. He was knocked to the ground. The blow left his ear's ringing.

Blood gushed out of a cut on the side of his cheek. Not waiting for the Sergeant to recover the Scarecrow Man reached both hands above his head. He interlocked his fingers preparing to bring the full force of them crashing down into Smith's head.

"Blam!!Blam!!!"

The two bullets from David's pistol ripped into the Scarecrow Man's left side. They had no effect, other than to make him furious.

He turned towards David and quickly charged. David fired two more shots, which missed. They ricocheted around the cavern one of them whining past David's head.

The Scarecrow Man crashed into David like a bull, lifting him off his feet. His momentum carried David a few feet before he lifted David and slammed him into the ground. The Scarecrow Man allowed his body to come crashing down on Dave's. The impact caused David to cry out in pain.

He was pinned beneath the madman.

Lying on top of David the Scarecrow Man lifted his head away from David's face. Their eyes locked on each other. David was a little groggy, but became fully alert. He realized the Scarecrow Man was gleefully looking into his eyes.

Opening his mouth, the gaping mouth filled with jagged teeth, the Scarecrow leaned his head back and laughed once more hysterically. He looked back at Dave preparing to bite down on his face.

"GET AWAY FROM MY DAD!!!!!" a voice yelled loudly at the Scarecrow Man.

Startled, the Scarecrow Man relaxed his grip on David, who was still struggling to recover from being slammed harshly to the ground.

He lifted his head and looked at Thomas who was standing about ten feet away. The Scarecrow Man stood up quickly. He spread his hands widely and started to slowly walk over to the teenager. The Scarecrow Man stopped abruptly as the elderly Indian, a man with no eyes and tear stained cheeks stepped around and stood at Thomas' right shoulder.

"Get away from my dad." Thomas repeated.

David had started to roll over wanting to yell for Thomas to run. He was unable to do so.

He noticed the elderly Indian, the one who had been in all of his dreams, step around Thomas. He wanted to scream for that Indian to help Thomas escape, but the words couldn't come out. The most he could do is watch in horror as the Scarecrow Man closed the distance between the three of them.

Thomas had stood in the cold wind guarded by or guarding, he didn't know which, the wolf and the buck. It had only been a few minutes when he noticed the elderly Indian man standing silently near the mouth of the cave.

The Elderly Indian stared at Thomas quietly in the darkness. His buffalo skin clothing whipped in the wind as the snow flurries swirled around his legs.

At first Thomas thought he was dreaming. Maybe he had fallen asleep standing up. He had read about people who could sleep sitting up or standing, but had not really believed it was possible.

He lowered the barrel of the rifle, fully aware the elderly Indian was not a threat to him, even if he were real. The wolf and the buck took notice, too. They both stood and looked into the direction Thomas was staring. Slowly, the Indian with bloodstained, eyeless sockets moved away from the cave and walked over to them.

Thomas watched in fascination. The Indian made a direct path to the three of them standing in the middle of the snow-covered field. He stopped a few feet away looking into Thomas' eyes.

"He's afraid of you," the Indian repeated. He had said this so many times in Thomas' dreams Thomas had expected it to be his first words, now.

"My dad told me to stay here." Thomas said quietly.

The wolf and the buck looked back and forth at these two humans. Neither animal made a sound, but both were waiting to see how the conversation played out. "He told me not to go there."

Thomas was startled to hear the Indian say, "I created this monster, years ago. In my anger and my sorrow, and in my wrath, I set this creature loose upon the world." He looked back over to the cave, fresh tears of blood streaming down his face.

"I even tried to bring this weather, with the hopes of slowing him down." The Indian gestured with his head towards the sky and the falling snow.

He paused waiting for what he was saying to sink in to Thomas. "None of it has worked."

"He's afraid of you," he whispered into the wind. Even without turning and looking at the Indian Thomas had heard and understood.

He subconsciously tapped the flint-knife in his right pocket. Putting down the M4 onto the cold ground Thomas turned his flashlight back to the mouth of the cave.

He looked down at his feet realizing the wolf and the buck had no intention of going any further. "I'm ready," he said.

Thomas walked over to the mouth of the cave with the elderly Indian close behind. The buck and the deer did not follow, both choosing to stay where they had waited with Thomas. Thomas whispered quietly to himself offering words of encouragement and began climbing down into the cave.

He had climbed down the fallen logs and glanced back only to see the Indian was no longer behind him. He cursed a little under his breath and continued picking his way among the fallen debris. He reached the cave floor his flashlight gave him enough light to see the elderly Indian was waiting for him a few feet away.

The two of them began following the cave into the darkness, though Thomas wasn't completely sure the Indian was really there. Part of him felt like it was still a dream.

"*Maybe a hallucination caused by standing out in the cold.*"

They followed the light which helped guide them along the main cavern, around to the left. Thomas did feel some comfort in knowing someone was with him down in the darkness of the cave. Even if the other person were only a figment of his imagination created in his mind to try to find a rational explanation for everything.

They rounded the first bend and paused. Thomas heard the echoes of two shots being fired. He sped up walking at a faster pace, worried something might have happened to his dad. The elderly Indian continued to walk a few steps behind him, gliding along in silence.

Turning the last corner, it had been an easy task to follow the light provided by the lanterns; Thomas was shocked to see his father lying on his back beneath the Scarecrow Man.

Instinctively he yelled, "Get away from my dad!!" The strength and depth of his voice shocked him. It seemed to anger the Scarecrow Man.

Initially, the Scarecrow Man stood and began walking towards Thomas only pausing when the elderly Indian stepped out from behind him. The mask on the Scarecrow Man's face contorted with an array of emotions as the eyeless Indian stopped at Thomas' shoulders.

Fear. Sorrow. Anger. They swept across his features quickly and were replaced by hatred and fury. Spreading his hands the Scarecrow Man closed the distance between himself and Thomas. Completely ignoring the elderly Indian the Scarecrow Man reached Thomas in a few steps and grabbed him by the shoulders with both hands.

In those few split seconds, a deep sadness swept over Thomas.

Visions of a father, a son, a brother, and a mother, all Indians rushed into his head. Laughter and wonderful moments of friendship flooded through him. The feelings of unimaginable sorrow and pain, as well.

Thomas looked quickly at his dad lying on the cold hard floor a few feet away. He finally realized why the elderly Indian had brought him down into the cave. The Scarecrow Man leaned his face towards Thomas, widening his mouth, intent on biting Thomas with his cold sharp fangs.

Thomas reached into his right pocket and brought out the flint-knife, the one his uncle had found years ago in a field. The Scarecrow Man clamped his mouth down onto Thomas' left-shoulder, blood gushing out of Thomas into his mouth. Gleefully the Scarecrow Man kept his mouth on Thomas' shoulder drinking in the blood.

Thomas hugged the Scarecrow Man closer, lifted his right hand with the knife behind his back and stabbed it into the back of the Scarecrow Man. The serrated edges of the flint knife pierced the whole from back to front where the Scarecrow Man's heart would have been.

Searing pain shot through the Scarecrow Man as he tried to push himself away from Thomas.

Thomas squeezed tighter, fighting to hold on. He wrapped his legs around the Scarecrow Man forcing his weight onto the already weakening legs.

Silently, almost in a whisper, as the Scarecrow Man fell to his knees, Thomas on top of him, Thomas said, "I give you back your heart my brother."

Falling forward, the Scarecrow Man pinned Thomas underneath his body. The weight of his lifeless-body made it difficult for Thomas to breathe.

Thomas lay dying a few feet away. David Dryver tried to roll over. He forced himself up onto his hands and knees and began to crawl to his son.

The elderly Indian kneeled down and touched Thomas on the forehead. An expression of sadness in his features he lowered his head and prayed to the Great Father.

"I thank you for your sacrifice. Now our family can truly be at peace." The elderly Indian stood up at the very moment David made it to his son. Shoulders sagging in the darkness, the Indian turned and walked away into the darkness, never to be seen or heard from again.

TWENTY

—— THE WOLVES THAT HOWLED ——

DEATH

David Dryver sobbed loudly into the dimly lit darkness, his tears staining his cheeks and dropping onto the muddy floor of the cave. He kneeled over the lifeless body of his son Thomas and was crushed by the overwhelming feeling of sadness.

His shoulders rose and fell deeply. His body reacted to what his mind had already told him. His son's eyes were opened slightly as if Thomas were looking at the darkness of the ceiling of the cave. David knew, though, these eyes saw no more. Thomas was dead.

Smith had run over to David to help him stand and half carried him over to Thomas. Together they rolled the Scarecrow Man over and pulled him away from Thomas. The flint knife had done its job. The tattered shirt was dripping with blood. The flint-knife had punctured a hole into the left side of the Scarecrow Man's chest.

Once Smith had realized Thomas was dead he left David to grieve in private and moved over to both the Private and to Chief Watson. The Chief was sore, his back having been thrown-out, but he could walk, even if barely.

It took a few minutes to revive the Private, but eventually he started to wake up. "What happened?" he said, groggily.

After Sergeant Smith was sure both men were going to be okay he helped them over to David and Thomas.

Smith put his hands on David's shoulder. He had witnessed bits and pieces of what had happened, but wasn't sure he had not blacked out and missed parts of it. He clearly remembered the elderly Indian kneeling over Thomas and whispering something to him then standing and walking away into the darkness.

"Dave," he said softly to his friend. "We need to go. I will carry him." Smith didn't know what else to say. His heart ached at the loss he knew David was experiencing. He was sure they were all still in shock from the events which had just occurred. The four men had just had the hell beat out of them, which was nothing compared to what had happened to his best friend's son.

"No." David said flatly standing up. "I will carry him. You help the other two."

Smith didn't argue. He knew David needed to do this. He needed to be the one to carry his son out of this cave. He turned away as the tears stained his own eyes.

The four men hobbled slowly back to the mouth of the cave. Each moved slowly for David's sake and because the Chief and the Private were in pretty bad shape.

When they made it to the mouth of the cave David waited at the bottom while Smith took both the Private and the Chief to the top, one at a time. Once both were out, Sergeant Smith climbed down once again and helped his friend move Thomas' body up out of the cave.

"It's stopped snowing," Smith said at the bottom of the cave before they began the effort of moving out of the cave and into the coming morning light.

He was not sure if it had stopped because it was a new day or because the Scarecrow Man was dead. They would have to wait until this evening to find out.

The events of the last evening played out over and over in his head. He deeply regretted having allowed Thomas to come along

Once out of the cave, Smith offered to go to David's house as quickly as possible and bring a vehicle to them. All three of the other men disagreed.

They wanted to walk, even if it were slowly, back. The Private and the Chief were still intent on no one finding out about the dead children down in the cave. They reminded the others of the pact they had agreed to down in the cave.

Smith glared at them, initially, but the reality of what would be found down in the cave returned. He nodded in agreement and looked to David for his reaction. David shrugged and nodded, also.

David, with the help of Smith, lifted Thomas into his arms and began walking towards Okawville. He had walked about five or six steps when the big buck and the wolf moved to block his path.

"What?" David said aloud.

The other three men paused watching the two animals. They had clearly moved to block David's path. Staring at the men silently, the buck kneeled down in front of David.

The wolf looked at David silently. He thought he noticed it gesture quickly with his head to the buck. David started to walk around the two animals cradling his son's lifeless body up against his chest.

The buck jumped up and repeated what it had done before. Both animals moved again to block David's path.

The buck knelt again in front of David, obviously trying to get him to do something. Slowly, finally understanding what they wanted, David draped his son's lifeless body over the back of the buck. Gently, as if it were aware of the precious cargo on its back, the majestic buck stood and turned towards the town.

Sergeant Smith and David took up positions on either side and the seven of them began the long-trek back to Okawville.

The seven entered Okawville the moment the early morning sun poked its head above the trees in the east. Crossing an overpass over Interstate 64, they walked slowly down route 177 passing the Dollar General and the Road Ranger to their left.

A State Police patrol car pulled up, the occupant having sat at the Dollar General for a few hours. The officer rolled down his window and looked at them. He recognized the Chief and Sergeant Smith from briefings they had all held on guarding Okawville.

"Chief, stop. I will call for an ambulance." Watson stopped to explain to him they needed to walk all the way home. He mentioned to the State Police officer he could radio ahead to let all of the others patrolling the town not to try to stop them.

He wasn't sure how the wolf and the buck would react. The Chief turned and walked as quickly as he could to catch up to his friends.

The four men, the buck, and the wolf, along with Thomas' lifeless body, turned into the asphalt driveway of David's home.

The buck veered to the left stepping off the driveway and into the grass. It knelt down and allowed David and Sergeant Smith to lift Thomas off of its back. Standing up, the buck and the wolf walked together towards the back of the house.

David continued kneeling near his son's body. The Chief and the Private walked to the police cars which were just pulling up. Sergeant Smith put his hands on David's shoulders hoping to help alleviate some of the heart-ache he knew his friend was experiencing.

The front door opened slowly as David's wife looked out of their house. "Dave, is everything okay?"

David's heart wrenched when she looked down beside him and realized that Thomas was lying on the ground. Screaming his name she ran over to the two men. Sobbing, she leaned down and picked up Thomas into her arms.

She sobbed saying softly, "My baby…my poor baby?" David sat on his knees in silence allowing her to grieve as he had done.

She was still cradling Thomas, Smith was still standing over David's shoulder also crying, and both the Chief and the Private were pointing back towards them explaining something to a few of the State Police Officers and some FBI agents, who had just arrived.

A few minutes later, everyone stopped, as the sounds of hooves clicking along the asphalt driveway came to their attention.

Even David's wife stopped crying. The deer walked down the driveway towards the front of the house. The big buck was in the lead with the others following close behind.

The buck paused and turned towards David and his wife. Slowly, it knelt down on its front legs. It held that pose for a few seconds, stood, then turned towards the highway. The police officers and FBI agents watched in fascination as the deer picked their way through the cars with the flashing lights and walked together down the middle of Front Street. They headed south past the local tractor dealership and once into an open field started to run as fast as they could.

David watched the deer disappear down the road and turned back to his son Thomas and his wife.

He was startled to see the Alpha female wolf and the rest of her pack standing closely behind. They had walked silently to the front of the house and now stood in front of David and the others only a few feet away.

They glided silently over the grass and came closer. David's wife started to panic, trying to pull away from the animals, until he reached out his hand and placed it on her forearm.

"It's okay. They don't mean any harm."

He was not sure how he knew. These were wild unpredictable animals. But, David felt he knew that at this moment everyone was completely safe.

The female wolf walked over timidly. She bent down sniffing Thomas and licked his cheek. The ice-blue eyes locked onto David's for a few seconds.

Leaning her head back the wolf opened her mouth and began to howl.

One by one, the other wolves of the pack leaned their heads back mimicking their leader and howled loudly into the morning light.

After about fifteen seconds she looked down at Thomas one more time and looked over at David. Their eyes locked and she whined as if to say, "I'm sorry for your loss."

Silently, the wolves turned and walked across the grass of the front yard moving in single file down Front Street. They moved out of town the same way they entered, silently. The pack followed the path taken by the deer. Once out past the railroad tracks to the south of town, past the tractor dealership, the wolves found the open fields. Just like the deer they broke into a trot and then into a run.

EPILOGUE
DOMINANT

LOCAL TEENAGER LAID TO REST

"It was pure magic," long-time family friend of the Dryer family was quoted as saying. He was referring to the outpouring of love the family received at the funeral services for their son Thomas William Dryver, age fourteen.

Thomas was killed exploring a cave outside Okawville on August 3rd, 2018. His mother and father reported he had left a note stating he was going to help find the missing children. Once receiving the report Chief Watson of the Okawville Police Department, also a long-time friend of the family started the search. They found the teenager at the bottom of the mouth of a cave. The cave, which had apparently never been discovered before, was about twenty-five feet deep. Chief Watson reported the most recent earthquake probably caused the collapse of some rocks which resulted in the exposing of the cave to the surface.

The Chief oversaw the filling in and covering of the cave with concrete. He reported wanting to prevent any other kids from accidentally falling down into the cave.

The funeral services for Thomas Dryver were held at the local high school. Thousands of people attended to pay their last respects to the beloved teenager.

Excerpts from an Article in the **West Washington Gazette**, August 6th, 2018.

DOMINANT

Two animals, one **predator**, one **prey**, met in the open field just before the coming of dawn on a warm, summer morning. They met to end a truce made by the two of them, a truce which had been born out of necessity, brought on by the arrival of the Beast, the demon, the Wendigo, which had entered these woods un-announced, bringing death and destruction in its wake. That alliance was now coming to an end.

A peaceful silence hung in the air, battling the chirping of the morning cicadas. The woods had returned to a balance which had vacated it for the past month or so.

The orchestra of insects sounded their calls in unison, raising and lowering in volume and tempo. They sounded off in anticipation of what might happen when the two animals faced each other in the morning light.

The insects, the only true witnesses to the timeless ritual of nature's hunt, believed their silence was a required part of the dance. While they waited in anticipation watching the events play out, the insects were unaware the two animals were meeting in peace, one last time.

The two animals felt an innate obligation to meet, in order to pay homage to the fourteen-year old human who had sacrificed himself so they might live.

Staring at each other, with unblinking eyes, both realized their survival, and the survival of their descendants, was owed that boy, the one who had given his life, the one who had sacrificed himself in the ultimate way. Without that boy, without that sacrifice, the Beast would have continued to hunt, the Beast would have continued to kill, and the Beast would have continued to feed.

Shadows both increased and decreased in length as the sun began its ascent above the vast horizon. White clouds, speckled with a serene azure continued their endless trek across the sky and into the depths of the vast ocean above.

The meeting place had been agreed upon in the voice-less fashion of animals, but communicated nonetheless through the necessity of ending an alliance which had been created out of dire necessity. Unable to articulate the magnitude of what had recently transpired, both were content with spending the last few moments of this alliance with each other.

The Alpha Female wolf and the large fourteen-point buck gazed at each other each acutely aware the next time they met nature would drive one to hunt and one to be hunted. One would make every effort to hunt, to kill, and to feed on the other. This hunt had been a part of nature many eons past. The drive to hunt passed from one generation to the next, in the voiceless, almost innate way animals passed on their skills.

The other would make every effort to flee, to fight, and to maim the other; at least to the point the hunt would be abandoned. This innate ability to flee, to try to preserve oneself for the purpose of passing dominant traits for survival to the next generation was just as important.

Without both, without both predator and prey, without wolf and deer, nature would not survive. That is what had been so disconcerting about the Beast. It did not differentiate between animals. Between predator and prey. Between wolf and deer. Between fox and rabbit. Between hawk and snake. To the Beast, every living thing was fair game. Every living thing was something to be hunted, something to be devoured.

It had moved on to humans which was an almost welcomed relief to the animals of the forest. The respite, while short-lived, had provided them the opportunity to seek out protection from their two legged neighbors.

Lowering their heads, in a bow to one another, the wolf and the buck gazed at each other for one last time, turned away and walked in opposite directions.

Each was no longer worried about the unseen eyes hidden within the woods. Each was no longer worried about the odor of death and decay which had permeated the woods with the arrival of the Beast.

The natural smells of the forest had returned.

Peace had been achieved.

In their voice-less fashion, the animals knew the natural balance of the woods, the endless serenity of the forests, the slow, flowing water of the creeks, and the endless bounty of the fields, had been restored.

The buck disappeared into the fields of ripening corn and did not glance back. There was no need. The Alliance was over.

The hesitancy necessary for survival had returned. Never again would the buck look to the wolf pack for protection. Never again would it lay down its own life, as it had done when it rescued a pup from the Beast. The scars on its side were proof of that. Never again would it be necessary to protect one of the members of the pack.

Entering the woods, on the opposite side of the field, the female wolf also did not hesitate to look back.

Immediately, it began to weave between the trees, hopping over rotting logs and picking its way through the yellowing shrubs, the wolf headed in the direction of its den.

Work needed to be done. The pack needed to be brought back to its original strength. That would take years, but nature demanded it be done, for the good of the pack, for the good of all the animals, both predator and prey. It had to be done for the good of the natural balance to the woods.

As it picked up its pace breaking into a full sprint, the wolf fought against the desire to howl.

It took a few minutes before the female wolf allowed the realization to sink in that at long last, the wolf pack was once again the **dominant** predator in the woods.